HARM'S WAY

Anna, at eighteen, is unquestionably confident in her attractiveness to men, she's never been hurt. After going to work and live in Paris, she strikes up a close friendship with Beth, a woman twenty years her senior. While Beth enjoys Anna's girlish enthusiasm for Paris life — Anna is drawn to Beth's warmth and grace, and her intangible air of loss. When Beth meets Christian she is besotted. But Anna cannot be happy for her friend: bitterness about the new lovers tests their friendship — and her own fledgling powers of seduction. But who is her real rival: Christian or Beth?

Celia Walden was born in Paris in 1975 and lives in west London. She edits the *Daily Telegraph*'s 'Spy' column, having previously worked as a feature writer for the *Mail on Sunday*. She writes a monthly column for *Glamour* and *GQ* and appears regularly on national television. This is her first novel.

CELIA WALDEN

HARM'S WAY

Complete and Unabridged

ULVERSCROFT
Leicester

First published in Great Britain in 2008 by
Bloomsbury Publishing Plc
London

First Large Print Edition
published 2009
by arrangement with
Bloomsbury Publishing Limited
London

British Library CIP Data

Walden, Celia.
  Harm's way
  1. Young women- -France- -Paris- -Fiction.
  2. Paris (France)- -Social life and customs- -Fiction.
  3. Large type books.
  I. Title
  823.9'2–dc22

  ISBN 978–1–84782–747–0

Published by
F. A. Thorpe (Publishing)
Anstey, Leicestershire

Set by Words & Graphics Ltd.
Anstey, Leicestershire
Printed and bound in Great Britain by
T. J. International Ltd., Padstow, Cornwall

This book is printed on acid-free paper

To my mother and father

1

It was on my way home from the dentist, nearly five years after we first met, the left side of my bottom lip numbed, that I saw her. Portobello Road was teeming with Christmas shoppers who moved in predictable lines, never varying from their tasks: an army of coloured ants. The crowd was beginning to suffocate me, but the winter air crystallised any ill humour into the freezing tips of my fingers.

I had, over the years, imagined a hundred backs to be hers, the same thick ponytail on a dozen different heads. Once, after hearing a voice which I thought must be hers, I waited patiently at the swimming pool for a woman in the cubicle beside mine to emerge. This time I was sure.

I stopped, tempted to follow her but suddenly afraid. The rain had shrouded her hair in a veil of crystal drops, and I watched as she disappeared into a side street towards Westbourne Grove. I found myself moving forward, hastening my pace. At the mouth of the narrow street cluttered with market stalls I caught sight of her again. She was also walking fast, and I struggled to keep up. In front of me, a woman swept a dog into her legs, giving me an accusatory look as I stumbled past.

'Watch where you're going, will you?'

A group of youths ahead of me broke apart and, as though sensing my presence, she suddenly swung around.

People were jolting our elbows, bags catching each other as they passed by, but Beth just stood there facing me, in everyone's way, waiting for me to make the two steps that would take me to her.

'Hello.'

'Hello.'

'You live in London now?' I heard myself ask politely.

'I have done for the past two and a half years.'

We were by a pub with outdoor heaters like a Parisian cafe, and I wondered if she too had made the connection. So despite the December chill, the chairs and tables outside were full of people, packages between their legs, coddling pints with their gloves on.

'Shall we sit, for a moment?'

It was only then that I saw the child. I had at first assumed that it belonged to someone else, but I could see now that it was hers, from the pale freckled nose to those translucent blue eyes.

'We'll be late, Mummy.'

'No we won't, tiger. We're picking up a hamster,' she explained.

Clumsily, I indicated a recently vacated table.

'Shall we?'

'Yes, let's.'

It was perhaps the one conversation in my life to date with no room for pretence. Beth spoke first: 'You look well.' She smiled her saintly smile, flecked with sadness. 'You haven't changed a bit.'

It sounded like an insult.

'And you look beautiful — as always.' I said.

'What can I get you?' A round-faced teenager — probably a student earning a bit of extra cash during the holidays — looked down at us expectantly.

'We'll have two glasses of rosé.' And then turning to me, 'Who says it has to be a summer drink, anyway? And — what would you like, darling? No, no Coca-Cola — and an orange juice, please.'

'Exactly.'

'Sorry?'

'You're right. About the rosé, I mean. It shouldn't have to be a summer drink.' I felt young and gauche again; Beth was in control.

'What are you doing now?'

'Oh, I work for a gallery. It's not one of the big ones, so the pay's no good, but, well, it's a bit more interesting than what I was doing before, when we . . . in Paris, I mean.'

I saw her cheek twitch. She put a suede-gloved hand to it, brushing away a fallen eyelash, and with that small movement the rush of memories came back so strongly I felt dizzy.

★ ★ ★

When I'd first left Paris I had nurtured the pain I was experiencing, addicted to the sadness I could evoke with the simplest recollection of the months we'd spent together. I'd dreaded the moment when that response would no longer come, knowing that as time went on I might have to drag the match not once but twice, then three times against my heart to spark the familiar flame.

We had met in a very prosaic Paris. Not a set from a Godard film where elegantly disabused girls sat smoking outside cafés, but against a backdrop of tedious days and squinting mornings. To prepare me for my history of art studies at university, my uncle, a museum curator in London, had secured me a position as a guardian at the Musée d'Orsay

— a cavernous converted railway station on the left bank. I had always wondered about those people who sat in rooms filled with paintings by dead artists, listening to the embarrassed whispers of dutiful visitors in search of self-improvement. Perhaps these guardians were life's observers, content to sit by while others engaged with the world. I was initially unexcited by a job whose only purpose in my eyes was to give me a reason to be in Paris and to wait, as I had waited for a long time, it seemed, for my real life to begin.

From my first day at the museum, when I'd seen Céline, the head of personnel, take a silver package from her bag and open it to reveal a perfectly cored apple cut into sixteen segments, I'd suspected I might have trouble fitting in. The thought of that apple has stayed with me as an example of the alienating precision of some Parisian women.

My first week was spent in a flat belonging to a friend of my mother, who was out of town. Neither a stranger to Paris nor habitually shy, I nevertheless felt intimidated by the prospect of getting to grips with a city that was less like London than I had expected. I'd finished my A levels assuming there would be a greater buffer of TV days and pub nights than the few days I had been limited to. But my father, with uncharacteristic firmness, had casually mentioned the job in Paris on the very morning I lay recovering from the school leavers' party held in our honour. 'And don't you dare start trying to sort out her accommodation too,' I'd overheard my mother telling him late one night as I tiptoed down the hall to get a glass of milk. 'We've got Anna this job and we'll subsidise her while she's there but after that,' I heard the sound of her boot coming off and a shallow exhalation of relief, 'she'll just have to fend for herself, like I did to get myself through law school.' I couldn't remember a time when her voice hadn't been shot through with weariness. Rarely home before ten, my mother's devotion to her job meant that my father and I usually dined alone — something I was more than happy with.

★ ★ ★

I moved to Paris two weeks before my job at the museum began to give me time to find a flat and explore the city, but the oppressiveness of my own company took me by surprise. Choosing to be alone can be poetic, but when there is no other option, solitude is less enticing. I took refuge in a stack of Georges Simenons I'd found in the guest

6

bathroom and sank with alarming speed into a static existence, not bothering to change out of my dressing gown and eating dry cereal straight from the box. In my loneliness I became aware of every noise, even the sound of my own jaw masticating those flakes of corn. It was only towards the end of the week, when I had reached the bottom of the pile of books, that I decided to be brave and start looking for a flat.

Fusac, a magazine for English and American students distributed free in Parisian pubs, had been recommended by a friend for its small ads, but it took an entire afternoon of roaming from the Frog and Lettuce in Saint-Sulpice to the Irish pub in Bastille, where the walls are papered with jaundiced postcards, to locate a copy. When I did I was disappointed to find that it seemed aimed primarily at American students looking for non-smoking flatmates. I rarely smoked, but hated the idea of being told not to. Then a notice at the bottom of a page caught my eye. The American Church, it said in bold print, was the place to find temporary jobs and somewhere to stay in Paris.

Enjoying the trail I was following, which had, at least, given me a reason to get dressed that morning, I made my way to the church, an uninspiring mottled building on the left

7

bank. Foreigners surrounded the notice-board, and after taking down a whole page of possible flats on the back of my curling Paris guide, I arranged four appointments for the next day.

The first two studios I saw made one thing painfully clear: anything described as 'un loft' was for me, at five foot eleven inches tall, a physical impossibility. The second landlord hadn't even let me see the flat, bursting into a large, humourless laugh as soon as he'd laid eyes on me.

'*Ahhh non, Mademoiselle*,' he'd smirked, looking from me to the invisible person beside me in disbelief, while wagging a fat finger inches from my nose, 'this one is not for you.'

The third flat was perfect. A box-like studio in the Marais, it was less than half the size of my bedroom in London, and slightly more expensive than I'd budgeted for. But it was exactly where I had imagined myself living. The pink-grey buildings of the Marais — the gay quarter of Paris — leaned towards each other the higher they rose, as though com-plicit in the promiscuity of the streets below. It seemed as if people living in the apartments at the very top could reach out and touch one another from their opposing windows. I was charmed by the fact that in Paris, even in wealthy areas like the Marais, houses had peeling façades and shop fronts bearing their original 1900s lettering.

There seemed no affectation, none of the frenzied desire for modernity that is evident in London, just a natural stylishness. Many of the 'men-only' bars had frosted windows to a foot beneath the awnings, so that all you could see if you glanced inside were the crowns of scarred, shaved heads tilting towards one another, below a thick, blue layer of cigarette smoke. Once I noticed a man dressed in a corduroy suit with patches on the elbows shuffle his little boy uneasily across the street when about to pass by a shop window filled with sex-aids.

In what I already thought of as my street, many of the walls were decorated with ribald hieroglyphics. The imperious green door of the building with its defunct bronze knocker broke open to reveal a pretty hidden square where the windows — joined diagonally by a web of washing lines — refracted prisms of sunlight on to the cobblestones. My landlady, Madame Guigou, was a petite, nervous woman who suffered from acute psoriasis. Her neck always bore an imprint of the latest, violent scratch, so that one could see the blood humming beneath the surface. She spoke in a series of breathless gasps, spitting out her words as though fearing they might run out, while spasmodically running veined claws through her brittle hair.

'It's not been available to rent for a long time,' she explained hurriedly, 'because of all the renovations. The building's quiet and the neighbours are *assez sympathique*.'

I wondered at the '*assez*' and cast an eye over the water-stained ceiling and well-used furniture, reflecting what it could possibly have been like before the 'renovations', but not much caring either. It would be the first time I had lived alone and the rush of excitement I'd been holding in since arriving in Paris finally came.

*   *   *

There had been nothing to keep me in London, no boyfriend or friendship serious enough to anchor me to the city. At eighteen my few, brief relationships had been no more than a succession of passing sensations. Nothing seemed to cohere. I can still remember the exact moment, a month before my fourteenth birthday, when I understood the power maturing within me. During the previous two years my body had undergone a series of humiliating changes for which I wasn't ready. Then suddenly harmony was re-established. We were on a family holiday in Pescara, an uninspiring seaside town near Abruzzo in Italy, and I'd run down to the beach opposite the hotel for an early morning swim. Family groups were already laying out their paraphernalia, and as I pulled my dress up over my head, I noticed a group of slightly older Italian boys looking at me, their brown skins still with that peculiar oily luminosity that is subsequently matted by age. At first, I couldn't decipher their looks — and then I knew. I remember that the feeling of their eyes on me as I arranged my body on the towel and tucked my thick dark hair behind one ear was at least as enjoyable as the sun against my skin. I had a premonition that the sensation might be addictive, and, surprised at how delicious it was to luxuriate in someone else's gaze, hoped fervently that I would grow up to be beautiful. When I got back to my hotel room that night I stood in front of the mirror for a long time, newly in love with myself, examining the gentle roundness of my breasts and the nascent curve of my hips, savouring it all through the eyes of the boys on the beach. The next morning, I'd awoken to find a small patch of blood on the hotel sheet.

I hadn't grown up to be beautiful; at best, I was occasionally described as 'pretty'. I was too tall and boyish in figure, with deep-set eyes and my dark, messy features lacked the symmetry that traditionally defines beauty: the 'before' picture in a women's magazine. The realisation caused me a moment's pain, a snarl in the skein of my perfect existence, but I had one consolation: boys seemed to like me, and then men. In a mirror-like response to their collective gaze, I developed my own fascination with them. From puberty onwards — and this was a fault of mine — the only thing that secured my lasting attention was the opposite sex. Neither animals, landscapes nor objects held any value in my eyes. But my father, the look on a woman's face when she speaks of a man, and the sinewy forearm of the bus conductor as he took my change — these things captivated me.

Leaving the few girls I saw as friends posed no problem. Until that year — until I met Beth — my female friends had counted for very little. As an only child I had always found it hard to have the generosity of spirit that my friends demanded of me, assimilating myself more easily into large groups that I could drift in and out of. When people asked me how I felt about a particular subject I could never quite believe they cared what my answer was. I assumed that it was all a charade, that people only feigned interest in others so that they, in turn, would be indulged. I had always supposed that the kind of selflessness which made you interested in other people's emotions would occur naturally in adulthood. Selfishness, at that time, seemed to me to be a good thing, making you act on your desires and achieve them faster than those who check with everyone before going after what they want, and as a result are too late to get it.

★ ★ ★

My new apartment building was flanked on the right by a popular launderette, where men sat around pretending to read *Wallpaper** magazine, pausing to tease designer briefs from the jaws of the machines while critically observing their neighbours' laundry.

To the left of number 35 rue Sainte Croix de la Bretonnerie was an even more surprising sight: the Sun Café, a bar and sun-bed centre where you could enjoy a frozen margarita from the comfort of your slippery-with-sweat glass bed. But my real joy, and the reason I had rented the flat, was the tiny balcony, just large enough to fit a flower pot and the skeleton of a chair I'd found on the street. Overlooking the blue slate roofs of Paris, it was a perfect spot. The only eyesore was the blackened plastic tubing of the Centre Pompidou, visible in the distance, like a mass of cancerous entrails.

When your spirits are uplifted you want to tell someone about it, but after twice dialling my father's number (my mother hated to be disturbed at the office) I hung up, knowing that his soothing voice would only induce the semblance of a complaint from me where there was none. At 3 a.m., I awoke to a banging noise coming from the flat next door: a slow, measured knocking on the wall. I waited for it to subside but instead it gradually increased in volume. Covering my face with my pillow and cursing French plumbing, I strove to sleep. Eventually the knocking stopped as abruptly as it started.

★   ★   ★

Despite the loss of sleep, the next morning I felt brighter. I bought a plant, attempted a French paper but gave up after a glance revealed an impenetrable thicket of statistics accompanying each and every article, and began to wonder how I would ever meet anyone in what I was starting to understand was a difficult city to break into. After the third day of speaking to no one, my cheerfulness receded and anxiety set in. A film was the only way to assuage the panic. While I was buying my ticket to the third part of a Hollywood trilogy, a teenage girl behind me in the queue tapped me on the shoulder and asked whether the first two had been any good. I walked into the cinema elated by the few words we'd exchanged, wishing I could somehow have extended the conversation, but left the theatre despondent that the prospect of any further human interaction that day was slim.

I am pleased now, for those days of loneliness, because it was only after being forced to stare down the intimidating colossus of Paris that — all of a sudden and quite unexpectedly — I fell in love with it. In many respects, it is a city built for the lost: taking a wrong turn leads to such enchanting discoveries that one soon begins to do it deliberately. The French even have a word for it, 'flâner' — to stroll aimlessly — which I would do for hours, from the rue de l'Échaude, past the sleepy bookshop L'Or du Temps, down to the more refined rue de Seine, turning off at the rue des Beaux Arts to contemplate the hotel where Oscar Wilde died in poverty and disgrace. Like that of a medical student handed his first scalpel, my curiosity to uncover the city's viscera knew no bounds.

Just when I began to revel in my solitude, an antidote to my loneliness came from an unexpected source: a schoolfriend, Sarah.

Sarah was the kind of girl who laughed differently in the company of boys. She'd rung to tell me about the last one she'd met, liberally interspersing her conversation with that large, slightly frenetic laugh, pausing only for the barest murmur of acknowledgement from me.

I let it all pass over my head until she suddenly asked, 'Did you ever meet Beth?'

'No. Why should I know Beth?'

'She's that great Irish woman I told you about. You remember. The one I met doing work experience with that dress designer in London.'

I vaguely remembered Sarah's exultant description of Beth, at the time putting it down to her hyperbolic tendencies, but was soon to realise how accurate it was.

'Anyway,' Sarah continued, 'she moved to Paris a year ago to work at some fashion house. Can't think which . . . but quite a famous one, I think. She's practically my mother's age, but she doesn't act like it, and if you want her to she'll happily take you under her wing. Anyway, you've probably already got yourself a little clique . . . '

I took down Beth's number: it would be a good place to start.

16

2

I hesitated to contact this unknown woman but out of a mixture of desperation and curiosity, did so a few days later. Low-voiced but welcoming on the phone, Beth soon dispelled my embarrassment. Still, I was convinced that at best our meeting could yield little more than a few tips on day-to-day life in a Paris that seemed increasingly impregnable.

She had set a date for that Sunday at the Marché aux Puces de St-Ouen in Clignancourt, which sold every kind of bric-a-brac from vintage clothing to antiques. Once a place where social rejects found refuge, it now featured regularly in French gossip magazines like *Voici*, with the likes of Juliette Binoche and Sharon Stone (when she was passing through) pictured chatting beatifically to ancient Algerian stallholders.

At the gates of the métro station at Porte de Clignancourt I spotted Beth immediately. She was petite, with shoulder-length hair the colour of partridge feathers. The translucent whiteness of her skin was as recognisably Irish as the watery blue almonds of her eyes.

She did not correspond to my childish idea of what a forty-year-old woman should look like for one simple reason: she was undeniably beautiful.

As I approached her I caught an impression of snug curves beneath flimsy linen trousers, hips jutting out exuberantly from a slim waist. Her eyes, flashes of colour in the grey of the underground station, flicked over the crowd before alighting on me.

'Hey,' she drawled with a lazy Irish lilt as I walked towards her with the fixed, determined smile you adopt when meeting someone for the first time. 'I've been looking at that girl over there wondering if she was you.'

Up close I could see that she was twenty years my senior. Time had sketched fine lines around her eyes, and two grooves, lightly charcoaled exclamation marks, were already forming between her eyebrows. We brushed our lips awkwardly across each other's cheeks (would we have done that if we had met in London?), and as we neared the market I found myself blurting out: 'God it's good to see another person. I've been going nearly mad since I got here. Isn't that pitiful?'

My speech sounded rushed, as though exhaling breath I had held in far too long.

'Not at all.' Beth gave a gentle smile

revealing small, curved white teeth, a smile which set off perfectly the lazy dance of her eyes. 'You should have seen me when I first got here. I remember trying to buy some green beans and walking out when the cashier asked me to weigh them because I couldn't understand what he was on about. That, my friend, is pathetic.'

The 'my friend' was a bonus, encouraging me to open up more. I began recounting some of my own, only slightly embellished tales of humiliation at the hands of Parisians. After a moment I became aware that I was sounding like a child, trying to match her experiences in a desire to make her like me. At first unsure of which tone to adopt with her (should I treat her like a friend or like one of my mother's dinner guests?) I was quickly reassured by her easy manner. I liked the fact that her attention to me was steady, undivided. As we wandered past a Rastafarian sitting cross-legged on the pavement behind a patchwork of DVDs, she bent down to look closer at one while I chattered on, throwing me a 'Really?' over her shoulder just as I began to wonder whether she was still listening. Beth's movements had a grace and fluidity which drew admiring glances from passers-by, without her seeming to notice.

'God, you've done so much already — and

you've been here less than a month,' she murmured, shaking her head at an over-zealous stallholder's advances. 'I've been so caught up in work that I've hardly had the chance to get to know Paris.'

'The thing to do is just to start walking and see where it takes you. I'm only just beginning to find my way around but I feel I have to investigate every passage I see, you know? Just in case I miss something.'

She smiled, amused by my enthusiasm. 'I'd never thought of it that way — but you're right.'

By the time we had walked past the long line of street sellers that led, like scattered human crumbs, to the real market, I felt proud: a schoolgirl who had made her first friend, and I suddenly recalled the special sense of privilege and prestige friendship brings in the eyes of children which, perhaps, we lose as we get older.

Together we weaved through the rows of stalls, so deep in conversation that we obstructed other buyers, who reminded us of their presence with a dry smack of the tongue to the upper palate. I bought a set of six 1930s-style Perrier glasses Beth had found hidden behind a cracked basin. I still have them today. I know exactly where they are: on the left hand-corner of the shelf beneath the kitchen sink, but I would never use them again.

'Where the hell did you learn to speak French like that?' she said, grabbing my elbow and leaning in towards me after her darting eyes had registered my bartering exchange with the stallholder. 'I just can't get to grips with it — it's still a relief when people see me struggling and answer in English.'

I shrugged, pleased. 'I did it for A level, and we've had quite a lot of holidays here, so . . .'

Beth blew a silent whistle through pursed lips, and I had the absurd thought that the gesture was too young for her. 'Of course I might have learned more if I wasn't sharing a flat with an Irish bloke. Stephen's my best friend's little brother,' she explained. 'He's from the same village as me, Skibbereen (you won't have heard of it), but he did French at university, speaks it perfectly, which means he really doesn't see the need to practise with me. Of course it might also have helped if my father had forced me to sit down and do my homework at the weekend, instead of helping him out on the farm.'

Seven years her junior, Stephen had witnessed every adolescent folly Beth and his sister, Ruth, had committed, and was able to remember them all with the disconcerting clarity of youth.

'Stephen works for a big magazine company in London, and so when he was moved to their Paris offices a few months ago, I was hoping he'd be keen to share a flat with me. I just get lonely otherwise, on my own, you know? It takes much longer than people expect to make friends in a new country, don't you think?'

Beth had related all this before we'd chosen what we wanted from the handwritten blackboards adorning the walls of a crêperie in the hub of the market.

I liked the sound of Stephen, and began trying to formulate a question that might tell me how attractive he was. I was still too excited by men to be able to imagine them purely as friends. But the interest I had in the opposite sex had one, vital clause: it must be reciprocated. The second I arrived in any given place I would scour the room for the responsive gleam in a man's eyes, a reflex of mine that showed little sign of passing.

'He's single and great-looking, in case you're wondering,' Beth said with an indulgent smile, looking above my head at the menu and then back, fixedly, at me. 'But you've probably got someone, haven't you?'

I laughed. 'Actually no.'

'I can't believe that: why not?'

'I suppose I rarely find people that I like.'

This wasn't true. I liked men all too easily: little men who looked up at you admiringly, big men who cradled your head in their hands, clever men, stupid men. I liked them but I was never affected by them.

'You seem to be a pretty self-reliant person, one way and another.'

'Oh I am,' I agreed. 'Very much so.'

'I'm not,' she rejoined easily. 'I'm the worst kind of woman. When I like someone I can't help making it far too obvious. I call them constantly, try to book them weeks in advance, neglect my friends for the duration — which tends to be short — and generally become this terrible, fawning Irish mam. Naturally they end up running a mile.' She smiled to herself, amused, but seeking no kind of reassurance from me. 'You'd think I'd learn, wouldn't you? You'd think it was something you'd get better at as you got older, but the funny thing, Anna, is that you never do.'

One of my biggest faults was my capacity instantly to dislike people, writing them off for making a single statement I didn't agree with. So I found it hard to rationalise the immediate warmth I felt towards Beth. Yes, there was a complete honesty about her which was very appealing — a lack of undertones in anything she said or did that made any *arrière-pensées* impossible — but it was more than that. With friendships, as with lovers, there is always one who is keener, more impatient to reach the point of intimacy than the other, and at that moment I felt that I needed to seduce Beth, to convince her of my worth. When I questioned her about her reasons for coming to Paris (how could a forty-year-old woman not have strong enough ties to make such a move impossible?) it surprised me to discover that I was genuinely interested in her answers.

Cheeks flushed by the heated lamps above our heads, Beth told me — halfway through another anecdote — of her mother's death from cancer when she was only eighteen and the onset of her father's Alzheimer's several years later. Being forced to look after her little brothers and ailing father had ripped a hole in her youth, which she was clearly trying to fill here in Paris. I gained the impression that there was more to it than that. But when, with the flourish of a pink-knuckled hand she suddenly exclaimed, '*Et voilà!*' I knew that despite her apparent openness, that was all I would find out that day. Avid to find out everything about her by now, I hoped that the bruised quality I sensed beneath her cheerfulness would be explained as I got to know her better.

Looking back I can only compare the way I felt when I left Beth later that day to falling slightly in love. Here was a conduit for my experiences and feelings, and I adored her for it. My life in Paris, hitherto filled only with my burgeoning love of the city, suddenly seemed filled with possibility. Beth and I could discover things together, share experiences, get bored *together*. I fell asleep less nervous about my first day at the museum than I had been, and looking forward to dinner at Beth's the following evening.

★   ★   ★

I was at once relieved and disappointed when Stephen opened the door to the flat on the top floor of a building in rue des Gravilliers, an insalubrious street off the rue de Turbigo. When I had read, too young, Flaubert's *Madame Bovary* I'd been struck by the accuracy of his description of her — of all women perhaps — as '*voulant retirer de tout quelque profit personnel*'. As soon as I saw Stephen I recognised him as one of those men from whom I would be able to draw no profit at all. Tall, dark blond and blandly

25

good-looking, with a strong forehead but a certain weakness around the lower part of his mouth, Stephen was one of those rare men for whom on a sexual level I felt absolutely nothing — not even my usual desire to have him fall in love with me.

Perhaps he felt the same. As he struggled to shut the door, still sticky with fresh paint, and commented on the powerful fumes ('Try not to breathe too deeply or you might keel over') I saw his eyes flit over my body approvingly, but not lingeringly.

Beth was in the kitchen, stirring something sweet and meaty in a large saucepan. My first impression on seeing them together was that, had they not looked so different, one might have mistaken them for brother and sister. They had adopted many of each other's mannerisms, especially the way Beth had of nodding slightly when she laughed, as though confirming her own joke. I watched from a high stool as they laid the table and bickered over which herbs to season the salad with, waiting until I had an audience for my description of my first day at work.

★   ★   ★

It hadn't gone badly. I'd pushed through the revolving doors into the grand atrium of the

Musée d'Orsay feeling no great trepidation, only a growing curiosity to discover the details of my daily routine. I had dressed carefully, and felt smart in my new suit, wearing just enough make-up to look like I was wearing very little, with my hair tied in a low ponytail. My pride in this attention to detail was overshadowed by the clicking arrival of Céline, the impeccably dressed small-boned woman of uncertain age I could see coming towards me, a purposeful expression on her face. She walked briskly, though with downcast eyes, in the manner of someone with a very specific, emotionless job to do. The tap of each heel sent a reverberation of efficiency through the halls of the museum, enough to make the figures in the Impressionist portraits sit up straight within their frames.

'Anna?'

'Yes,' I had said, as brightly as I could.

'*Bienvenue*,' she pronounced, with anything but a welcoming expression on her face.

And therein, I thought, lies the talent of that certain breed of Frenchwoman: the words the circumstances demand are there, but their meaning is somehow lacking. Holding out my hand I remembered, too late, that the customary British gesture could provoke embarrassment and a faint irritation in France. My hand wavered a split second too long in mid-air before she took it, with the gracelessness of a teenage boy holding a baby.

'Follow me and I'll show you where you can hang your coat. Then we'll have a little chat about what you'll be doing.'

In some indefinable way Céline made it clear that I was to follow behind, not beside her — perhaps as a gentle payback for the moment of discomfort I'd caused her when I held out my hand. She took me to the staff room: a smallish locker-lined space with high frosted slit windows beneath the ceiling through which one could decipher the mottled greys of Paris. More civil than friendly, she explained my duties and hours, never pushing the boundaries of conversation so far as to enquire about my living arrangements or what had brought me to Paris. It took me a few more encounters to register that Céline smiled only when she wanted to, never out of decency like everyone else. Introducing myself to two of my co-workers — a dark-skinned girl in a voluminous smock and a tall, shaven-headed man who were neatly stashing their possessions in lockers — I noted a similar abruptness of manner which fell slightly short of rudeness. It was a Parisian trait I was going to have to get used to, a world away from the instantly indiscreet confidences exchanged in any office by the supposedly stiff and inhibited British.

All this rang bells of recognition over dinner. The Frenchwoman's most outstanding talent, Stephen assured me as he picked a piece of *mâche* off the tablecloth, lay in her genius for silently undermining any surrounding females. Since these were national characteristics that could never be changed, the only way to handle them was to develop a tough exterior that guaranteed instant respect. Gratuitous kindness in Paris was not a quality; it was a weakness. I nodded agreement, remembering a cautionary tale the mother of a Parisian-born friend had told me. In the playground the Englishwoman had been in the habit of telling her little boy, 'Now don't push forward. Be nice, and let the other children have a go on the slide before you,' until she overheard French mothers berating their neat and polite-looking offspring for letting others push ahead of them. As I was quickly to discover, it all made perfect sense.

★ ★ ★

The gallery each guardian invigilated was always the same: gallery number fourteen was my lot. The most famous painting in my room was Manet's *Le Balcon*, flanked on the left by his arresting portrait of Berthe Morisot. Insofar as I had anything to do at all it was to make sure no bored child or ignorant tourist touched any of the paintings, spoke too loudly, or attempted to walk round an exhibition in the wrong direction — a misdemeanour of which Céline particularly disapproved. There was only one way of viewing an exhibition and that was in the order established by authority. For me the worst thing about my new job was that it was forbidden to read. And of course I was to become an unperson — something I was unused to and initially found it hard to live with. Very soon, however, I realised that being invisible had its advantages: I was able to overhear intimate conversations and study the people engaged in them. That first afternoon I had watched with a mixture of amusement and mild indignation as couples dressed in subtly gradated shades of black ignored me with the same studied dedication they devoted to the Impressionist works lining the walls.

Beth grinned into her wine as I finished my account of the day and paused to take a mouthful of my now luke-warm *poule au pot*. They seemed genuinely entertained but I was keen not to appear self-obsessed. Had I been talking too much?

'Your boss doesn't sound like a barrel of laughs,' said Stephen sympathetically. 'Still, it must be fun people-watching all day.'

I had the impression Stephen wasn't too keen on the French, but Beth told me later that it was French men he had taken against. For all his mocking, the women he went for in a big way.

He and I soon became what I could only, at my most generous, qualify as 'companions'. Like many supple-minded young men I have since come across from the world of magazine publishing, Stephen's interest in the surface of things was almost feminine — and something which, at that time, I could relate to. The slight campness of his manner seemed to be at odds with his love of women. Later I realised that these two carefully cultivated sides to his character worked harmoniously towards the same goal. We huddled together with the lazy ease of expats, but I doubt whether even if things had turned out differently I would still be in touch with him today. My friendship with Beth was something deeper. During those first few weeks it was a rare day when we didn't see each other, either for a quick coffee or for dinner at her flat before a night out. Her advice was always sane, tempered and completely selfless; my admiration for her grew with every hour we spent together. Still, I was beginning to learn that beneath the surface there was a disquiet which gave her an edge she might otherwise have been lacking.

Perhaps I listened when she talked more than I would have done with my contemporaries, and asked many more questions, but otherwise I behaved almost exactly as I might with friends of my own age. Gone was the initial restraint, the swallowed swear words. Still, Beth had a disconcerting way of making me realise before I said something that it was childish, brash, or simply calculated to achieve a reaction. The first time we got drunk together I enjoyed watching the alcohol take effect, softening the more authoritative aspects of her manner, deflating her serenity, and giving me an inkling of the messier human being she must have been at my age. I wished then that I could see my mother, just once, in that same malleable state, and that we might share such an intimacy.

To begin with, I suffered pangs of guilt about not devoting more effort to making French friends, but my absorption with Beth quickly immobilised me, rendering virtually everyone outside her small circle worthless in my eyes.

I was fascinated by the dichotomy in her personality. Professionally, she could appear terrifyingly grown-up, but with me, although her opinions were more mature than mine, no subject seemed too juvenile to discuss. I had never been interested in fashion as a concept, not through any aversion to clothes but simply because I was reluctant to bother educating myself in trends I would never follow or dresses I was too young to afford. Yet after hearing Beth describing a Jean Paul Gaultier show she'd attended the previous week — she liked to check out the competition — I happily accepted her invitation to the Ungaro collection for the following season.

It was staged in a disused monastery in the Latin Quarter, now part of the Sorbonne University, and I drank in every detail of the cluster of industry insiders gathered outside. The women seemed to me dressed with studied negligence, the men in a deliberately outmoded manner as if to elevate themselves above the world they inhabited. Once inside we were seated on velvet-cushioned chairs to observe the procession of limp-limbed models saunter by, their blank eyes fixed on a distant point, like over-made-up sleepwalkers. Earnest-looking journalists from *Le Monde* or *Le Figaro* made incisive scribbles in notebooks to praise or dismiss in a single, devastating word the quality of a certain style or cloth, thereby establishing a whole psychology of fashion for the year to come.

Fashion in Paris, Beth explained later in an overflowing brasserie on the carrefour de l'Odéon, was not the frivolous pastiche it had become in London. It was seen as a valid art form that serious men, as well as women, talked about over dinner. People laughed at fashion for being out of touch with everyday existence, but a deliberate sense of dissociation from reality was what these shows were really about: an entire industry built not on the way people actually lived or behaved, but on their aspirations.

Later she took me to the after-show party held in Les Bains Douches, so called because the premises were in a converted public baths. The bovine bouncer at the door, standing with his legs apart as if braced for a stampede, grabbed our invitations and surveyed them with indifference.

'*Allez-y,*' he relented, having impressed upon us his all-encompassing power. We stepped into a roaring din of fake laughter and the resounding smacks of air-kissing. As I listened to men with spray-on T-shirts discussing the benefits of cardio-vascular activity, I began to see what Beth had meant by dissociation from reality. My lack of attraction towards Stephen meant that I had begun secretly to resent his presence on our outings. I wanted Beth to myself, and disliked the habit he had of turning our conversations away from us, as if determined to rob us of our companionship. When we were alone, Beth with her face propped in a frame of freckled hand, I found her willingness to listen to whatever I had to say infinitely reassuring.

'You look quite lovely tonight . . . ' she'd interrupted that night, eyes lazy and dark with drink. 'I do wish you'd let me dress you next time we go out — I keep seeing things at work which would look great on you.'

I was unused to compliments from women, and took another sip of my drink.

'Do you want to know a secret? This is the first time I've been to one of these 'after' things since I moved here. I was dreading it,' she continued. 'I only came becasue I thought you might enjoy it, but it's turned out to be quite good fun, hasn't it?'

'Is that true?' I replied.

She was charming in the blue light, unaware of how beautiful she was, and I watched out of the corner of my eye as two men at the bar looked appraisingly in her direction.

'I swear. I've always felt, well, a bit awkward about coming to these places that are always filled with beautiful young things.'

'And by that you mean beautiful young men?'

'Yes,' she flushed, 'I suppose I do. I can't help but imagine that they must wonder what someone of, well . . . '

' . . . of your age is doing here? Beth, look around: there are people of all ages. And isn't it just a question of confidence?' I added, touching her finger lightly with mine across the table. 'I always think that if you walk around thinking you can have anything you want, you usually can.'

Beth gave me a brief look, ironical but indulgent, before breaking into a laugh made up of a trio of ascending notes, which didn't quite ring true. 'I'm sure you're right, Anna. Let's drink to that.'

★ ★ ★

That night, not wishing to be alone, and feigning excessive drunkenness, I contrived to spend the night with Beth.

'The sofa's not very comfortable, but my bed's massive, so you're welcome to share it

36

with me as long as you don't wriggle.'

As she tripped gently back and forth across her room, with the hooded eyes and stupid smile of the inebriated, I slipped quickly into bed and waited for her to join me, surprised by the bite of disappointment I felt when, after emerging from the bathroom ready for bed, she turned the light out and promptly fell asleep.

* * *

Waking beside Beth the next morning, I leant across her to switch off the alarm clock, smiling at the creases the sheets had made on her sleeping face. Ignoring the fact that it would make me late for work, I sank back down and allowed myself ten more minutes. Asleep, she looked half her age, with a faintly questioning expression about her eyebrows which made me smile. Her lips were closed, but a steady and invisible vent rhythmically tickled my propped forearm.

'Is it time to get up?' Suddenly, she was awake, although her eyes still struggled to focus. I sat up quickly.

'I'm afraid so. I'll grab the first shower, shall I?'

* * *

37

Wearing one of Beth's jumpers over the previous night's outfit, I tried to shuffle into the vestibule of the staff entrance as inconspicuously as I could. Avoiding Céline's gaze, I deposited my bag in the staff room with what I hoped was aplomb. The besmocked girl I'd met on my first day looked up from her book.

'It's Anna, isn't it? We met the other day. I'm Isabelle.'

Isabelle was half-Romanian and had moved to Paris from Lyon a year ago. A dark fringe of hair and glasses disguised the pretty face of a girl in her mid-twenties: a dusky complexion, full curved lips overshadowed by a slight down. Yet there was an insecurity in her eyes that, had I been a man, would have immediately put me on my guard. As a fellow history of art student, Isabelle was one of the few who found themselves working at the museum through vocation. I earmarked her as a possible work friend, someone to while away my empty lunch breaks with, and thought nothing more of her.

★　★　★

I had begun to settle into my flat. The nocturnal knocking had eased — it now troubled my sleep only one night in three

38

— and although my job at the museum still seemed a world away from the nightlife I was discovering, come six o'clock I could retrieve my belongings from my locker and wind my way slowly home through the back streets, pausing from time to time to catch a glimpse of enchanting secret courtyards behind slowly closing double doors. And Stephen was right: there was a lot to be said for my occupation, the educational solace of watching.

I had been instructed, for one day only, to sit in on an exhibition of photographs by Henri Cartier-Bresson. Robert Doisneau I'd always found a little too posed, but I loved Cartier-Bresson. Living in Paris had heightened my appreciation of his work: it occurred to me that, were it not for changes in fashion, I could still have been observing the city through his delicately angled lens. A wan-faced businessman with a blonde prone to splutters of laughter were first to arrive. Then came an old man with birch-silver hair who, in his green-flash trainers, squeaked gently from photograph to photograph, taking care not to get too close to the prints, lest the images should fly away like rare birds. When he reached the penultimate exhibit — a picture of a soulful young man sitting outside a Bastille café clinking a cloudy glass of Pastis with a young woman — he stopped and

39

looked around nervously. The picture had done what only a photograph of genius can do; it had captured the essence of life at the very moment it expired, like the last dance of a butterfly. It was the millisecond of anticipation prior to the first sip of a shared drink; the instant two people lean a fraction closer, that moment somehow encapsulating all that was most intimate and exciting about human companionship. The old man sighed and turned abruptly towards me, the frayed corners of his mouth approaching a smile. It was then that I understood his veneration.

'*C'est moi.*'

I rose from my chair, unsure of what he meant and a little apprehensive. Then a closer inspection eliminated all doubt: the man in the picture was him.

'It's exquisite,' I told him, touched by his look but conscious of the banality of my words. Having nothing more significant to add I directed him to the gift shop, telling him he could buy a copy of the picture there. I watched him grow smaller and smaller as he walked jerkily through the atrium, rendered a little pathetic by the surrounding grandeur, occasionally pausing on his way, as though to contemplate in silence this miraculous recovery of a moment in his past.

★ ★ ★

That night I moved restlessly in my sleep, my dreams overrun by armies of Cartier-Bresson images. At five in the morning, rather later than I had become used to, I was awoken by the now familiar sound of a fist pounding against the wall. This time I got up determined to find out the cause of the knocking. After a fruitless phone call to Madame Guigou, I went to the boulangerie beneath my flat to buy a *chausson aux pommes* for breakfast.

'*Vous avez l'air fatigué, Mademoiselle*,' the florid boulangère reflected.

I reached for my paper bag, transparent with seeping butter, and told her about the knocking that had been keeping me up every few nights since I'd moved in.

'Which flat are you in? Not the sixth floor?'

I nodded.

'Ah,' she exclaimed with a dismissive gesture, as though the reason was self-explanatory. 'That'll be Monsieur Abitbol. He's a troubled man. In fact,' she added brightly, 'the last girl who lived in your flat, poor mite, had such a terrible time she had to move out.'

I wanted to discover more, but a small and impatient queue was forming behind me, so I

41

left. No wonder my wreck of a landlady had neglected to tell me that I was renting a property next to a well-known sociopath.

Beth looked concerned when I recounted the exchange, while Stephen, caught in the vortex of his own laughter, rocked back and forth on his chair, helplessly trying to bring himself back from the brink.

'The thing is that I'm not even surprised,' he finally managed. 'The French go about in that decorous way of theirs, as if their lives were perfectly normal, but I swear this city is full of madmen. It comes from them living on top of each other. And all that self-control: it's got to crack sometime.' The impact of this remark was diminished when he reached for a cigarette and ran his index finger and thumb down the length of it before lighting up, a gesture I suspected he had only acquired since moving to Paris.

Stephen was right. Paris had little of the space or greenery of London, added to which the sense of people being piled on top of one another intensified the general mood, from the scowls on pedestrians' faces to the angry behaviour of the drivers hunting them down. But there was a fruitful nervous energy I had never come across in London, as though the annoyances of city life conspired to create a general sense of purpose.

I dragged Beth to one event after another, ignoring her pleas for a quiet night in. After her initial reluctance subsided, she displayed a boundless energy which, exceeding even mine, left me bemused. I never even considered her age a factor — something she sensed and which, she once told me, set me apart from everyone else she knew. A condition of our jaunts was that she be allowed to dress me, forcing me to parade back and forth across her sitting room in sample garments brought back from the office until she found something she was satisfied with.

The weekends were my favourite time. I spent the week mapping out our pleasures, gratified by the look of wonder on her face as I guided her into Delacroix's studio, off the lovely place Furstenberg, hidden behind St Germain des Prés. 'How did you know about this place?' she would ask. 'I must have walked past here a thousand times without even knowing it existed.' In a Saturday ritual she claimed to look forward to all week, I would text her a house number, street name and a time, like an old-fashioned telegram, punctuated only with full stops. Like lonely heart assignations we would meet, without any prior phone calls, but with the certitude that hours of enjoyment lay before us. Sunday afternoons were spent sitting by the fountain in the Jardin du Luxembourg reading, with barely a sentence exchanged between us.

Once (on Beth's insistence) we even joined the little children at the puppet show. I liked to buy French gossip magazines, peopled with characters I neither cared about nor could identify. I would thrust their sleek pages under Beth's nose, pointing out the celebrities. Bemused by my interest in such trivia she would glance from the page to me, shake her head with a half-smile, and return to her book. We had built up a sense of complicity which relied for its intimacy on us being utterly different. Beth was the kind of woman who, when she asked someone a question cared about the answer. She was gentler than I, wiser and less impulsive, which made it easier for her to tolerate my bouts of egoism. Only rarely did she ask for something in return.

Her father's health, I soon discovered, was a serious source of concern.

'He has his sister there with him, but I can't help thinking that I should be there too.' She looked at me entreatingly. 'The thing is that I spent years with him, *years*, and in lots of ways they were just a complete waste of time. He didn't even know I was there, you see. I do pay my aunt — she used to be a ward sister in Dublin — to look after him, and Ruth pops in on him most weekends, so he is well catered for. And, well, I can't just leave all this, can I?'

There was nothing I could say to assuage her sense of guilt. I would appease her as best I could, tell her that — unlike her siblings — she had already devoted years to him, done what she could and should, and that she only had one life to live. But I could see she was only voicing an ever-present fear about his precarious health, and that many of her nights were troubled by the decision not to sacrifice what remained of her life, her work and her youth to his illness. One of the most chilling aspects of the disease, she had explained, was that it was so alienating to loved ones.

'I remember seeing the world from the top of his great strong shoulders as a child. Now he looks like an old woman, and when I try to have a conversation with him all I want to do is scream, 'Stop pretending not to understand!' It's as if he's acting a part, deliberately, to annoy me.'

But Beth's father was old, and as anyone with elderly relatives can testify, it is not so much laziness or lack of feeling that resists contact but rather the reverse. It is the horror of seeing the face you know best afflicted by the whimsical deformations of senility.

'It's funny,' she once said, 'because even when my mother was alive, I somehow always felt closer to my father, you know? I suppose most people find that odd.'

'I don't,' I had replied. 'My mother . . . ' and suddenly I couldn't think what to say about her. 'Well, she's very busy, and when she's not, she's tired, so . . . It's been that way as long as I can remember. Still, Dad always says that if it weren't for her job I wouldn't have gone to such a good school — or be here now, I suppose.'

'Or met me,' Beth added with a calm smile.

Our discussions about heartbreak were similarly lopsided. I had never lost anyone, always lived in a womb of comfort sheltered from pain and loss. Of course I'd split up with boyfriends; most of them were an obvious reaction to the one before: if one had been wild and jealous, the next would be understanding and quiet. But to date no one experience had given my character the roundness and depth I admired in Beth: I had not once cried over another human being.

I didn't hanker for suffering, but I was impressed by the effects it could have. And there was something else. I had noticed the physical change such experience can bring. Nothing as brutal and disfiguring as scoring lines across a face, but a certain sharpness about the eyes that my face lacked. It was there in Beth's eyes, and in the resigned expression on Berthe Morisot's face. Its absence in my own made me scowl at the mirror with perverse frustration.

★ ★ ★

That Saturday Stephen was unable to convince me to join him at Queen, a vast gay club reminiscent of a sado-masochistic multi-levelled car park, with oily-skinned men in overhead cages undergoing live nipple-piercing, their pupils avid and dry with drugs they'd taken. Beth was easily won-over, impatient to fully embrace the Parisian nightlife she had shunned for so long, but I declined, spending the evening reading the first chapter of a novel on my university syllabus and waiting for the call my mother had promised me before falling asleep with the phone still in my hand.

When Stephen answered the door to their flat late the following afternoon, damson thumb-prints pressed into the grooves beneath his eyes, I was surprised to find Beth still in bed. Wearing only one of Stephen's old T-shirts, the cotton rendered almost transparent with age, and in that quietly voluptuous state that too much alcohol and too little sleep can induce, she recounted, squirming girlishly beneath the duvet, the events of the night before. Queen had been so packed at first that she had wanted to leave. But Stephen, with the mixture of petulance and voracity Beth and I had often noted whenever there were possibilities of new sexual encounters, had persuaded her to stay on for an hour, buying her a drink to cement the deal. She caught the first words of an eighties song that she loved (discussing music, I had realised, always made Beth's age shockingly apparent) and the next time she looked at her watch it was two in the morning. The dance floor was thinning out. Making her way towards the bar to get a glass of water she had walked past two men: an Arab with long black hair that curled around the nape of his neck and a scar under his eye, and a serious-faced thirty-something man in a short-sleeved grey shirt and low-slung jeans.

'I just couldn't stop staring at him,' she said, laughing at the blandness of her forthcoming description. 'He had one of those faces that I could just look at for ever — sort of weirdly perfect, with something a bit sad in his expression.' The fact that the evening had ended well was becoming increasingly evident. The preamble and upwardly twitching corner of Beth's mouth conspired to create an itch of impatience in my stomach. What next? To distract herself from the man's looks, Beth had moved quickly to the bar: one last drink. Waiting for the barman to notice her, unable to resist another glance, she had turned to find this vision standing directly behind her.

'Do we know each other?' he'd asked in a slightly aggressive manner.

'No.'

'So what's with the staring?' He broke into a smile, not waiting for an answer. 'They're going to kick us out in a minute. Come and have a last dance.'

'So I followed them on to the dance floor,' Beth continued with slow satisfaction, reaching for a tissue, moistening the edge with her tongue and moving it gently along the mascara-ingrained creases beneath her left eye, 'and I'm thinking: why the heck are all good-looking men gay?'

That was the rudest Beth got: heck; my initial impulse not to swear in front of her had been right.

Somewhere in the next hour, she went on, time had speeded up. The Arab had left, and it emerged that his 'beautiful friend' — *quelle surprise* — was not gay at all. Beth had asked him back to the flat for a nightcap which still stood, untouched, on the coffee table, and

49

after a kiss and an adolescent fumble the pair had fallen asleep on — but not in, she took care to specify — her bed. She'd woken up, less than half an hour ago, cursing the ineffectual blind for allowing the sun to stream in, just in time to hear the catch on the front door click as he let himself out.

'You just missed him,' she concluded. 'But my God, Anna, I wish you'd seen him. And do you know what the worst part is? I didn't get his number and I can't even remember his name.'

With a theatrical muffled cry she disappeared into a quilted ball of duvet.

★ ★ ★

Beth wasn't keen on one-night stands. She'd spent most of her twenties trying to be like other girls — who themselves tried to be like men — unsuccessfully attempting bravado comments like: 'I don't care if he doesn't call. I just needed some sex,' before hunching with embarrassment at the sound of her own words. Now Beth was pleased that the evening's outcome had been fairly innocent. It meant that she could replay the night's events without any sense of having compromised herself. On the few occasions she'd actually slept with a virtual stranger and

50

never heard from him again, far from being able to shrug it off, she'd been left feeling brittle and ashamed. More than her Catholic upbringing, it was the result of a natural desire to be honest about her own emotions.

'Wasn't he something, Stephen?' she shouted into his room, where a pair of anonymous women's legs were just visible through the open door. There was a pause long enough for us to think he hadn't heard before the weary reply, 'How the hell should I know, Beth?'

'Ugh, that's such a cop out,' she muttered to me.

At this point I stopped listening, bored by the topic of a faceless clubber Beth would doubtless never set eyes on again, and slightly dismayed at seeing the woman I admired beyond all others behave like a naïve young girl for the first time. In her I had observed and sought to emulate the self-assurance, elegance and intelligence of a grown woman. This feeble brand of a would-be youthful sensuality had no place in my perception of her.

Later, of course, I told her what she wanted to hear.

'Of course you'll see him again. Paris is such a small place; just think of all the people you and I keep spotting everywhere. Tell me about Hélène?'

Hélène was the most famous drag queen in Paris, who spent her time flitting from club to club, stealing garnishes from barmen and throwing straws at bad dancers. Beth laughed grudgingly, like a child emerging from a fit of tears but not wanting to make it too easy on the parents. And I happily assumed that was the end of that.

As it turned out, she did see him again, less than a week later.

* * *

Beth and I had had dinner at Le Café, a little restaurant whose importance was explained by its definitive pronoun. Loud techno was blasted from speakers half the size of the place, and you were forced to wait patiently for the waiter to stop finger-drumming on the side of your table before he took your order. Subdued by an enormous slice of tarte tatin each, we trudged up the six floors of my apartment building a few hours later to retrieve a belt of mine Beth had insisted on borrowing. Breathless, and pretending to look forward to a night out when I secretly suspected we both wanted to stay in, we spotted a squat, slack-featured old man coming towards us down the stairs. Although I'd never met my infamous neighbour,

52

Monsieur Abitbol, I knew without a doubt that this man with eyes like old marbles — so buried were the pupils beneath layers of cataract — was him.

He must have been a different size once. Although he was barely five and a half feet, beneath his shabby linen jacket were shoulders you could sense had been wide. Now that his outline had softened he appeared to be wearing another man's clothes. His skin, too, seemed to have become too big for him, and I could imagine it hanging in folds beneath his shirt. Not knowing what to say, and wishing to avoid looking directly at him, I mumbled a barely audible '*Bonjour*', only to be stunned by the tirade of abuse that streamed like bile from his thin-lipped mouth.

'How dare you say hello to me when you're the reason I haven't been able to sleep for weeks. Would you STOP that infernal banging, for God's sake!'

With that he pushed past Beth and me. We heard the rustle of his K-way, like emptying sacks of sand, gradually fade as he stormed down the stairs. I lowered myself on to a step, and stared at Beth before we both dissolved with laughter.

'He, he, he,' Beth wheezed, 'was accusing *you*!'

Incapable of speech, she was still clutching a rib when the well-groomed mother of three from the floor below opened her front door and stuck her head round to see what was going on. Three neatly spaced parallel lines appeared on her forehead, her eyes flat mirrors of colour repelling all humour. I apologised in between hiccups of laughter, and let us into the flat.

That evening we had decided to try somewhere new: a place called Le Baron. As Stephen was to bring along Christine, a features editor from *20 Ans* — a cleverly marketed magazine aimed at oversexed, underactive teenagers aspiring to the grand old age of twenty — he was determined for us to go somewhere a little more straight. Le Baron was on Avenue Marceau. After paying fifteen euros to get in, the women were served free alcohol all night, while the men were obliged to pay. In Britain the place would have gone bust within a couple of hours, with ambulances queueing up to remove the intoxicated bodies of young females. Here, Parisian girls in tops just the right side of provocative sipped kirs, mindful not to raise their voices. They were precisely the type of women who brought out the British *salope* in me, and while I started dancing with a group of Belgian stag-nighters, Beth went to the bar to collect the first of our free margaritas.

It was only when I began to feel the stiff leather of my shoe cutting into my toes that I realised how long Beth had been gone. I finally spotted her crossing the club towards me, empty-handed, and smiling like a lunatic.

'Where are our drinks?' I shouted, surprised by the annoyance in my voice.

'Guess who I just saw?' Beth replied.

It was the man from Queen, standing several feet in front of her in the queue for the toilets. They'd chatted and exchanged numbers, but by the time she had come out he had gone.

'His name is Christian,' said Beth gleefully, 'and I've invited him to my birthday do next Friday.'

3

The following week passed effortlessly. I had difficulty believing it was already a month since I'd moved to Paris. It was the beginning of July, and the nights were long and balmy. June had been relatively mild, and being able to sit outside after work for the first time that year made it feel like evenings had just been invented. Girls wandered serene and beautiful through the streets, gracefully accepting compliments. A crop of new films appeared in cinemas, all of which I wanted to see, and unknown songs made me turn up the radio. Life was laced with idle pleasures.

At work there had been a groundbreaking moment: Céline had volunteered some information about her private life. She showed me, with a perfectly buffed almond nail, a magazine picture of a handbag, which she had instructed her boyfriend to buy her for her birthday. I did my best to display interest. Not only did Céline have a boyfriend, one who perhaps was in the habit of buying presents for her, but she also liked handbags, a facet of her life which aligned her with roughly ninety per cent of the female population.

After work on Thursday, I ran down to Colette on rue Saint Honoré, managing to slip through its forbidding doors five minutes before closing time. The doorman let me in with a blind tilt of his head and a subsequent, imperceptible shake, as if to say: 'Lady, if you're not going to devote proper time to your shopping, I'm not sure we can help you.' Spotting the cream silk camisole that had enraptured Beth the week before, I pulled it off the hanger and over my head. Its broderie anglaise straps came down far too low in front, but would be ideal for Beth's fuller chest. Stores in Paris are not invariably friendly places, especially when you are keeping the staff there after hours. Unable to bear the glare of the assistants any longer, I made my way swiftly to the till.

★   ★   ★

It had taken longer than usual for the museum galleries to empty that Friday, and by the time I'd gone home and changed, Beth's party had long since started. In a sepia-coloured dress with thin straps that Beth had given me, I'd climbed the five floors of her building buoyed up by the appreciative glances I'd received in the street.

'It looks perfect,' said Beth seriously, pointing a dangerously slanting glass of Pastis at the outfit. 'Turn around.'

She was already well on the way to being drunk, and more striking than I'd ever seen her.

'Is he here yet?' I whispered.

Beth mouthed 'No', a fraction out of sync with the movement of her shaking head. 'I don't think he'll come.'

It was a question — and one that I couldn't answer. Her mouth was wet and shiny, with tiny crystallised clusters at the corners indicating an earlier *friandise*.

'Just assume he won't and anything else will be a nice surprise,' I suggested, giving Beth's shoulder a reassuring squeeze and enjoying the fact that for once it was me playing the sensible, advisory role.

In the kitchen Stephen was taking out of white paper boxes intricate petits fours from the patisserie across the street. I perched on a bar stool and quizzed him about his evening with the magazine editor.

'Ugh. Remind me never to get involved with anyone in women's magazines again,' he moaned. 'Just when you think they're actually interested in what you're saying, you realise they're plying you for information about what it is to be a man so as to have something to take in to a conference on gender issues the next day.' He licked a piece of jellied salmon off his thumb dejectedly. I laughed.

'So do you reckon this Christian guy is actually going to turn up?'

'Doubt it,' said Stephen, impassively, 'I just hope it won't ruin her entire evening if he doesn't. She gets like this: sort of . . . ' I sensed he wanted to say 'desperate', but was trying to find something less harsh, ' . . . over-excited.' Then he brightened. 'But the ukulele player who lives opposite and cooks naked said he'd come.'

The doorbell rang and more guests appeared, the last of them the ukulele player, dressed in printed Indian trousers which tapered at the ankles. No sooner was the door closed than the bell rang again. It continued to do so for the next hour, each peal promising the excitement of a new arrival. As there were no chairs left I lowered myself on to the floor, next to Nathalie, a work friend of Beth's about whom I only knew one fact (gleaned from Stephen): that she smoked in the bath.

Beth had sprung up animatedly from her position on the couch and was guiding someone proprietorially by the arm through the room. His features were hidden by a mass of other, already less important faces, and I found myself craning my neck to catch sight of the man I knew must be Christian. He was standing in front of me now, smiling politely at Stephen, and I worked my way up from the battered trainers to a flash of jawbone, catching a snippet of strongly accented English. Then a voice said: 'Anna, *je te présente Christian.*'

I struggled up, pulling my dress down clumsily, conscious of how much I despised that gesture in other women, and gave him the automatic kiss on the cheek. Still the intimacy of that act did not come naturally, and I felt that he must sense my awkwardness.

An hour, several bottles of wine and one spillage later, a discussion about the differences between France and England was in full flow. Nathalie and Marie, a friend of hers, were the instigators. Their comments on British girls' tendency to wear short skirts and no tights, even in winter, had prompted a surge of moralising interest from the women, and a more basic enthusiasm from the men. Christian had disappeared from view but was, no doubt, still either in the room or out on the balcony. I felt a sudden rush of desire for attention — to see every face turned towards mine — and feeling forgotten down on the floor I joined the realm of the standing and embarked on a well-used diatribe about how the French see the English, knowing that Beth had heard my turns of phrase before, but that the rest of the room, and Christian, had not. Gratified by the laughter I was getting, and the gradually expanding group around me, I started on an anecdote, knowing that the outcome painted me in a flattering light. It occurred to me that if an outsider had been observing me they wouldn't have liked me much. Christian's eyes flew into focus, and I felt them on me for a split second, while Beth's lingered on me a second longer.

As the evening wore on I realised that, though I had not yet been brave enough to look at Christian's face full on, or stand near enough to overhear his conversation, I had somehow taken in the fact that one of his front teeth came forward a little more than the others, forming a broken triangular shape which forced his top lip to protrude slightly, and that his voice went up half an octave when he spoke English. His eyes were a dark-green colour flecked with gold, and slanted sharply at the edges, giving him the appearance of being either bored or amorous. I couldn't be sure whether he too felt that we'd been walking in circles around each other all night, but was determined to find out. Around one in the morning I found Stephen and Christian in the kitchen, laughing over a photograph of Beth pinned to the noticeboard.

'My sister says that at university Beth was always the one to suggest something really stupid at the end of the evening, something they would both regret the next day,' Stephen was saying.

They laughed indulgently. I felt sick — and very young. I'd drunk too much red wine, my teeth and the roof of my mouth coated in a metallic layer of it, and suddenly felt *de trop* in my dress. Sitting down too heavily on a bar stool I looked up to see that Stephen had left the room. I knew Christian was still there, leaning against the sink, and could feel his eyes on me.

'Are you OK?' he eventually asked in a strong *banlieue* accent.

'Fine,' I answered, too quickly. 'I shouldn't have had that last glass.'

Only then did I take the opportunity to look directly at him, drinking in the tortoiseshell eyes and dark strand of hair that lay like a scar across his forehead. He complimented me on my French, and I reciprocated on his English ('ten years in the Parisian service industry is the best way to learn a language'), and when he asked, I began to recount how Beth and I had met. He was sitting at the bar now, leaning forward on his elbows, listening. He said my name with a soft inflection on the final a, as though scared to break the vowel. How nice it would be, I thought, to hear him whisper it. That instant, Beth appeared, placing her hands on her hips theatrically and scolding: 'What are you two doing in here? Come through next door.'

Back in the sitting room a group of people were arguing over the music, brandishing CDs they each wanted to hear. The ukulele player was asleep in the corner with his mouth open, two fillings discernible in the shadowy recess of his mouth. Opposite him, Nathalie gesticulated wildly to Marie about something neurotic. I looked at Beth and Christian, seated in the corner of the room. They were facing each other on the sofa, Beth pushing a strand of hair out of his eyes. Her sucked-in waist and extravagantly emphasised breasts betrayed the lusty confidence of alcohol. Who could resist her? But before I could break their intimacy by going over and announcing my intention to leave, the pair stood up and wordlessly made their way towards her bedroom, leaving the party in full swing.

I awoke twice that night. The first time nagged by a needling sensation so akin to jealousy that I refused to subject it to full consciousness; the second feeling petulant and dissatisfied. I'd always despised girls who flirted their way through insecurity. Although in my view, even the worst behaviour could be excused by lust, any other motivation was deeply shameful. Pulling on a pair of shorts and a T-shirt, I left the flat thinking I might go for a run, but instead weaved my way disconsolately along the already bustling river banks in search of equilibrium. I had counted three bridges, a dozen sun-glazed second-hand bookstall owners and five posters of Freud's profile — 'What's on a man's mind?' — before a reassuring thought edged itself to the surface.

It was the intensity of my friendship with Beth that made me want to feel involved in this new relationship she was forming. My thoughts were simply a reaction to being marginalised. I wanted to call Beth and hear in her voice that I had betrayed none of my emotions the night before. Perhaps I might even admit how attractive I found Christian, laughingly tell her how lucky she was. Saying the words might erase all this negativity. Then the image of them both breakfasting, enjoying that indecent hunger that the first night brings, blackened out all my reasoning.

I dived into the nearest métro and made my way to the Musée Rodin in the seventh arrondissement. Rather than go inside (I had already been there twice since my arrival in Paris) I found a bench to sit on in the gardens behind it, and watched a student drawing the limbless copper statue which rose from the middle of the pond on a plinth stained jade-green by years of rain water. But the convulsed, naked figures around it only reinforced the sensation that everyone was revelling in an intimacy from which I was excluded. And no matter how many times I re-ran the evening in my mind, the truth was that when Beth had interrupted my conversation with Christian, ushering us out of the kitchen, for a split second I had hated her.

* * *

When she called by the flat on Sunday night looking pallid and wanton after a weekend spent in and out of bed with Christian, I noticed that her eyes had acquired a glaze nothing could penetrate. We sat, shoulders touching, on my window-box-sized balcony. And while Beth kept her excitement warm by recounting snippets of her conversations with Christian, compliments he had given her ('He says he likes the birth mark I have on the inside of my thigh; he says it looks like Italy') and described, with a complete lack of modesty, the sexual epiphany she had experienced, I stared across at the dirty plastic tubing of the Centre Pompidou, wondering how on earth they would ever clean it, and how dull women can become when speaking about the objects of their affections.

That evening something in our friendship was displaced, though only one of us felt it.

4

Summer was in full flow, and Paris was heady with expectation. Beth had kept her honeymoon period with Christian to an impressive minimum. Although the two had more or less vanished for ten days, her gregarious nature soon prevailed. When the four of us began to meet up again in the evenings I had felt as much excitement about our outings as a teenager preparing for a date; I never asked myself why, or whom I wanted to impress more: Beth or Christian.

I had not exchanged a single private word with him since the night of the party, having put the tensions of that night down to drunken paranoia. I knew no more about Christian than the little Beth had told me, but I did know that she, like all excessively kind women, liked to collect broken men. Christian was no different: his father had left when he was twelve, leaving him to support his mother and a younger half-brother, now a small-time drug dealer living in one of the vast concrete jungles on the outskirts of Paris that the government had built to deal with their immigration problem. Eyes glossy with

67

admiration, Beth had told me that every month, Christian sent his mother over half the salary he earned managing a large, impersonal restaurant in Bastille, subsisting on what remained by living in a tiny 'chambre de bonne' in the sixteenth. One night, when walking behind them to a café on boulevard Voltaire, I noticed Christian's gently tapered fingers, their tips iridescent on the naked small of Beth's back where her shirt had ridden up. I felt oddly indignant at their apparently genuine attachment to each other after so little time. Unable to understand the sourness of my emotions towards the first friend I had come to love, and increasingly crazed by the nocturnal banging on the wall, I decided to seek out a diversion.

That Thursday was funk night at the Rex Club. Stephen and I had arranged to join the others there after a brief catch-up of our own. A quick drink beforehand turned into several mojitos so strong they made your eyes water, and by the time we decided to leave, alcohol had stolen two hours from the evening. It was well past eleven. Conscious that my gestures were extravagant and my laughter too loud, I followed the blue strips of lighting lining the staircase into the club. Beth and Christian were standing, self-conscious in their sobriety, by the back wall. Annoyed by the obvious dislocation of our moods, I was pleased to spot Anne-Sophie, a girl from the museum gift shop, dancing with a large group of friends in the middle of the floor. I made my way over to her, and with a nod of recognition, placed myself on the fringe of their circle.

Opposite me was Vincent, a friend of Anne-Sophie's I'd met once before and registered as having something attractive about him, if only in the shadowed groove of the line leading from his nose to the central join of his top lip. Taller than most Frenchmen, and less slight-shouldered, he became an instant target. We danced a couple of feet apart — held together by our eyes alone — and when the DJ made a bad choice of record, I pulled back a little, checking an imaginary message on my mobile, and waited for his approach.

'I didn't expect to see you here,' he started in loud but unsure tones.

'No — I was bored and decided at the last minute to pop down,' I lied pointlessly.

Behind him a girl with a sticky aubergine bob and too much eye make-up appeared.

'Vincent,' she shouted, without acknowledging me, 'viens dancer.'

'In a second,' he replied into a curved palm

as he tried to light a cigarette.

Scowling, the bob approached and blew out the flame before he was able, then disappeared into the crowd. I laughed.

'Sorry about that. She's an ex-girlfriend: I guess she felt threatened by you.'

Making any French girl feel insecure was so flattering as to be worth celebrating, so I let Vincent lead the way to the bar where we downed bitter cocktails from tall glasses. Our conversation was dull, but its subtext, adolescent in its essence, kept me interested. Spotting an opportunity I pulled Vincent over towards where Stephen, Beth and Christian were half-swaying, half-chatting on the dance floor. Vincent moved in behind me, linking his arms loosely around my waist, his breath warm against my bare shoulder. Beth was oblivious, lids semi-closed and arms held high above her head, too intent on keeping moving to notice. And while Stephen interrupted his conversation with Christian long enough to lift an eyebrow suggestively in my direction, a flicker of sobriety crossed Christian's face as he took in the picture. One tiny glance, if you're looking for it, will tell you all you need to know: those quiescent eyes were unmistakable.

A little before five we stumbled into the

dark-red shadows and sobering chill of boulevard Poissonnière, where cackling parties dispersed throughout the street. Beth had been desperate to leave for some time, but stood alongside the others, hugging herself as Vincent and I exchanged numbers and a forgettable parting kiss. Left too late in the evening, it had inspired only a kind of enjoyable indifference on my part. As our shared cab sped across a Paris still glittering with timid lights, our ears ringing, a silence descended. Wedged in between Stephen and Christian, his arm protectively around a somnolent Beth leaning her forehead against the window, I suddenly felt that the evening had ended too soon. Christian stared ahead, seriously, but as we neared my flat, where I was to be dropped first, he turned and, so close I could smell the alcohol on his breath, whispered, 'I didn't realise you were the kind of English girl who kisses anyone who asks.'

The taxi had stopped, and Stephen was holding the car door open for me. I might have thought I'd misheard, were it not for the feel of Christian's cool eyes on my back as I climbed out, without even a polite kiss goodnight.

★   ★   ★

Next morning, not wanting to get hold of Beth on the phone, I called Stephen's mobile and suggested brunch at Le Café Charbon in Oberkampf. We sat on the over-heated terrace discussing the events of the previous night, pausing with closed lids to absorb the sunshine pounding our faces. I felt grateful I hadn't mentioned Christian's comment when I saw him and Beth weaving their way through the tables towards us. Pale-faced and smiling, Beth led the way. Christian followed with downcast eyes.

'Did you ask them to come along?' I whispered to Stephen, angered by the ubiquitous couple.

'Well, I mentioned we were coming here,' he replied defensively. 'Why? Shouldn't I have?'

'I just thought it would be nice to . . . ' but before I could invent an explanation, Beth was pulling iron chairs gratingly across the pavement from an adjacent table. She fell sensuously on to one, obliterating our sunlight.

'What a night that was, eh? What kind of state were you in Steve!' Kicking the leg of his chair teasingly, she scolded him for ignoring a mutual friend of theirs in the club, with whom he'd had a romantic dalliance several weeks ago.

I stole a sideways glance at Christian. With one brown elbow on the table, he was studying the menu, his eyelashes hard black fans against his cheeks.

'What are you having, darling?' Beth asked softly in French.

Both Christian and I looked up.

'Anna.' Beth smiled at my confusion. 'You'll have the 'orange-scented' madeleines, won't you? Just to please me? Oh to have the metabolism of an eighteen-year-old again — and you, Christian?'

'I'm not that hungry. I'll just have a coffee and a bit of whatever you're having,' he answered in French.

The intimacy of his reply irritated me like an itch beneath the skin. And since when did Beth understand French so well? Complaining of a headache, and ignoring the three surprised upturned faces, I left.

That afternoon I walked from République to the pont de l'Alma, willing every step to alter my mood. Instead, I felt more alone than during my first two weeks in the city. Even the river, glinting placidly in the sunlight like a young girl unaware of her own attractions, served only to heighten my sense of irritation. I was not an envious person. Nor did I normally covet other people's happiness. And yet something about Christian had upset the balance of my friendship with Beth, bringing my nerves up like a rash.

★ ★ ★

During my lunch hour the next day, I pulled a folded flyer from my pocket and dialled the seven-figure number scribbled in the corner, conscious of my motivations, but prepared to try anything *'pour me changer les idées'*. The pleasure in Vincent's voice was audible in the first sentence he uttered, and I appreciated his easy phone manner. He suggested booking a table that night at a seafood restaurant in the eighth arrondissement and I agreed. Over a tiered platter of shellfish, a little embarrassed amusement over the plastic bibs and a bottle of Riesling, I was surprised to find myself enjoying Vincent's company. His features were finer than I'd remembered: a high forehead tumbling into deep-set eyes fringed with donkey-straight lashes. A self-deprecating humour gradually emerged which would have been more attractive were it not for the occasional downtrodden expression betraying various neuroses I had no intention of exploring. Simultaneously I decided two things: that I could never feel anything other than fondness for Vincent and that I would take him home that night.

★ ★ ★

The following week took an unexpected form. Vincent and I spent nearly every night together. I was taken aback by his ardour, by the pleasure I derived from him in bed, and found the almost daily gifts of flowers and eighteenth-century novels — love and intellect are symbiotic forces in France — both baffling and amusing. One of the things I have always felt alienates me from most of my sex is the lack of excitement with which I receive flowers. For me the problem lies in the implicit emotional pressure in that seemingly benign gift. If presented to you with a flourish in a restaurant, the gesture is enjoyable for him, but leaves you burdened for the rest of the evening. They betray a kind of desperation in the giver — and remind me of our neighbour back in London, who bought his wife a puppy when he found out she was having an affair.

The determination of Vincent's attack bore results of a kind. I began to adopt the language and gestures of passion, without experiencing any of its emotions, marvelling at my lack of feeling, like a child who runs his finger quickly through a flame and is astonished to feel no pain. I learned then something that has been of value ever since:

if, during a relationship's initial stages, one side is too consistently proactive, the other becomes emotionally lazy. Why let yourself feel when someone is doing it for you? I savoured the ease with which I behaved like an object of love, feeling that the role suited me. But there was more to it than that. Beyond the physical satisfaction of this relationship, I experienced a kind of clinical, intellectual pleasure in thinking about love, or rather the lack of it. I had read too much de Beauvoir not to interest myself in its very essence.

★ ★ ★

Looking back I think I must have behaved like the perfect lover: one's gestures are always more measured, with less chance of bungling, when they are false. Just as adults, sitting silently in their cars at the end of an interminable dinner party, must compliment themselves on their pleasantries — remembering the name of their neighbour's third child, enquiring about a recent job change — I relished pretending to care. The ease with which I could respond to Vincent's romantic pronouncements shocked me. As I soon discovered, however, life has a habit of throwing up scenarios that are difficult to play out with any semblance of feeling.

* * *

It was just over a week into whatever it was that Vincent and I were doing together. On that febrile Tuesday, the covered sky, a low, insistent ceiling above our heads, crushed the spirits of Parisians desperate for air. After much prompting from me, Vincent had bought tickets for Ionesco's *Bald Prima Donna* — Paris's answer to Agatha Christie's *Mousetrap* — which had been playing for forty years at a charming little theatre in the sinuous back streets of the Latin Quarter. I'd skipped up the two flights of stairs to his flat that afternoon feeling almost fond of this man I barely knew, only to find him pale and prostrate on his sofa: a migraine. He might as well have told me he had bowel problems, I could not have found the condition more repugnant. Migraines? Weren't they the fragile woman's affectation? I sat down limply by his feet, conscious that I should touch him in some way, looking at my hand lying useless and upturned in my lap, and willing it to somehow give the required sympathetic pat.

'I didn't realise you got them. How . . . ' I tried to clear the hostility from my throat, 'long have you had them for?'

'God, as long as I can remember,' he winced melodramatically. 'I used to have

77

these amazing painkillers the doctor pre-
scribed for me but I'm out. You couldn't run
down to the chemist over the road and get me
some Migraline, could you? It's not great, but
it'll help.'

'Of course I could,' I smiled, relieved to
distance myself, if only for five minutes, from
the sight of his feverish eyes and the scaled
track of dry skin on his bottom lip.

But an hour and two tablets later Vincent's
headache showed no signs of abating, and I
wondered whether he might be thoughtful
enough to suggest that I go to the play with
Beth instead, so as not to waste the tickets.
The vulnerable silence emanating from his
huddled figure was getting tiresome. Massag-
ing his temple feebly with my finger, I
whispered: 'Do you want me to leave you
alone so that you can get some sleep?'

He shook his head and gave me a
martyr-like smile tinged with tenderness. In
my (admittedly limited) experience, relationships had always run up against one, tangible
moment of disgust from which there was no
return. It could be provoked by a comment or
a seemingly harmless gesture, but once it was
there, it festered until the faint revulsion, the
sheer disrespect, outweighed every other
aspect, eventually forcing me to break it off.
Occasionally — through boredom or lethargy

— a length of time would pass between the moment of realisation and the end of the relationship. I might have felt more optimistic about Vincent, but for a story my mother once told me about a friend with an adopted baby. The woman had invited my mother round to meet her new child, but later, while making them both a cup of tea, had suddenly dissolved into tears. Empty words of comfort and diffident back-stroking from my mother had eased out a confession: in a dry whisper, her friend admitted to feeling nothing for the child. Four months later she had rung my mother to tell her that as she'd nursed the baby through a fever, she'd felt love for the first time. But just as vulnerability can be the catalyst for love, where there is no love it simply highlights the lack of it.

With Vincent, I was worried that the whole episode might have entrenched terminal disgust too soon, and determined to keep it at arm's length while I still needed him. I did, however, have one thing to thank him for: although he had failed to banish thoughts of Beth and Christian, I felt that he was, at least, endowing me with weapons with which to fight back.

Over the following weeks, I used Vincent, knowingly and without bad conscience. His presence alleviated my nerviness around Beth and Christian, four being so much more comfortable a number than three, and his docile nature nearly always ensured that he didn't overplay his part.

That Friday afternoon was a rare exception. I arrived late outside the only cinema in Paris still showing a Hollywood blockbuster we had all somehow missed. Its obstinate presence in theatres across Paris and its posters in métro stations meant that we had, at first, systematically expunged it from our thoughts. But the film's PR machine continued to chip away at our defences until one by one we succumbed, finally agreeing to endure the thing together.

Stephen was already inside, buying popcorn with Beth, and as the cab drew up outside, I could see Vincent's back, irritating in its familiarity, as he stood chatting to Christian. I had deliberately engineered to be late, but the arrival was not as I had planned it: none of the men — because of Vincent's stupid positioning — were able to witness my approach.

'Ah, there she is,' Vincent eventually said, smiling in what was meant to be an affectionate way, but which looked to me like more of a queasy sneer.

'Here I am.' I leaned in and kissed his

cheek tenderly, to his surprise. 'Hello, Christian.'

I was beginning to enjoy the greeting kiss charade.

'Where are the others?'

'Inside, stocking up on nibblies.' Vincent used words like that, fey diminutives which emasculated him even further in my eyes. 'Shall we?'

Christian said nothing, as was his wont. And once inside, the chorus of chatter from Stephen and Beth drowned out his silence. Forcing our little throng to sit in the correct order — with me in between Christian and Vincent, where I wanted to be — had not been difficult. People flail around helplessly when facing the most trivial decisions and are always secretly pleased to have someone take over. Vincent, in the last seat on the row, exhaled with satisfaction as he extended his legs into the aisle, while on the other side of me, Christian was reaching over Beth to help himself to Stephen's popcorn.

'Why are we here?' I whispered, trying to detect even the faintest glimmer of tension in his demeanour. But his shrug and its accompanying mumble were lost in the dimming lights and inappropriately loud majesty of the opening credits. Ten minutes into the film I was still asking myself that very question.

'*I do this for a living, Mrs Van Den Broek, and the FBI know that I'm damn good at it. I suggest you have a drink: something strong. I'm going to do everything I can to get your son back.*'

I wanted to catch the scathing expression I imagined must be present in Christian's eyes, but having him close had contracted the muscles in my neck so tightly I felt unable to move my head. I risked a glance at the hand, which lay on the arm rest, an inch away from mine, as though discarded by the rest of his body. Its stillness seemed a gesture of such defiance that I resolved to block him from my mind, and concentrate on the film.

'*I want this son of a bitch nailed and I'm feeling like I'm on a roll. Friday is pay day.*'

Four men had been shot, and Christian's hand still hadn't moved. The paralysis seemed to have pervaded the rest of his body, so that I wondered hopefully whether he might have fallen asleep. But no, nothing about those knees, the caps pronounced cleft domes beneath his jeans, could possibly be relaxed. Someone's arm, Vincent's, was winding itself around my neck now, lightly passing over my right shoulder before alighting on a curling strand of hair tucked behind my ear. Fingers, grotesque tentacles in my mind, filled the corner of my vision with a flesh-coloured haze. The knowledge that Christian was witnessing the whole scene caused me such a sense of mortification I could almost hear it in the darkness.

'Stop it: you're tickling me,' I hissed, trying to keep the anger from my voice.

'Am I, baby?' He mistook it for teasing. 'Do you want me to stop?'

'Yes. I do. I'm trying to watch the film.'

Giving me a final squeeze of the neck as he withdrew his hand, Vincent put both hands back in his lap and laughed suddenly, too loud, at one of the protagonists' witticisms. Beth hadn't so much as chuckled: having seen her kick off her shoes at the start, I imagined her seeking Christian's feet with her own. During quiet moments in the film, when neither of the actors spoke and the incidental music was kept to a minimum, I could hear my neighbour's shallow breaths punctuated by the occasional swallow.

'*This is surveillance, not narcotics. Shit like this is what makes people hate cops.*'

Around us was a plethora of movement: for the past hour people had been wriggling in their seats, sucking sweets, clearing their throats, rustling wrappers and sneezing. Christian and I were a static island, shadows frozen like Hiroshima victims. Finally, having contained itself too long, my discomfort came to the fore, manifesting itself in a hollow twinge down my left leg: cramp. I reached down to rub the offending calf, forgetting that this would instantly rekindle Vincent's attention.

'You OK, darling? You got cramp?'

'Yes, just a little,' I whispered, 'but . . . '

'Shhhh!' came an imperious order from the row behind. It broke the paralysis. I turned towards Christian. Where was the harm in looking? But to look was everything. His face — bisected into a Pierrot-like mask by the screen lights — eventually succumbed to my unspoken plea. His soft sigh of frustration had just cemented my sense of victory when he leant abruptly towards Beth, whispered something in her ear, muttered 'excuse me' to Vincent and me, and left the cinema.

'What was up with him?' I asked twenty minutes later as, with that peculiar sense of disorientated despondency specific to cinema leavers, we trudged silently through the foyer.

'Oh, he wasn't feeling too great, so he's gone back to mine. What did you think then? It wasn't as bad as I thought it might be. In fact . . . '

Our conversation, and that of the two men, was arduous. The evening ahead now appeared charmless to me, and I tugged Vincent's hand discreetly.

'Well, I'm going to get this young lady into bed,' he responded obediently, kissing Beth on the cheek.

My goodbyes were cut blessedly short by the arrival of our bus, but once aboard I heard Beth's voice shouting after us: 'Anna, I almost forgot to tell you: Ruth — Stephen's sister — is coming to stay on Sunday for the week. I can't wait for you to meet her . . . ' the rubber-sealed doors of the bus wheezed shut and the final part of her sentence reached me as if from under water, ' . . . you'll love her! Let's speak tomorrow to arrange supper.'

I took my seat at the back of the bus, unexcited by the information I had just received.

'That should be fun — to meet her friend, this Ruth girl — shouldn't it?'

I hadn't addressed a word to him since the credits had rolled, and took this as the pathetic attempt at mood-gauging that it was intended to be.

'Why should it be fun? You've never met her, and nor have I. She could be a nightmare for all we know.'

'Anna.' He was smiling down at me complaisantly, my appalling behaviour apparently serving only to endear me further.

'What's all this about? Is it because of this girl, Beth's friend? Are you jealous?'

His face was close to mine, and I channelled my momentary dislike of him into the beauty spot which protruded, like a murky spent tear, from his left cheek.

'For God's sake, Vincent,' I jeered, with a laugh that sounded sour even to me. 'You just have no idea what you're talking about — do you? Why would I be jealous of some middle-aged woman?'

'I mean jealous because of Beth. Anyway I'm joking, baby. Why don't you calm down?'

'I am calm: you're just talking rubbish, that's all.'

He wasn't, of course. The very idea of this woman's presence annoyed me — and I hadn't even met her yet.

★ ★ ★

'La Péniche, that's the name of it. It's not far from where you are, just past the Musée d'Orsay as you go down on the right hand side towards the river and under the bridge. Christian suggested it.'

'Can I borrow a pen, Isabelle?' Clamping my mobile phone to my ear with my shoulder, I lost the second part of Beth's instructions. 'And it's a restaurant on a boat? La Péniche?'

Isabelle, sitting in her usual chair in the staff room, had put her book down the second my phone had rung, as though the conversation included her. She mouthed 'Yes it is', and gave me a thumbs up.

'Great. But please don't worry if you and Ruth fancy a night catching up together. I know it's been a while since you last saw her.'

Beth's aptitude at saying the right thing was beginning to rub off on me. The only difference being that I didn't believe a word I was saying.

'Don't be stupid, we sat up until 2 a.m. last night catching up after she got in,' Beth assured me, 'and she's dying to meet you.'

I ended the call and put my mobile in my bag.

'It's great fun — La Péniche.'

I looked up absently at Isabelle.

'The boat. You'll love it.'

'Oh. Yes, it sounds different.'

She seemed to be waiting for something. Suddenly, I realised what it was.

'Would you like to join us? I mean, you're probably busy, but if not, well . . . '

'I'd love to. Thank you.'

★ ★ ★

I dressed up for Ruth that night, not Christian or Beth, but a middle-aged doctor I had never met. It was she I thought of when I pulled the low-cut red silk dress over my head and belted it tightly around my waist. I thought of her, too, when I wound the cotton ribbons of my espadrilles around my calves. Surveying my reflection in the métro doors as we passed through a tunnel, I wondered why I was putting so much effort into making a woman instantly dislike me. The answer was obvious: so that I could be allowed to hate her.

'Anna — what a lovely dress.'

They were all standing to meet me, Christian looking embarrassed by such formality, as I walked up the gangplank on to the picturesque wooden boat moored to the bank of the Seine. Ruth was taller than I'd imagined, almost six foot in the sexless flat sandals she was wearing. As pale-skinned as Beth, she had neither her poise nor beauty. She had Stephen's mouth, but her face, cut into sharp angles like a cubist painting, had as its centrepiece two triangular nostrils, which, hoisted high, gave her a permanently austere look, like a governess from a nineteenth-century novel. Beth was a decorative collection of organic shapes next to this ungainly string of limbs.

'It's a beautiful dress,' said Ruth, with a touch of disapproval, 'what's it made of? Now, Christian, move out the way, I want Anna to sit right here, next to me.'

She patted the chair next to her ominously, while he got up and seated himself beside Beth.

'Anna is the pefect shape for my designs, Ruth. I'm always getting her to model things for me, aren't I?'

I noticed Isabelle, standing awkwardly by the bar.

'Hey, Isabelle — I hope it's OK, Beth, I invited this girl from work — we're over here!'

She had seen us, of course, but was too shy to come and introduce herself. Her leaf-coloured smock had been swapped for a brown linen dress, and her face was lightly but meticulously made-up.

We were on the top deck, and the tables were quickly filling up before, at eight o'clock precisely, the boat loosened its moorings and began its gentle tour of the city. It was still bright, with the hum of summer exuberance drifting from the banks and bridges. An industrial-looking bateau-mouche sailed by noisily, spraying neon lights against the quais of Île St Louis as it passed, lighting up people's dining rooms with a sudden flare as they sat down to supper.

'We're moving. Look!' Flushed with excitement, Beth winked at me across the table and I felt my clenched hands relax beneath the table.

'Great idea,' I mouthed at her as the boat gained pace and Christian waved at a group of musicians setting up on the bank. But already, anxious to make Isabelle feel at ease, she was pouring her a glass of wine and asking her about herself.

'Anna.' On Ruth's lips my name sounded like a reproach. 'Beth tells me you work at the Musée d'Orsay. That must be fascinating. When did you decide that you wanted to work in the art world?'

I turned reluctantly towards her.

'Oh, I don't. I mean, I don't really know where I want to work yet, but I'm going to study art history at university next year, so this seemed like the best place to spend my gap year . . . I'm only eighteen,' I added, by way of an explanation.

'At your age I had already enrolled in medical school.'

'Just like my mother — only she's a lawyer. And do you have children?'

'Two, yes.'

'Two . . . ' I nodded, reaching for the bottle of white that had just arrived (Ruth must have ordered it before I arrived: Beth and I always drank rosé). 'That must be difficult — having the time to see them, I mean. My mother seems to find it hard coping with just the one.'

Conscious of the vulgarity of my gesture, I filled both of our glasses to the brim.

'Ah, ah, ah. That's plenty for me: I'm not a big drinker. But you seem to have turned Beth into quite the party girl.'

We both looked over at her. She was telling a joke with both hands on her hips and the corners of her mouth twitched in anticipation of the punchline. Both Christian and Isabelle waited, spellbound.

'I'm not sure I've 'turned her' into anything — that woman has more staying power than I do most of the time.'

'Oh she's never been short of that. But I think she's gone out more in the past few weeks than she has in a long while — since leaving Ireland really, and Johnny.'

'Yes, she told me about him.' I was determined to let Ruth know that I knew all about Beth's past. 'Sounds like it was a good thing that they didn't go ahead and get married.'

'It probably was. He was a great local lad,' she added disparagingly, 'but as it turned out, he hadn't quite got all that fun out of his system.'

Unwilling to show up any gaps in my knowledge, I turned towards Stephen, and was surprised to find him engrossed in conversation with Isabelle, who had taken her glasses off and put them beside her plate.

Having nothing else to do but act out my role for Ruth as the immature little girl of her expectations, I turned the conversation to trivial matters, refilling my glass so often that, when Ruth went to the toilet, Beth laid a hand on my wrist and whispered, 'Steady: there's no rush.' There was nothing lyrical about Ruth's Irish accent: her questions were statements, her small talk openly judgemental. After Christian's fourth cigarette downstairs (despite being in the open air Ruth had made her feelings on smoking quite clear), it became obvious that he, too, had taken a dislike to her.

'So you've been managing this place for nearly three years now? And is that how you two met: Beth came to your restaurant?' she'd asked with the smile one reserves for elderly relatives.

Under the guise of politeness, her tone towards both of us had been consistently derogatory. She would know full well the circumstances of their first meeting, and be using this to make some kind of a point to Beth. I had little life experience but enough imagination to see that Christian would hardly conform to Ruth's ideals for her best friend. As a result, I had temporarily absented myself to join in a toast to the birthday boy on the opposite table, and Christian's seat was once again empty.

'Well he's certainly a looker Beth, there's no doubt about that.'

Beth shifted in her chair. 'Yes, he is, but, Ruth,' she had to stop her saying something irreparable, 'it's more than that. He's snapped me out of a mood I feel like I've been in for a long time. Everything about him is just so fresh, if that makes any sense.'

Beth was scared of her: it was pathetic to watch.

'I'm off to get us another bottle of wine.'

'Anna, wait, I'm not sure we really need one. Ruth, will you be drinking any . . .'

It was too late, I was already squeezing past the handful of people cluttering up the narrow wooden staircase which curved down from beside our table into the underbelly of the ship. Downstairs, bordering a tiny dance floor, was a larger bar than the one on the top deck, and one without a queue. Christian was nowhere to be seen. I had felt myself losing sync with the others, the grown-ups, an hour ago, but was powerless to stop it. It was on my way back up the stairs that I heard a deeply familiar voice, cutting across the discord of a hundred others.

'You're quite wrong, Ruth. She's a sweet girl.'

Despite the Gypsy Kings from above curdling with some French rap from the deck below, despite a second rendition (French this time) of 'Happy Birthday' and snatches of five different conversations, all I could hear was Beth.

'Headstrong is the word I would use.'

'Yes she is. She's a stubborn little thing and I think it's great — I'd want any girl of mine to be just like her. Plus,' there was a pause and I could hear her smile, 'Anna's just so bloody excited about everything — it's wonderful. And I'll tell you another thing: it's catching.'

I had known they were discussing me, of course, but hearing my name made me start.

'Excuse me. You going up?'

A waiter pushed past me, and I flattened myself further against the banister, waiting for something, I knew not what, to be said.

'I can see that — and I love hearing about you doing all this stuff, sounding so . . . energised, I suppose. Look: she seems fine, it's just that . . . does she care much about anything except having a good time?'

Beth snorted with laughter.

'Probably not! She's eighteen, Ruth. Can you remember what you were like at eighteen? I can, and God, it was a good place to be. And there's another thing: she . . . '

'What are you doing, Anna?'

It was Christian, bringing with him a breeze of cold tobacco.

'Jesus, you made me jump. I'm just checking out the music down here.'

'You go first.'

I made sure that Ruth knew, by my smile as I poured her a glass of rosé she didn't want, that I had heard everything. Something had crossed her face when the two of us had appeared from below, and I felt confident that she would be less vocal with some of her opinions during the rest of her stay in Paris. I fell asleep that night wondering how Beth had ended her sentence, replaying her words in my head, and imagining the rise and fall of that lightly freckled shoulder beside me.

★ ★ ★

The biggest celebration of the French year, Bastille Day, fell on the Saturday that Ruth went back to Dublin. My sense of jubilation was increased by the knowledge that I would be spending it with Beth and Christian, among others. The whole weekend was a *fête nationale*. The streets were lined with red, white and blue, and after the presidential parade down the Champs-Elysées, every bar in the city opened its doors to revellers, serving up trays of *eau de vie*.

Vincent and I joined the rest of the group after lunch, and our small party began to straggle up the banks of the river towards the Champs-Elysées. Beth had had the foresight to arrange for us all to go to the Bastille party being held at the Salle Wagram, a huge eighteenth-century converted theatre and music hall. Nearly a thousand people were expected, and the dress code was strictly red, white and blue. I'd bought a blue dress that buttoned down the front, retouched a pair of battered red Minnie Mouse-style shoes found in a bargain basket at a second-hand shop, and completed the outfit with a white ribbon in my hair.

As usual, the men had made the minimum effort, simply wearing striped shirts and jeans, but Beth drew glances in the street, fresh and beautiful in a 1950s-style blue and white polka-dot dress with a red sash that enticed the eye to her neat waist. I could smell the heat of the midday sun in my hair, rich and pungent like a sunbathing cat's fur, and a rivulet of perspiration had already formed between my breasts. Although Beth,

96

regretting her choice of shoes, clung to my arm through the crowds, her skin was not clammy like mine, which stuck to hers, reawakening waves of her scent with every perspiring step. Even in pain, she was dignified in the animalistic way that only women can be, and I felt weak in the face of it. There was something about Beth that made you want to feed off her strength: I derived more pleasure looking at her than I did watching Christian that day.

Instinctively we both stopped walking as we saw that the normally uniform grey upward expanse of the Champs stretching before us was filled with an impressionistic mass of daubed colour, cluttered with people of all sizes.

The men carried children on their shoulders, while rows of damp, pink faces shone around steaming crêperie stalls. Periscopes being sold on street corners, in order to afford onlookers a better view, captured solid gold prisms of light and projected them randomly across the crowds. Stephen had made sangria in an old two-litre Evian bottle which began to be passed around as soon as we'd found a spot by the roadside. Standing in front of Vincent I could feel his body giving off heat, while the arms around my waist could have been anyone's for all the emotions they stirred in me. The procession seemed interminable. Nobody noticed or cared when Chirac finally passed by.

'Remind me again why we didn't watch it on telly?' said Stephen as we fought through the slowly moving crowds to seek refuge in a nearby café.

'Oh come on Stephen. You're just grouchy because for once you haven't got a date,' I laughed.

'Something I'm going to deal with pretty swiftly,' he rejoined easily, pinching the skin on the back of my arm.

Inside it was cooler, and the crispness of the gin and tonic cut through my stomach, unsteady and thick in the heat. Thankful that the group was large enough for me to allow myself to watch Christian unnoticed, I deliberately placed myself on the fringe of a discussion which required only the occasional nod. Vincent was discussing the pros and cons of de Villepin with a slight, pretty friend of Beth's, so I permitted myself a few moments of sensual contemplation. Talking casually to Stephen, and dressed in a white cheesecloth shirt pulled tight against his broad shoulders, Christian had his sleeves rolled to the elbow, yet there were dots of dampness beneath his right armpit that merged into a small, transparent oval. There

98

was something so sensual, so base in the suggestion of the warm body under that shirt that I had to look away. I needn't have bothered: he'd barely glanced at me all day. Stephen had rapidly turned his attention to an elfin girl on the adjoining table, and I leant forward to ask Christian whether his restaurant would be full that night.

'From the looks of things earlier on, I guess so. The place is crammed full of bloody Americans at the moment,' he replied. 'All they ever want is a beer for themselves and a cosmopolitan for the wife. Still, it keeps things ticking over nicely and the staff are grateful for the tips.'

His was an apparently unexceptional life, yet there was nothing about it that didn't interest me. I wanted to discover whether he liked Beth for the same reasons I did, what position he slept in, and what his school reports had said about him as a child. As soon as Christian stopped talking, the expression drained from his eyes and was replaced with a vacuous glaze. He looked stupid and beautiful, like a model in a magazine.

By the time we left to make our way to the Salle Wagram, the streetlights had turned the café's white awning a burnt orange colour. After queueing round the side of the building, we were greeted by a sight I would never forget. Ushers in wigs and Napoleonic costume were taking people's coats, while a ten-foot drag queen dressed as Marianne, the emblem of France, complete with stilt-like stilettos filled with gloopy glitter, inspected the outfits before allowing people into the main room.

It was a quarter to twelve, yet everywhere bodies gyrated to an insistent Raï beat and the mournful cries of an Arab woman, sun-flushed faces miming words to songs they didn't know, smiles going cheap. Sucked into the whirlwind of dancers, Vincent and I soon found ourselves swaying together. Had he always been this keen to touch me? His arms were everywhere, whistling around my hips, brushing against my shoulders, detaching damp hair from my neck. The tiny kisses he inflicted on each inch of bare flesh were leaving trails of saliva down my arms, his stubble irritating my skin. I pushed him back roughly.

'I'm going to get a drink!' I shouted across the din, desperate to escape from him and thankful that he made no attempt to accompany me. By the time I'd reached the bar my dress was sticking to my back, and I could see that there were people four deep waiting to be served.

Turning, parched and exasperated, to go back the way I came, I registered Christian alone, standing a little way off by one of the carved stone columns. As I approached, he saw me and smiled. He was holding a large ice-filled drink which glowed turquoise in the strobe lights.

'Want some?'

He held it out to me and I sucked half of it up, gratefully, spilling a few drops down my dress.

'I was trying to get a drink at the bar but . . .'

My back was against the column, and in the instant before his lips were on mine I recognised them as being as familiar as my own. It lasted a mere second, but as he disappeared through the oblivious crowds I looked down to see that my dress was undone, and felt the delayed sensation of his hands against my exposed breasts. Fumbling to button myself up, and moving sharply away from the column, as if blaming it in some way for what had happened, I began to laugh with surprise, with horror, with longing. Then I saw Vincent, a few feet away, looking at me with the mute stupidity of an animal.

5

Paris was hung-over. Shopkeepers took down the battered flags from their awnings, and swept up dirtied strings of multicoloured paper from their plots of pavement, muttering *'Bonjour'* to each other quietly, as though fearful of waking the sleeping city. It did not surprise me to see, when I woke, that Vincent was not lying next to me. From the look on his face the night before I'd known that I would never see him again. I didn't care; I felt only relief at his disappearance, now certain that he would never tell Beth what he had witnessed. At first I'd thought he might do just that: walk over to her on the dance floor of that heaving club, whisper in her ear and watch as her expression turned to disbelief. The kiss had left me limp enough not to have cared if he had. But instead Vincent had turned and left. I hadn't even tried to go after him, preferring to lose myself with strangers the rest of the night. I left around 5 a.m., without saying goodbye to anyone.

The phone rang and I extended my arm just as far as I needed to unhook it with a finger. It was Beth, hesitantly asking if we could meet. After replacing the receiver, I remained completely still, my arm in mid-air, paralysed by the thought that somehow she knew. We met on the Pont Neuf, where a model in a transparent raincoat and black underwear was being photographed for a fashion magazine, and walked through the side arch of the Louvre into the main courtyard. Did she know? She was as talkative as usual, but there was tension in her demeanour. On either side of the Pyramid, shards of refracted sunlight danced on the sheets of surrounding water.

Sitting wearily on the low marble border, I heard myself ask, 'So what's going on?'

'It's Christian.' Beth ran a pale hand through the water. 'He was in a weird mood when we got home, well, this'll probably sound stupid to you . . . '

'No,' I urged, my voice metallic, 'go on.'

'Just that he seemed, I don't know, distant — or something. The way we are together, in bed, Anna,' she looked at me and shook her head smilingly, 'it's like nothing else I've ever experienced. There are no boundaries, nothing we can't do in front of each other.' She stopped, noticing my reddening cheeks. 'Sorry — am I embarrassing you?'

'No,' I urged, wanting to know every detail now more than ever.

'Well, last night it was different.'

'You slept together last night?'

'Yes.' She seemed surprised at the interruption. 'It was brief and, well, rough, then as soon as it was over he shrank away from me and fell asleep on the other side of the bed. I'm sure I'm reading too much into it, but it was just a bit disconcerting — as though he were angry with me about something.'

I had difficulty hiding my smile of relief.

'Is that all? My God, Beth, he was probably drunk — and tired. It was pretty late by the time we got home.'

She was beaming, relieved. 'I'm sure you're right, but — and don't take this the wrong way — I've slept with a few more men than you over the years, Anna, and trust me, you can tell a lot from the way a man behaves in bed. Normally, we can't get enough of each other. It's like both of us have the same compulsive need to just touch each other; sometimes we just do that, and nothing else, for hours.'

I swallowed hard and waited for any trembling in my throat to vanish before attempting to speak. I had slept with two men, three now, counting Vincent, none of whom had provoked anything like the feelings Beth had described to me.

'Still,' she went on, 'if there were anything

104

wrong he'd never have suggested we go away together, would he?'

'Go away together?' I managed feebly, my smile a painted grimace on my face. 'Just like that? I mean — you haven't known him that long . . . Do you think it's a good idea? Where would you go?'

'His uncle's got a little house on the Île de Ré that we can use,' she explained absently.

I was shocked. The kiss must have been fuelled by alcohol, or perhaps to test whether his instincts about me being an 'easy English girl' were correct. And I'd unquestioningly accepted his advances, despite having every reason not to.

'Well,' I said, feeling the stone walls of the courtyard vacillate around me, and knowing that I should talk, say something. 'That sounds pretty exciting. And it couldn't have come at a better time: you were just saying the other day how tired you are; how badly you need a break. You should definitely go.' This last phrase reinstated me in my important position as her friend, I felt, giving me back a vague sense of power.

Beth looked surprised.

'Oh, I'm going to.'

Pure happiness broke out on her face. She put her arm around me and squeezed my waist tightly.

'I should trust youth over experience,' she laughed with delight. 'Because it's just like you've always said: I should stop questioning things and just go with them.'

I couldn't remember saying that, but if I had I wished I hadn't.

'I know it's still early on, but I've never met anyone quite like him, Anna. I can't even find any points of comparison with other men because it's all so different. And I know the fact that he's French plays a part, but the important thing is that he feels the same way about me, which I think he does — otherwise he wouldn't have suggested this.'

She was silent for a while, pushing back the cuticle on her thumbnail as though the action might help quantify in some precise scientific way just how dear she was to Christian.

'But Jesus, here I am going on about my life and I haven't even asked how things are with Vincent.'

'Oh.' I cared about as much about Vincent right now as about the line of ants weaving their way behind my left foot. Less, in fact, as they at least gave me a reason not to look at Beth. 'Well, I'm not that keen on him,' I said, angling the tip of my flip-flop on a wayward member of the procession and pushing gently down on it. 'In fact, I doubt I'll be seeing that much more of him.'

Beth looked shocked. Even the closest friends, I reflected, fail to notice what is going on around them when caught up in their own relationships. As if to confirm this she stood up, brushing imaginary dirt off her skirt.

'Really? I'm surprised. I thought you two were quite good together. I even thought maybe he might turn out to be your first love.' She smiled, leant forward and tucked a lose strand of hair behind my ear.

I was irritated by the maternal nature of the gesture, the tantalising waft of her scent, everything. Until that moment Beth had never adopted such a tone with me. Now, there she was, smugly pushing me towards this insignificant person, this nothingness. And all so that she needn't feel guilty about her own liaison, about leaving me behind as she went off with Christian. I bit my lip to avoid spitting out the few words it would take to wipe the smile from her face.

'I'd better go home and pack.'

'What, now? When were you two thinking of leaving?' My words stung, made me feel like an outsider looking in.

'Well, that's the thing. Christian wants to leave first thing tomorrow morning. And actually that suits me too — it's all pretty quiet at work at the moment.'

We walked silently back across the bridge

and I found myself disliking it for being quite so picturesque, so smug and consistent in its own beauty. Beth was musing out loud about which clothes she should pack, and I, unsteady on my feet, tried in vain to decipher the whole turn of events. Was Christian doing this because he felt guilty? Or was it because of a genuine fondness for Beth? As I darted a sideways look at her happy profile, my heart lifted. I alone knew that what made her look older that day were the wrinkles of joy sharpening her eyes, that because she'd once had to let out the skirt that she was wearing, it was only ever worn on 'fat days'. He couldn't love her like I did.

The photo shoot was finished now, and a browbeaten photographer's assistant was busy clearing away what seemed an unnecessary amount of equipment. I spent the remainder of the day pacing my flat, berating myself for having let a Parisian backdrop temporarily erase the cynicism I was so proud of.

★ ★ ★

An interminable succession of covered, over-ripe days followed. In the evenings I tried to keep busy, spending one suffocating night with desiccated friends of my parents, another accompanying Isabelle to an art launch, and the rest of the week insatiably drinking in the lesser-known parts of Paris. But my discoveries were less exultant without Beth by my side: standing before Moreau's lurid depiction of Salomé in the eccentric one-man museum it had taken me nearly an hour to find, I half turned to share my thoughts with her, only to find that she was not there. I found squares, shops and lost corners of Paris so wonderful that I would pretend to discover them weeks later with Beth by my side, simply to be able to relive the moment with her. I was dismayed when, having sent her an excited text message about a period costume shop behind the Place Monge that I had chanced upon, I received a perfunctory 'sounds fun' in return. Since she had left, her messages had been short and sparse, with a ring of politeness about them I couldn't stand. And yet the information I crammed into my otherwise empty days failed to block her out. Still I found time to picture Beth brushing a strand of hair out of Christian's eyes, imagining, with a shiver, his hands on her hips, the way, she had once blushingly told me, he liked to hold her steady.

★　★　★

Vincent never called again. But Stephen was not so easily dismissed.

'What do you mean *nothing*,' he said so loudly in the halls of the Louvre that a far more conscientious guard than I immediately shushed us.

'Just that nothing's happening there. We haven't spoken to each other in a while. It was never a big deal.' I shrugged.

'Oh, I know what's going on here.' He grinned, inadvertently obscuring *Rubens' Wife* from the collective gaze of a group of Japanese. 'I was the same at your age — too many temptations out there to stick to just the one person.'

I laughed, thinking how little he knew me, and how our friendship would probably not exist if it weren't for Beth.

'So you've changed a lot over the years,' I murmured sarcastically. 'Seriously, though, I just didn't particularly like him. He was wet . . . you know I can't bear that.'

We went on to Georges, a new restaurant that fascinated us both on the top floor of the Centre Pompidou. The waitresses, in skin-tight leather trousers, were so beautiful that nobody cared if the service was a little slack. I was unable to concentrate on the conversation, waiting in vain for Beth to reply to a message I'd sent hours earlier. Despite my best efforts, the subject turned to Christian.

'So come on: what do you think of him?' Stephen leant forward expectantly across the white Formica table. 'Because I thought he was OK when I first met him, but now I'm beginning to wonder. I mean, Beth's no fool, I know that, but she's at the time of life where she wants things — things I can't imagine he's going to give her. And you want to see some of his friends.' His face was lowered to within an inch of the table. 'They look like the cast of *La Haine*.'

Stephen was a snob, which usually amused me, but this time I decided not to give him the answer he wanted.

'Maybe she's just enjoying herself.' I got a kick out of saying the exact opposite of what I thought. 'Do you know any other forty-year-olds like her? Because I don't.'

'Yes, but don't you think there's something dodgy about him?'

I thought for a second before answering with total sincerity: 'No. I think he's had a messed-up childhood, a bit like Beth, but otherwise he seems to be a pretty gentle guy.'

'Look, I'm not saying he's sleeping around but none of us know anything about him. And Beth's gone into this thing head on.' He paused. 'Anyway, who am I to judge? She said she was having a great time a couple of days

111

ago, so unless they've got sick of each other since then . . . '

'She rang you?'

'No — just sent a text saying she was having a ball. Over here!' he cried out to a lost-looking pair of leather trousers carrying our two drinks on a tray, and changed the subject to women.

I walked home incensed by the fact that Stephen came first in Beth's affections, especially when there appeared to be nothing he wanted more than to see her relationship fail. Stephen had grown up with Beth, watched her go through all that had made her what she now was, yet he begrudged her this happy episode. Because that was undoubtedly what it was in my view: an 'episode' — not something for us to start theorising about. I had connected so little with his concerns that I hadn't even felt tempted to tell him about the kiss. Back at the flat I put the telly on mute and sat on the floor eating leftovers from my fridge and watching the images move on the screen. I missed Beth. For the third time that day I ran my eye over the pencilled list of places for us to visit which I had drawn up in a fit of excitement at the prospect of her return. Embarrassed by the childish optimism in each rounded letter, I screwed it up and threw it in the bin. I wanted to make her laugh with tales of yet more banging on the wall during the early hours, tell her that I suspected Isabelle had a crush on Stephen. It was also, absurdly, to her that I most wanted to confide about Christian. 'Like a Virgin' was playing in a club across the street and as I washed my face I could hear Monsieur Abitbol enjoying an abusive phone call on the other side of the wall. Didn't he ever tire of swearing? It soon transpired that the abuse was directed at me.

'She's a bitch, keeping me up all night with her knocking. I'm going to get the police round, that's what I'll do. Bitch. And if that doesn't work I'll go around there and sort her out myself. That's what I'll do. Bitch.'

'Just you try,' I mouthed to myself in the mirror.

★ ★ ★

I knew that the next day, no matter how hard I tried, would be spent awaiting Beth's return. Might she have fallen in love with Christian? Surely she would be cautious, and not become too attached. Did she really, as Stephen had insinuated, want to settle down and have children? Perhaps, but it was hardly going to be with Christian. No, this was an

113

insignificant fling, something to boost her confidence.

Leaning from my balcony watching families in the street making their way home after extended Sunday lunches, I felt I'd been offered a view of life that helped put things into perspective. Later, I went to see a French film whose only point lay in giving the semblance of significance where there was none. The protagonist, a sultry French girl prone to spouting tiresome oxymorons — 'I love you, but I hate you' — sat in a series of identikit Marseilles cafés smoking, eventually killing herself over her love for an uninspiring flower-shop owner. Back at the flat I sat in my tiny Parisian bath watching the skin on my feet whiten and shrivel. The purr of the phone made me slop bath water on the floor, drenching the mat, discolouring the grooves between the tiling. It was Beth, every syllable she uttered plumped with happiness. I didn't dare ask too many questions. Besides, she promised that when we met the following evening she would tell me all about it.

★ ★ ★

As the machine spat out the purple tip of my métro ticket the next morning, I decided that the only way to break this gathering storm

114

cloud was to tell Beth everything. The underground stops flitted by and I covered every eventuality in my mind at a furious pace. The two of them had not been together long enough for a split to be traumatic. Christian would disappear into the Parisian suburbs, like one or two of the boys in my short past, leaving me with only the odd pinch of regret. Beth would forgive me because of the generosity of spirit that was her very essence. It would, perhaps, even bring us closer. One day, soon, we would laugh at the ease with which we'd both been taken in by this man.

Besides, my fixation with him and the memories of that night had left me feeling humiliated. There was no room for him in my vision of this year in Paris, the first of my real years — no room for him in Beth's future or in mine.

Content with my lightened conscience, I found that my working day unfolded easily. At lunchtime I ran into Isabelle in a cheap Chinese restaurant decorated with paper tigers, a place I thought I was alone in having discovered, and we talked about Stephen, her plumbing difficulties and the museum's measly pay rates over dim sum.

Mid-afternoon I rang Beth's office and arranged to meet her at the Lizard Lounge, a hectic bar in the Marais I knew she liked, though it was largely populated by Brits behaving as they would do in their front rooms. Still, it was somewhere I could count on for enough background noise to dilute the seriousness of the discussion we were about to have. As I made the arrangements with Beth, I felt a pang of guilt about Isabelle, who was pretending to read in the corner of the room, the velvet Chinese slippers she always wore turned inwards in the attitude of a penitent schoolgirl. Another time, I thought to myself. This was not set to be a pleasant evening.

By the time I got there, Beth had two kirs waiting on the table and was sitting back in her chair, radiant and relaxed, her breath shallow in the heat, the blue material of her dress stretched into a series of neat, horizontal lines across her lap. As she fanned her face with a flyer, I noted that she was as fair as when she'd left, and that her hair — with all the liberated confidence of a woman sure that she is loved — was less groomed than usual. When she saw me, she smiled with such utter, warm sincerity that I adored her all over again. As soon as I could disengage myself from her embrace — the warm length of our bodies against each other like a testament to a friendship I was about to forsake — I sank down into a chair.

'You look great,' I said, as airily as I could.

'Really? It poured with rain the whole week.'

'You're joking.'

For a second I thought I might be spared: the week had been a disaster, her fantasies of a romantic beach idyll dashed by bad weather.

'Of course I am. Although it wasn't actually that hot, which was fine really, because you know what I'm like in the heat,' she went on, 'but God, did we have fun.'

She launched into an effusive account of the holiday, sparing no detail, from the exact layout of Christian's uncle's house to the exhausting cycle rides they endured to get anywhere on the island, and for a moment I found myself enjoying it with her, encouraging her description of their long siestas every afternoon. And then the loud chunterings of a group of Englishmen at the bar distracted me.

'Hey — boring you, am I?' Beth joked.

'No, no, sorry. I was just thinking what idiots the English always are abroad.'

I smiled weakly, gesturing with my chin towards the group of men and wondered if now was the right time. Beth made a small, acquiescent 'o' with her mouth and in its hardened contour I read disappointment at what she had interpreted as my lack of enthusiasm. I encouraged her to continue, fixing on a tiny scratch by her mouth as she told me that she was in love with Christian, that she felt closer to him now than she had ever thought possible. I realised in an instant that I could not tell her. I remember, at fifteen, breaking a boy's heart while he was halfway through a bowl of spaghetti carbonara. He'd stared at me incoherently, tears welling up in his eyes, while I'd wondered whether to point out the creamy smear on his chin. I didn't, and he will have returned home, bruised, to discover it himself in the mirror.

Until that moment I'd imagined that my confession to Beth would come easily, a simple person-to-person discussion about a man neither of us even knew two months ago. It would have been uncomfortable, but honest, and the idea of honesty appealed to me with such sudden force that it might just have been invented. The incident would, perhaps, even bring us closer than we had been before. Besides, I was not too young to appreciate the transience of someone like Christian in both of our lives. But my logic had omitted those details that made Beth, like everyone else, human, fallible — able to bleed

118

and hurt. In the face of that small, hurt mouth, I felt weak. A second round of drinks arrived and I brightened: it had only been a kiss. Why on earth did I feel I had to tell her? I would forget about Christian — let this thing go. After all, it wasn't as if I was in love with him. The trouble was that at eighteen, I'd never renounced anything in my life: I just didn't see why I should have to.

* * *

My resolve was aided by the arrival of a childhood friend, Kate, for the weekend. The truth was that I had forgotten all about her coming until a knock on my door late that Friday night. It had been impossible for my heart not to miss a beat; I was foolishly hoping that it might be Christian. When I saw Kate's expectant face, masking her weariness from the trip, I nevertheless felt a rush of happiness. Like cicadas, we spent the following days engaged in the sort of meaningless patter that is incomprehensible to outsiders.

'So how's X? Is she still with Y?'
'Oh yes.'
Languidly drawn circles on the sand, their only purpose was to maintain a current of inconsequential chat. The weekend had flown

119

past this way: in a blizzard of semi-confidences. Kate had been curious to meet Beth, joking that she'd felt increasingly put out by my emails, which were peppered with references to 'my friend Beth'. And she was intrigued by the age gap.

'Isn't it weird going out to clubs and stuff with, well, a much older woman?'

'No,' I countered. 'She's not like anyone else I know. She's . . . ' I felt powerless to describe her. ' . . . so wise about life. But she's fun too. You'd understand if you met her.'

'I'm dying to, but you say she's busy this weekend.'

I had no desire for the two to meet. I welcomed this calm period like shade after the midday sun, and ignored Kate's requests. For her last night in Paris I'd booked us a table at my favourite restaurant, Le Gamin de Paris, a candlelit brasserie with poorly executed amateur frescoes adorning the walls, and where, until they were able to seat you, they provided free aperitifs at the bar. That night Bertrand, the manager whose face was an intricate map of spider veins, kept us waiting for the best part of an hour. Whenever he passed by, juggling a pile of empty plates, his thumb in someone's unfinished carrot purée, he would bark out to the bartender:

'*Encore deux kirs pour les belles Anglaises*.' We stood contentedly, our backs pressed against the glass, the sweet cassis taking the sting out of the table wine it was mixed with, while Kate nattered on, her soothing continuity echoed by the credit-card machine on the counter as it chattered out receipts. Outside, a streetlamp lit up menu readers' faces from above, flattening the edges of their features, reducing noses, chins and foreheads to plains of yellow flesh.

I had stopped listening to Kate. After spending three days away from Beth and Christian, my feelings of deprivation, like those of a dieter, had swollen until the prospect of abstaining altogether had become untenable.

6

It was the 1st of August and the whole of Paris had shut down. Shops were boarded up or displayed scrawled notes in their windows saying: 'Back on 5th September.' Even the patisserie beneath my flat had Sellotaped a fragment of lined paper to the door that read: 'Taken the kids to the seaside. Back in September.' It was as though the holidays had come as a complete surprise, causing everyone from bank managers to street cleaners to hurriedly pack a bag and head for the coast. The few remaining shopkeepers perched in their doorways, scanning the pavements left and right for potential customers, before flicking their consumed cigarette stubs dejectedly into the gutter.

The city felt like a department store after closing time, the streets indecent in their bareness, and I loved it all the more for the sense that it now belonged to me. The museum's staff was not among the sudden exodus, but nowhere else on earth would I have rather been, at that moment, than Paris.

★   ★   ★

I hadn't seen Christian for over a week, and Beth only once for a drink and a stroll through the Luxembourg, cut short by his telephone summons. Still my sense of quiet anticipation wore on. As a heat wave took the city to thirty degrees, Stephen was the first to interrupt the static glaze of high summer by suggesting we join the masses in abandoning the stifling city. Pierre, one of his company's executives, had a villa just outside Deauville, and we were all invited to spend the bank holiday weekend there. The question Beth immediately asked was why we had not been told this earlier.

'Because,' he answered, his words laden with joking condescension, 'I usually wait to be invited before taking a whole troop of people to someone's house. It's a courtesy thing: you wouldn't understand.'

'You mean he'll actually be there?' I asked, dismayed.

'Yep, but he's fine.' Stephen banished our concerns with a movement of his hand. 'He's one of those fifty-something divorcés who like having a bunch of young people around. You'll like him: he's a nice bloke, probably a bit lonely, but perfectly nice. I think there's a kid somewhere in the equation ... but it won't be there,' he added in response to our appalled faces. 'Anyway, he's got a pool and a wine-cellar, so whatever happens we'll have a ball.'

I nodded agreement, my head buzzing with mischief, and looked over at Beth, who was looking at Christian. The idea of spending four days with them both was delicious. I was already planning outfits, and conjuring up languorous positions in which I would be surprised, immersed in a book.

I spent the days leading up to our departure oblivious to the Velcro-packaged American tourists hampered by prodigious backpacks who tiptoed reverentially around the museum. Isabelle was curious to know what was making my step so light.

'I just can't wait to get away,' I smiled secretively. 'I haven't seen that much of France and, well, you know, it's exciting.'

I was lying, of course, having spent most of my summer holidays in France as a child, but Isabelle wasn't to know that.

'I suspect there is, perhaps, something more to it than that?'

Her tone grated, and I stared blankly back at her.

'No,' I replied. And then, in an attempt to modify my previous tone, 'There really isn't, Isabelle.'

'I just thought that,' she pulled her sleeve over her hand and looked down at her feet, 'that maybe you and Stephen . . . '

I burst out laughing, relieved without knowing why.

'Oh God, Isabelle — is that what you think? No.' I leant over and rubbed the billowing tube of black fabric encasing her arm appeasingly.

'Hey — look at me. I really don't . . . Stephen really isn't my type.'

I paused. Then I said, 'Is he yours?'

She looked embarrassed. 'I like him. Yes. But I'm not sure he . . . well . . . '

'Rubbish.' I cut her off, bored. 'You should have said. Why don't you just come out with us when we get back; flirt with him a bit?'

The idea of Isabelle flirting with anyone was laughable, and I doubted Stephen would be interested, but our foursome was in danger of becoming stale, and I welcomed the idea of a fifth party.

★   ★   ★

When the date of our departure — circled in red on the calendar on my kitchen wall — finally arrived, I could barely stand still. Beth and I had spent the past two weeks in delightful preparation, spending hours in Galeries Lafayette choosing bikinis, and an afternoon in the bookshops of the boulevard

Saint Germain buying novels to read while we were there. Afterwards we drank bitter hot chocolates in the Café de Flore next door, while laughing at the pseudo-intellectuals in thick-rimmed glasses discussing the state of French film at a neighbouring table. Beth had spoken a great deal about Christian, admiring the discreet kindnesses towards his family she was forever discovering.

'I suppose we've both been forced to take responsibility very young,' she'd explained. 'Do you know that his father hasn't given his mother a penny since they've split up. Isn't that disgusting? Poor thing's had to support his mum since he was fifteen.'

While I wasn't thrilled by this increasingly close bond, the pleasure I derived from being her confidante, and the sense that I was being included, prevented me from taking her emotions as seriously as I should have done.

★ ★ ★

That Friday, I watched the ornate gilt clock in the museum atrium — half visible from where I sat — as the hands, so heavy with gold that they scarcely seemed able to move, limped towards five o'clock. Stephen and I had arranged to meet at La Défense, at the furthest Western edge of Paris, to pick up the hire car. I made the forty-five-minute journey in twenty.

From the other side of the car park, where reflections from lambent rows of red cars created a liquid metallic gleam, I could see Stephen being handed the keys by a man in a luminous tank-top. By the time I reached them, the forms had already been filled in, and we were off, Stephen at the wheel, I in charge of the map. There was only one thing to stay clear of: the Arc de Triomphe. Anyone in their right mind avoided that roundabout as though their life depended on it — which it did. It was only when we found ourselves racing towards it up the avenue de la Grande-Armée that I realised my error. Stephen fixed widened pupils on me for an instant as he realised what lay ahead. Any motoring rules the French ordinarily follow were disregarded here in a whirlpool of egos. The cars moved in short, brutal spurts towards the maelstrom like a shoal of vicious fish. After some shouted abuse and accusatory looks, we made it out of there. Having extricated ourselves alive, it seemed pointless to worry about taking the wrong exit.

We picked up Beth and Christian from the flat, where they had been waiting for us for over an hour. Stephen slammed a tense fist down on the horn so hard that I suggested he might let me take the wheel. Christian was the only name omitted from the insurance forms so there were three of us to share the drive. He accepted more readily than I had anticipated, and as I hopped out of the passenger seat, Christian appeared, followed closely by Beth. A shadow of something akin to embarrassment passed across his face as he saw me, and I didn't like it. It was the kind of look you give someone you would rather wasn't there.

With a sinking heart, I took the wheel and manoeuvred us out of the small streets of Paris and on to the périphérique. Only then did the atmosphere in the car relax. I hadn't dared look at Christian in the rear-view mirror, but when I did, I saw that his arm was around Beth, and her body curved towards his. A few minutes later he pointed at a grey enclave of housing blocks, just visible in the distance, and whispered something in her ear. As Beth turned to look at the dark mass, I remained transfixed by Christian's slow blinks: waiting for any perceptible emotion to fill the vacuum of his face. Their voices, murmurous and uninflected, reached me in snatches from the back seat.

'If you ever did want to go and see him, we could do it together,' said Beth.

I didn't catch his reply, but I recognised the

reverential way in which he looked at her as she spoke — as though she knew all the answers. I looked at her the same way.

⋆ ⋆ ⋆

Although enjoying my role as driver, I had made little contribution to the conversation so far and, after nearly an hour, was beginning to feel ignored.

'Does anyone mind if we stop for a coffee?' I asked hopefully, spotting cryptic French signs, which I took to indicate a nearby petrol station. There was a murmur of approval and minutes later we pulled in to a service station. Leaning against the wall by a cash point flashing the word 'defective', the yellow letters bleeding in the heat, we sipped shots of coffee from plastic cups. Christian was wearing a flecked grey T-shirt and low jeans above which, when he ran his hand across the back of his head, as he sometimes did, a flash of hipbone jutted. When I looked at him squarely, which I rarely allowed myself to do unless I was talking to him, I felt a dog-like hunger. Perhaps it was because I now knew things about his body, through Beth, which only a lover should know. The skin around my eyes felt dry and tight from squinting at the road.

'I'll drive now if you want, Anna,' said Beth, as though reading my mind.

I forced myself not to appear unnaturally happy at the thought of being crammed in the back seat alongside Christian. As the engine started up, shoving the case of Sancerre we'd bought as a present for Pierre into my thigh, I felt my left hipbone slam against Christian. After an initial tension I could not believe I was alone in feeling, our bodies began to ease against one another. With every speed-bump, every traffic light that suddenly turned red, the corner of the cardboard box dug deeper and deeper into the soft flesh of my thigh, yet still I had no desire to push it away. The drive seemed eternal, soothingly rhythmic, and eventually I fell asleep, waking only once, to a wave of night air as Stephen took over from Beth in the driving seat.

The car finally climbed a dirt track through a pine forest, and we soon pulled up to what was clearly Pierre's house. Before us, in the headlights, stood a man in camel drawstring trousers and espadrilles. Framed by the open door and silhouetted against the pink light within, he gave a large, theatrical wave.

'Welcome! Welcome my friends,' chuckled Pierre, rubbing his hands in anticipation and gallantly taking my case as we walked up the stone steps. The four of us stood inside the house, bags hanging listlessly from our fingertips, wearily entranced by the sight that greeted us. A mosaic floor tiled in earthy orange and brown stretched towards an L-shaped staircase, curving enticingly into the upper levels of the house.

'Well, don't just stand there! Put your bags down and come and have a drink. You must all be exhausted. Is it too cold for you on the balcony? No?'

As Stephen and Pierre walked ahead of us, discussing the intricacies of our route in the way men do, Christian, Beth and I followed in silence. I circled her waist with one arm and wondered if Christian, at least, was preoccupied by the same thought: the proximity of our rooms. But once seated on the dusky balcony on a low wicker chair, I felt my mood lulled by the digital chanting of the crickets. I remembered, as a child, imagining the insects to be amorously inebriated by the heat. Years later, when it was explained to me that they were merely rubbing their legs together, I felt cheated.

'Ready money for your thoughts, Mademoiselle.' Pierre, who was sitting closest to me, leant forward and flicked a mosquito from my knee. 'I'm afraid there are rather a lot of them around here, and they seem to prefer the ladies.'

I felt prematurely fatigued at the idea of spending a weekend deflecting our host's advances. He was neither attractive nor impressive enough for me to use as a weapon of jealousy. True, he did not look his age, but his teeth had a peculiar brownish cast which bore testament to several decades of Gauloises Blondes, and the blue-blackness of his hair shone unnaturally in the porch light. His eyes were his most appealing feature: moss green with brown flecks, surrounded by a kindly mass of lines.

'Oh, I'm just suddenly quite tired,' I smiled apologetically.

'You probably haven't eaten. How rude of me. There's some cold chicken in the fridge, and some ratatouille I bought for lunch but could heat up. Would anybody like . . . '

But Beth, rising from her chair with a graceful yawn and motioning Christian to do the same, cut him short.

'Actually, I think we might turn in. It's been a long night.'

'No problem. Let me show you to your rooms. Stephen!'

Pierre shouted down to Stephen, who was smoking distractedly in the garden below. The *petit salon* on the ground floor had been transformed into an adequate temporary bedroom for him.

Pierre left the table and we followed him. As we reached the top of the staircase I felt my heart beat a little faster. The second floor was far from being the enormous space I had envisioned. The narrow strip of landing had just three doors, terrifyingly close to one another. Pierre leant forward and opened the door on the far right.

'Now this,' he announced, 'is your room, Anna. It used to be my daughter's. Well, when I say used to be . . . it still is, I suppose. But she lives with her mother now in Lyon and only comes here during the summer holidays.'

My curiosity aroused by the remaining two doors, I failed to register the significance of this information.

'And this,' he continued, flinging the middle one open theatrically, 'is the bathroom.'

I hadn't expected that: my own bathroom.

'Finally: you two lovebirds are in here.'

I wasn't able to see into Beth and Christian's room without appearing too obvious, but I caught the edge of a mosquito-netted bed covered in an elaborate *toile de Jouy* quilt. It looked idyllic.

'Now I'm afraid the house does have this

133

one peculiarity, which I've never got around to changing. Both of your rooms have connecting doors into the bathroom, so you'll just have to remember to lock them from the inside when you're in there.'

While Beth and Pierre giggled at this, I turned my head away slightly lest my confusion should show. Christian, as always, gave nothing away.

'I hope you're comfortable here, and if you hear any weird noises during the night,' grinned Pierre at me, 'I'm just down the hall.' An ambiguous remark that did nothing to raise my confidence in him. 'Well, *bonne nuit* you lot. I expect to see you all bright and early for a pre-breakfast swim.'

'Goodnight. Goodnight, Anna.' Beth kissed me warmly on the cheek. Christian gave me a half-wave as they disappeared into their room.

Undressing in the solitude of my room, I noticed a mulberry-coloured score, like a fingerprint in jam, smudged across my thigh. The friction from the case of wine had stopped just short of drawing blood.

Stretching myself on the slim bed, too short for my long limbs, I tried to place when I had first had this feeling. It was the sense of exclusion I had experienced as a child, when my parents disappeared into their bedroom.

Before children even have the most basic understanding of sex, they sense the otherness of *that* room: the indefinable scent in the mornings, the muted laughter that can be heard through the walls.

No laughter came from Christian and Beth's room that night, although I lay awake, straining to hear even the slightest sound. I longed to hear Beth moan — just once, just softly. Perhaps if I had, everything that followed might have been avoided. The reality of their unity might have cancelled out my childish desire to spoil things. But after twice hearing running water and the flush of the cistern before myself tiptoeing into the bathroom to wash, letting the tap dribble rather than wake them up with my painfully prosaic activities, the only noise was the rhythmical bleating of crickets.

Stirring restlessly in bed, trying to locate a fresh corner of sheet, I wondered how to turn our unexpected proximity to my advantage. A few feet away, Christian was lying next to Beth, both of them naked, perhaps, and my confused desire could not alight on one vision or the other.

My surroundings, too, conspired to haunt my dreams. A large one-eyed doll slumped in a deathly pose on the book-shelf opposite me, her remaining eye staring, infuriatingly, just above my head. The shelf itself was filled with oddly named children's books, and on the floor by the door lay a small pair of battered summer sandals, still encrusted with sand. I remembered the way Pierre had spoken about his daughter, in the deliberately matter-of-fact manner emotional men do, and the sight made my throat catch with sadness.

★   ★   ★

I awoke to the sound of water flushing somewhere behind my head. The pipes clanked louder and louder until I opened an eye. Someone, I suspected Beth, was brushing their teeth with an electric tooth-brush. In the foreground was the grid-work pattern of my cotton sheet. A little further off, the buzzing hesitations of a fly. I swivelled my head to look at the Mickey Mouse clock by my bedside: a yellow gloved arm pointed to eight-thirty. I had slept nine hours. Falling back into the pillows I breathed in the jasmine air, the sweet child scent that still hung about the room, and contemplated the slit of light above the shuttered window. It flickered intermittently, obscured every now and again by a travelling shadow — a swaying branch perhaps — and I smiled at the prospect of the days that lay before me.

Remembering the new bikini Beth had picked out for me finally acted as incentive enough for me to throw back the sheet.

Downstairs the house was cool and deserted, but I could hear Stephen's distinct guttural laugh, followed by a loud splash, coming from the back garden. Tiptoeing down a shallow flight of steps that led to the swimming pool, I began to add a touch more momentum to the swing of my narrow hips, seeking to emulate the lazy sensuality I had so often admired in Beth's own walk. I wandered over to the pool's edge and sat down, immersing my legs in the water.

'Good morning, sleepyhead.'

Stephen's face, level with my knees, rushed up through the water towards me, as he pulled my feet playfully to his chest.

'Don't you dare,' I warned. 'How long have you all been up?'

As he began detailing his night's sleep and the morning's discoveries, I took the opportunity to cast a glance around the pool. Pierre was nowhere to be seen, but Beth and Christian's tonally contrasting figures lay extended on parallel sunloungers on the far side of the pool. Beth propped herself on to an elbow and blew me a kiss. Christian lay on his front, a towel wrapped around his waist, apparently engrossed in a magazine. He made no move to follow Beth as she got up, stretched, and padded towards Stephen and me.

I'd all but seen her naked in the fitting rooms or whilst preparing for an evening out together, but had never had the chance to contemplate her body in its entirety. An expensive-looking red bikini — not the one we'd bought together — broke up her body into appealing segments, smooth elastic digging into her hips so that an enticing swell of flesh curved outwards above it. The milky skin of her thighs and stomach looked as unmarked as a twenty-year-old's. Beneath the sun's unforgiving electric glare, the brazenly seductive nature of that body was shocking. I glanced down at my legs — long, straight, boyish, every pore magnified by the water — and wondered whether Christian had ever compared our two bodies. A flash of white in the corner of my eye warned me of his approach.

'Morning, Anna.'

He smiled and knelt down by the pool, steadying himself on Beth's shoulder. As he did this, she inclined her body towards him in a movement so intimate that it seemed indecent.

'Ah, Christian,' exclaimed Stephen, letting go of my feet for a second to submerge his head in water. 'You'll come and join me, won't you?' he said as he resurfaced. 'I can't believe none of you have been in yet. You must be mad. It's gorgeous in here.'

Christian took a flying leap, clutching his knees to his chest, and landed with an impressive explosion in the middle of the pool.

'Jesus! I can hear you lot from a mile away,' boomed a voice behind us.

We turned to see Pierre's supercilious face advancing beyond the box hedge. As he turned the corner, I saw that he was carrying several small greaseproof bags and a baguette beneath one arm. After a series of trips back and forth from the kitchen, we seated ourselves by the pool at the iron-legged table, laden with a multitude of dishes none of us felt hungry enough to eat. I watched, entranced, as Christian's arm, still glistening with water, reached for the jam.

'So, what do you all fancy doing today?'

Pierre turned over-energised eyes towards us, eyes that perhaps lingered a fraction too long on me, as he thickly buttered a croissant.

'There's not that much to see around here. There's a beautiful castle about half an hour away which is worth taking a look at. Oh, and today's market day in Honfleur, so we could go and get some supplies, if that appeals.'

Rather than endearing him to me, Pierre's desperate desire to please was irritating and a little sad. The prospect of the market was greeted with greater interest than the castle, and it was decided that we would drive to Honfleur immediately after breakfast. Dismayed by the notion of having to do anything, and reluctantly pushing my hopes of a lazy morning by the pool aside, I nodded in response to Pierre's questioning expression.

'We won't all fit in to one car, so, Anna, why don't you come with me and you lot can follow in the hire car.'

While the others went upstairs to get their things, I helped Pierre clear the table and answered a few perfunctory questions about my life, unable to feign enough interest in him to reciprocate with some questions about his own.

Luckily the journey into town took a matter of minutes. The leather seats stuck to my thighs in the heat and I felt aggrieved at being coupled with this slightly sinister older man. As I had feared, by the time we had found a parking space near enough to the market, we had managed to lose the others.

'Let's start off with the fruit and vegetables, shall we?'

I followed Pierre down a narrow pathway

between the stalls, lagging a little way behind, wondering how easy it would be for me to accidentally wander off. It was then that I spotted Christian, alone, his head bobbing with laughter as he bantered with an Algerian man selling belts and counterfeit designer bags. Diving behind a white van selling pizzas, I walked deliberately towards him, taking care to look in the opposite direction. If he calls out, he's mine, was my simple thought.

'Anna! Over here!'

I turned with a look of surprise.

'Christian,' my tone was flat, bored even. 'Where's Beth?'

I looked around me for any sign of Pierre and prayed he would not suddenly appear, asking me to test the ripeness of a tomato, and ruin this precious opportunity to be alone with Christian.

'She's just gone to the chemist. We've been instructed to find her strawberries.'

'Ah yes, she's always going on about how you can't get nice ones in Paris,' I answered automatically, annoyed with myself for having turned the conversation to Beth.

The market was grid-locked with people trying to complete their weekly shopping at the myriad stalls filling the square. Assailed by a powerful combination of smells — chicken,

141

lavender soap and *moules marinière* — we stumbled on in search of the red fruit that had become our mission. A farmer selling eggs was bawling out the same refrain: '*Deux euros les six; trois euros les douze,*' until I began to think he was deliberately trying to provoke a reaction in me. A pair of hands, attempting to remove me from an alley I was blocking, placed themselves firmly around my waist. I turned to vent my anger about the heat, the egg-seller, the curdling odours fuelling my on-coming headache and saw that the hands belonged to Christian, who was smiling down at my mouth.

'Look.' I wondered whether he might lean forward just a fraction and kiss me. 'We're too late.'

To my left were piled crates of strawberries, the top punnets bubblegum pink and amorphous in the heat. And there, bent over change she was counting out loud in adorably bad French, was Beth.

'Ha! I knew I'd get there before you,' she smirked, pulling Christian towards her and planting a kiss on his cheek. 'Where are the others?'

I hoped that the fact we both rushed to answer that innocent question together might be significant, but doubted that it was.

'Stephen's having a coffee in a bar around

the corner . . . ' said Christian.

' . . . and I've just lost Pierre,' I added, as we began to seek a way out of the market.

'So, go on: what do we reckon about our host then? What do we think about Pierre?' Beth stuck her lips forward in a mocking French pout as she pronounced his name, fixing us both with eyes avid for gossip. The question and the look encompassed everything I liked about her. It was about genuine curiosity, yes, but it also bore testament to her ever-present generosity: the desire to pull me into a conversation, make me feel included. She would, of course, have discussed Pierre with Christian at length — the 'we' was simply for my benefit.

'There's definitely something creepy about him,' Christian muttered. Beth looked smilingly at him as he spoke.

'I think he's quite lecherous,' I said, seeking a reaction.

'Why? Has he said something to you?'

Both Beth and Christian had stopped walking and were looking at me, wide-eyed. My remark had been customised to provoke, but now that I had their attention, I felt unable to deliver the information they were expecting. At the far corner of the square, outside a café, I spotted the flaxen crown of Stephen's head bowed over a newspaper.

'Well, no, it's just something you can tell. Look: Stephen's over there. Beth, give me that bag, you always insist on carrying everything.'

But Beth was excited by the subject now, and refused to yield it to me, even though the plastic handles were digging sticky white trenches across her fingers.

'Leave these to me. Now go on: he must have said something. Or was there a midnight knock on your bedroom door last night?' She raised an eyebrow.

I tried to join in with their laughter, but it sounded hollow.

'Don't be ridiculous. It's just that he's very, well . . . tactile,' I attempted.

'Poor guy,' chuckled Beth, as we reached Stephen, 'he probably can't believe his luck having this nubile young girl around.'

Thankfully, the thread was broken by the kerfuffle of appropriating chairs from neighbouring tables, and the conversation moved on to Stephen's back; he was suffering a few twinges after his night on the sofa-bed, poor dear. No one seemed concerned about finding Pierre. We had all resolved to leave our mobile phones switched off for the duration of the trip, and I amused myself with images of him, red-faced and contrite, checking every sweltering alley of the market.

★ ★ ★

He reappeared in exactly that state. Limping towards us in the midday sun, a tiara of perspiration adorning his hair-line, one arm unnaturally extended with the weight of his packages, and a look of boyish excitement on his face. We, meanwhile, had moved from coffee on to small glasses of pastis.

'Ah, *mes amis*! I have some culinary surprises in store for you,' he exhaled as he sank into the chair next to me, hastily provided by Beth.

'Let's have a look,' pleaded Beth.

'Oh no you don't. You'll see what's in there later on. So, what have you all been doing?' And, not waiting for an answer, 'And what happened to you, Anna? One minute you were right behind me, then I turn around and you've disappeared into thin air.'

I glanced at Christian, hoping he would not draw any conclusions from this, but he was ordering a drink for Pierre and hadn't even heard the exchange.

'I know! Well, where did you dash off to?' I answered seamlessly. Making people think they were the ones at fault had always worked well for me at school. 'I was completely lost. I didn't know what to do.'

'Oh, Anna.'

Pierre leant forward and picked up my hand, raising it slowly to his bulbous, cracked lips. Beth and Stephen were leaning back in their chairs, watching the scene smilingly, but Christian's face displayed only a mocking lack of interest.

The journey back to the house was considerably jollier and I had decided that Pierre might be of some use to me after all. Our aperitifs had broken through the invisible barrier of tension that had been present ever since we had arrived in Deauville. Two bottles of rosé were uncorked one after the other as we unpacked greaseproof parcels on to the watermarked wooden table in the kitchen. We had decided to eat inside, as the mosquitoes were circling viciously in the garden, their heat-seeking radars whining through the air. Pierre had come to stand behind me as I separated layers of thinly sliced cured ham, strips of white fat undulating in parallel lines down the edge of each piece.

'Just leave them like that, I would,' he said, unnecessarily close, his breath tickling the inside of my left ear.

'OK. What else can I do?'

Opposite me, Christian was peeling an avocado to add to the salad Beth was silently making up beside him. With one ivory-tipped nail he slit straight across the emerald husk, holding the naked slick fruit in between his thumb and forefinger before sinking a knife into it.

★   ★   ★

You may wonder that my constant observation of Christian was never noticed, but I assure you that when I did allow myself to watch him, I assimilated the superficial details discreetly. I knew all his tics, his behavioural patterns, but the intricacies of his personality were still a mystery to me. None of the others had any idea of my fascination with him, I was sure of it. And Christian, I assumed, was the most oblivious of them all.

Lunch was a rowdy, four-hour affair. Stephen, having drunk a little too much pastis beforehand, descended into a full-blown rant about the thirty-five-hour week, eyes watery with his own convictions, which the rest of us gradually dropped out of one by one. In such instances women can sidestep political or social discussions if they feel inclined, as I certainly did, feigning house-work to remove themselves from the table; just observe a bored hostess after dinner clearing the plates before people have even finished eating. I am amazed men fall for this means of escape so readily. Pierre was alone in trying, valiantly, to ensure that everyone stayed involved in the discussion until its conclusion. But by the time I brought the lemon tart to the table, even his protestations had withered into assent.

Beth, I'd noticed, was quieter than usual. As the meal ended and each of us began to wander off in a satiated daze, coffee cups still in hand, I spotted her alone by the pool, fishing a rogue leaf from the water's surface.

'Hi.'

I crouched down gently beside her, tucking in a corner of the sarong that had begun to unravel around her waist.

'Hello.'

The mellifluous quality of her voice seemed to be more calculated for other people's enjoyment than ever. Was it hiding something?

'Are you OK? You were very quiet at lunch.'

She looked up at me, transparent blue eyes clouded with something akin to melancholy.

'Oh, I'm fine. I just find Stephen exhausting when he gets like that. I often wonder if he even believes what he's saying, or whether he just gets a kick out of making his point — any kind of point . . . It's pretty selfish: no one else can get a word in. Still, it doesn't matter.' She broke into a forced laugh. 'Pierre was pretty funny though, wasn't he?'

The backs of my thighs were aching. Beth's joke gave me permission to sit down, interrupting whatever thoughts she was having. But as soon as I did, she yawned theatrically, passed a freckled hand over her face, and announced she was going inside for a nap. I wondered if Christian, whose brown ankles tipped with cream espadrilles were just visible on the patio, might follow her. But when she passed him, bending down to whisper something in his ear, he merely nodded and kissed her on the forehead.

I slipped out of my shorts and top, extending my body on a sunlounger, and hoped Christian would join me by the pool. The heat of my flesh soon reawakened a powerful smell of suntan lotion from the towel beneath me, and I wondered hazily about all the bodies that had lain on it before me. Feeling my extremities become limp, I squinted into the sunlight for any sign of him. The effort, and the smacking white light of the sun, was too great, and I fell into an instant sleep.

Why is it that, as a child, you are always advised against falling asleep in the sun? Is it the practical concern to avoid sunburn or

149

sunstroke? Or is it to prevent the sense of vulnerable disorientation that greets you when you open your eyes? A dog barking in the distance, the groan of a door, the plaintive shriek of a bird above, and a gradually advancing bassline seemed, like an amateur orchestra, to be striving to harmonise me into consciousness. I focused on Christian; now lying on the next sunlounger, so close I could touch him. If only . . .

Then I understood the source of the low thuds: there, coming towards us, from the depths of the garden, was a man so old that his skeleton seemed imprinted on the surface of his skin. The colourless overalls he wore only added to his spectre-like appearance, and the advancing wince of his surgical stick sounded like a reproach, breeding discomfort in me. Through one half-open eye, I watched him advance, slowly and with a determination that seemed to demand greater and greater support from his cane. As he reached the tiled circumference of the pool, my heart missed a beat. He was coming towards me, looking straight at me. Turning my head quickly the other way, I saw that Christian was asleep. But when, filled with anxiety, I swivelled my head back around, I saw that the old man was crouching, a little further off, his overalls trailing through the dust as he fixed a hose-pipe to a rusty tap protruding from the ground.

Fully awakened by the moment of panic the old peasant had provoked in me, I sat up stiffly, edged off the chair and slid to the bottom of the pool. In the water, my feet skating across the aquamarine tiles, there was nothing. All sensations reduced to an infinite coolness, I watched the slow movements of my newly pale and bloated body, like an embryonic moonwalker. A cloud above me turned the world dark green, my flesh a moribund grey. I let the trail of my own breath propel me back to the water's dark surface. The sun, obstinately strong, broke through the clouds, gilding every hair on Christian's brown feet as he stood by the edge of the pool. There was something threatening about his stance: the slightly parted feet, the shadow between his frowning brows.

'I thought we'd lost you,' he said, sitting down by the edge of the pool and submerging his calves in the water.

'I thought you were asleep.'

I fought the impulse to swim up to the open space between his parted knees. Inside the legs of his trunks I could see the whiter, more transparent skin of his upper thighs where downier hairs curled and stuck to the flesh like question marks.

'Where are the others?'

'Beth's asleep and so is Pierre, I think. I have no idea where Stephen is.'

I got the impression that Christian didn't like Stephen much. He suffered his presence, yes, but there was never any sense that the two had a connection. One would have thought that two men thrown together in such idyllic surroundings — if only for a few days — might end up finding some common ground. Perhaps the nature of their relationship with Beth made a friendship between them impossible. Christian's air of indifference made it hard for anyone (except, apparently, Beth) to get close to him, and Stephen was too selfish to condone any liaison that affected his ties with Beth. Beth had created an entourage of dependants who refused to share her. She was the vortex around which we were all circling: because we all needed her — and I had never needed anyone.

* * *

When Beth finally joined us by the pool, followed closely by Stephen, the sun was peering out shyly from behind the house, the brickwork patterned with its dappled glaze.

Christian and I must have looked like companionable young lovers, lying, as we were, barely a foot away from each other, each (apparently) engrossed in a book. A sheet mark across Beth's left cheek and a slight puffiness around the eyes were the only signs that she had been sleeping. Perching on the edge of Christian's chair, she kissed him lightly on the cheek.

'What have you two been doing?'

'Just reading, and dozing.'

'I know, I suddenly felt completely knocked out. How long was I asleep for?'

'About two hours,' replied Christian, placing a firm hand around the curved white stem of her neck.

'Really? God. This heat just makes me want to sleep for ever,' Beth added quietly, for a second looking like a lost child.

Absenting myself to avoid any more signs of intimacy between Christian and Beth seemed like a good idea. On the way up to my room I came across Pierre, carrying a pile of children's books down the stairs. I recognised the title on the first as coming from the bookshelf in my room, and felt surprised that he had been in there without asking me.

'Oh, hi there, Anna,' he said uneasily. 'I thought I'd give you a little bit more room and move some of this old stuff down to the cellar.'

He was hovering on the step beneath me, the pile of books propped precariously against his chest.

'Don't worry, Pierre: they weren't bothering me in the least. Here, let me help you with them.'

'No, no.' He shook his head, pulling away from my outstretched hands, and proceeded down the stairs with a brave smile. 'My daughter's far too old for these now, anyway.'

Entering my room I had the sensation that nothing was quite as I'd left it. I could feel Pierre's hands everywhere: rummaging through my suitcase, riffling through my toilet bag. Extending the length of my body along my unmade bed, I folded my arms behind my head and allowed myself a few minutes of reverie. Replaying Christian's face in the second before he kissed me gave me an easy hit but when my imagination tried to take it further — taking in those parts of him I had only seen in the past two days, as though the sun had left the imprint of the downward curl of hair leading south from his navel on my retina — something curious happened. My limbs became paler, more voluptuous and then it was not me in my fantasy but Beth and Christian. I awoke to a tapping on the

154

door. It was Stephen.

'Are you in the bath? It's time for dinner.'

'Just getting ready now,' I shouted, surprised by the clarity of my voice. 'Be there in a minute.'

A second of dizziness as I stood up soon passed and I surveyed the contents of my suitcase for a suitable dress to wear. I decided on a simple lemon-yellow sundress. My reflection in the bathroom mirror exhilarated me: I was almost pretty. The sun had tinted the tips of my cheeks a burnt rose colour, and a sprinkle of wheat freckles had appeared on my nose. My eyes were even blacker than usual, the heavy dark curtain of my hair framing them perfectly. I parted my lips, softly at first and then dramatically, enjoying my own vulgarity.

In the evening light, the drawing room had turned the colour of an over-ripe peach. The old fruitwood furniture and polished candlesticks created the illusion of a perfectly ordered family life, where in fact there was only a disparate group of people filled with untold tensions. Beth was laughing at something Stephen had said. Rested and luminous from the day's sun, her placid beauty dwarfed my own efforts in an instant. Christian was enjoying the joke, but distractedly, seated in the corner and skimming through an ancient copy of *L'Express* with a glass of red wine in his hand.

'Aha! And here she is.' Stephen effected a mock bow as I entered the room.

I gave him my finest sarcastic look, and, unable to conjure up any suitable witticism, sank into a wicker chair on the balcony.

'Did you sleep well? That sun really knocks you out, doesn't it?'

Christian rarely spoke directly to me, and I wondered at the reason for these niceties. My self-absorption was so complete that I found it impossible to believe that he might, occasionally, talk to me out of simple politeness.

'It certainly does. I'm still half asleep.'

'And you've caught the sun. Hasn't she, Steve?' Did Beth always have to intrude into our conversations?

'You have; look how brown you are. You look like an Italian film star.'

It occurred to me from their simple-minded jollity and the relatively early hour that they must have been drinking since I'd gone to bed. Dinner promised to be fun.

'Right, now everyone sit down,' Pierre announced, pretending to stagger beneath the weight of an enormous cooked ham. 'And will someone give that girl a drink.' He angled the corner of his head towards me. 'She looks

156

parched — I'm assuming she's on the rosé. It's all you foreigners seem to want to drink.'

I gulped down a few mouthfuls of the pale liquid, feeling it tingle against the back of my throat and suffuse my stomach with excitement.

French meals go on for ever. Just when you think you are physically incapable of ingesting a single bite more, along comes another course. It stands to reason that after cheese there is dessert and after that, coffee and chocolates — not to mention cognac. The men all ate a great deal, but Beth picked at her food and didn't appear to be drinking as much as the rest of us. Pierre opened our third bottle of wine, and I laughed as, after two fruitless attempts to pull the cork out with an old-fashioned corkscrew, Stephen grabbed it from him and was instantly successful.

The two sparred continually and I suspected that a closer friendship between them was to be the only real development of the weekend. Stephen had worked with Pierre for almost a year, but claimed the two had only ever spoken at office parties, where there had been an instant rapport. I found it odd that he would then invite a work colleague and three people he didn't know to spend a long weekend with him, but as with anything that benefitted me, didn't question it too deeply. After dinner a ten-year-old bottle of Calvados was brought out, and my already humming head knew that all was lost.

The more Beth abstained from the general exuberance, the more I felt compelled to join in.

'Let's go and sit outside, by the pool,' suggested Pierre, running his words into each other.

The men began gathering up bottles of alcohol and ashtrays, while Beth and I were sent to a large engraved oak cupboard in the hallway to find two old quilted bed-spreads to lie on.

I can still remember the magic of that evening. It was so tangible, so genuine, that I felt any grievances dissolve in our apple-scented laughter. We lay out there, head to toe, staring at the moon and listening to Pierre become philosophical, in one grand life-affirming gesture succeeding in knocking over a half-full bottle of burgundy. As I watched the crimson stain spread like blood across the blanket, something inside me hoped that he would never be able to get it out. Perhaps it was because I knew, then, that it would be the only thing about this weekend to stand the test of time. Everything else, the setting, our friendships and our romantic entanglements, were transient and unreal. At some point in the not too distant future I would be back in London, a travelcard-wielding adult, efficiently carrying out a job I might even be good at. And I would remember with a smile that year in France. Beth, of course, was a different matter: I could no longer imagine my life without her.

The whine of the occasional mosquito pierced infrequent lulls in conversation, and Stephen had already been bitten twice on his shin — two white, perfectly delineated mounds of poison rising up beneath the skin — so Beth lit large citronella candles that we found in a cupboard beneath the kitchen sink and placed them at the four right-angles of the pool. I could have predicted what came next, yet still it made me jump when, returning from a trip to the bathroom, I heard the crisp smack of bare flesh hitting the surface of the water. I suspected, even though I could not yet see, that it was Stephen.

I was wrong. By the edge of the pool lay Pierre's striped linen shirt and shorts. He was bobbing proudly, his hair a shiny blue fin in the candlelight, the curve of a buttock gleaming yellow beneath the water's surface. Stephen was crouching by the edge of the pool, tittering like a schoolboy. One sharp tug on his arm from Pierre and he, too, fell in, pulling off clothes made heavy with water. I had never seen Stephen naked before and experienced a stab of predatory curiosity which was swiftly satisfied when, as he strained up by the tiled edge of the pool to retrieve his wine glass from Beth, I caught a glimpse of surprisingly luxuriant light-brown hair and everything it attempted to hide. Slightly repulsed by the sight, my wish not to be drawn into this puerile scene fortified, I continued to enjoy my detached position at the top of the stairs, where I had not yet been noticed.

'Hey, Anna, come down from there and have a dip,' cried Pierre. 'It's lovely in here.'

I tiptoed warily down the stairs, shaking my head.

'No way. I'm perfectly happy as I am: warm and dry.'

Beth was huddled against Christian on the blanket, inches away from the stain. Sitting there like that they looked like crash survivors; scared rather than amused, she clearly as anxious as I not to be drawn into the game.

'What are they like, Anna?'

I shook my head. 'They're lunatics.'

Christian stood up and pulled his T-shirt over his head.

'What are you doing?' Beth asked.

'What do you think I'm doing?'

Fingering the top button of his jeans, he looked down and laughed at the apprehension evident, for very different reasons, in both of our faces.

But with one sharp tug on his hand, Beth pulled him back down. 'Don't.'

And despite a twinge of disappointment, I was relieved: I did not want Christian's nudity desexualised.

* * *

Stephen tired of the game first, clambering out clumsily despite Pierre's playful attempts to restrain him. But whereas Stephen quickly dried off and dressed, Pierre, luxuriating in a mistaken sense of youthfulness, wrapped a threadbare towel hardened by years of beach use around his waist and lay back on the quilt.

'*Alors*, Anna, my dear? I hadn't put you down as '*une timide*'.'

'I'm not,' I replied defensively, feeling my humour gradually blacken. 'I just didn't feel like a swim. And I do like to keep a little dignity,' I smirked to avoid any impression of prudishness.

'Dignity? Did you hear that, Christian?' With considerable effort Pierre turned

161

towards him, dividing up his fat neck into five thick rolls.

'I'm going to bed,' exhaled Beth, as though she'd been trying to get the words out for quite some time, and Pierre's question had finally allowed her to do so.

'*Bonne nuit, ma jolie.*'

Pierre was becoming embarrassing now, leaning across me to give Beth a kiss goodnight, placing the weight of his torso across my lap and one 'steadying' hand on my knee.

'Don't get up, Anna,' said Beth as I tried to free myself.

'Oh, OK. Sleep tight. See you in the morning.'

I turned to Christian, concern for Beth surpassing my interest in him.

'Is she all right? She's been off-colour all day.'

'She's fine. Women's things, I think.'

'Oh. Right.' And then, more to myself than to Christian, 'Why didn't she say so?'

For almost an hour we stayed up, trying to revive the enchanted quality of the early part of the evening. When we discovered that it had quite gone, it was time for bed. But there was one last highlight for me. When Pierre finally fell asleep, with an empty glass of wine in his hand and a thread of saliva joining his parted lips, Stephen had been forced to break his slumber and take him to bed. Christian and I then shared a few moments of silence as we watched a moth dance around the only remaining candle, daring itself to swoop ever closer to the flame before fluttering away, delighted at having cheated death.

'I suppose we should go up.'

It was the kind of remark made by people when they do not wish to be alone with somebody. We walked silently up the stairs to the cooing sounds of Stephen's voice as he put Pierre to bed.

'There we go, *mon ami*. And I'll put your glass of water just here.'

Standing outside our two doors on the landing, I was drunk enough to lean in first for a goodnight kiss on the cheek, hoping, once I was back in my room, that he had missed the trace of supplication in my face.

'*Bonne nuit.*'

'*Bonne nuit*, Anna.'

★ ★ ★

Two days. We had only two days left. It was with this bleak thought that I awoke the following morning. My throat was dry and a fuzzy coating on my teeth reminded me of the previous night's excesses. I sank back,

163

demoralised, wishing for a second that I was back in Paris. Despite the idyllic surroundings, the weekend wasn't going as I had hoped. Beth and I had scarcely spent a second alone together, and Christian wasn't paying me the kind of attention I craved. Our host's solicitude, on the other hand, was almost insulting.

'Anna! Beth!'

There he was now, his voice booming up the stairs. Sticking my head out of the door I saw Beth's face appear directly to my right, her hair matted into a tangled clump at the back of her head.

'What does he want?' I whispered.

'Dunno. Whatever it is, it's way too early.'

'How do you girls fancy a trip to the beach this morning?' thundered the voice from below. 'It's beautiful out there.'

I perked up instantly. Getting out of the house was exactly what we all needed, and for me it offered a promising opportunity to be admired by the outside world. Beth, too, seemed to think it was a good idea: smiling and rubbing her eye with a fist she retreated into her room, where I overheard her putting the suggestion to Christian. Downstairs Stephen sat in the kitchen stirring a filter coffee and staring at the purple liquid as though incredulous that anyone could drink the stuff. Pierre appeared a few minutes later, and was greeted by Stephen with the ironic air with which one welcomes people who have drunk too much the night before.

'So where's the nearest beach?' I asked impatiently. 'And how long will it take to get there?'

'Trouville has got some lovely little coves, but they tend to get a bit crowded at this time of year.'

'Maybe we should try somewhere less popular then,' suggested Stephen.

'Oh Stephen — stop being difficult,' I cut in peevishly, pressing a finger to my throbbing temple. 'Trouville's obviously the easiest one to get to so let's just go there.'

'Well, I'm definitely not driving,' announced Beth, strolling in with her beach bag in one hand and dark glasses in the other. 'I feel bloody awful.'

'And you didn't drink nearly as much as I did . . .'

She ran a hand lightly over the top of my head. 'I presume you feel fine. I never got hangovers until my late twenties . . .'

'I'll drive, Beth,' volunteered Stephen. 'I'm sure we can all fit in one car.'

'Let's get a picnic together and head off there pronto. Where's Christian?'

'He's just showering now; he'll be down in a few minutes.'

'Excellent. Why don't you two sort the food out and we'll leave in half an hour.'

* * *

By the time we arrived at the opening of the winding track leading down to the beach, it was gone eleven and scorching. Enjoying the concentrated sun on my base of my neck where my hair was tied back, I strode on ahead of the others. Pierre, I could have guessed, was the type to overburden himself hopelessly for such excursions. When, with an infantile feeling of joy, I turned to point out the blue mouth of sea opening up before us, I spotted him lagging behind, struggling, camel-like, beneath raffia mats, a hamper of food and an inflatable dinghy too small to carry anyone in our group.

He had the residual impulses of a parent and no child with which to make use of them.

The length of the beach was already densely populated with people, a chequered pattern of garish towels placed alongside each other in a game of human chess. We settled on a shadowy place by a tree, so that Beth and I could prostrate ourselves in the full sun, while the men, feeling somewhat more fragile, were able to seek shade beneath it.

Directly in front of us, four teenage boys had looked up at Beth and me and whispered to each other in French. Stephen and Pierre ran straight into the water, spraying up sand with their heels as they went. Pulling his T-shirt off, Christian busied himself with the parasol. I could see the symmetrical lines of his ribs through the buttery skin of his back as he bent forward.

The heat of the sun seemed to be entirely focused on the top of my head now, as though a filter were conducting it straight into the back of my cranium. I sat down heavily on a towel, conscious that a few steps were all I needed to deliver me from the discomfort, but somehow reluctant to take them. Luckily Beth pulled me up roughly by the hand and led me into the sea. In an instant, the world went from unbearably hot to serenely cool. As I surfaced the noises around returned, the crying child who had fallen head first into the sand and was now rubbing gritty fists into her eyes, the Algerian selling cold drinks and ice creams a little further off, the scolding mothers. Beth, hazy in her blue swimsuit, was standing to my right, staring at me.

'You OK?'

'Yes.' I spat out some salt water. 'Is it me or

167

is it even hotter than yesterday?'

'I think it must be. Look, there's a thermometer outside the lifeguard's hut. Let's go and check it out.'

We hopped across the few metres of burning sand to find that it was forty-one degrees.

'That's the hottest summer in eleven years, in case you're wondering,' the lifeguard informed us. 'Old people are dying in Paris. It was in the papers this morning.'

I hadn't seen a newspaper since we'd arrived in Normandy, enjoying feeling cut off from reality. Even Stephen, who usually read *Le Figaro* every day, was too lazy to drive to Honfleur to buy it.

'Jesus. Is there a telly at the house? We'd better watch the news when we get back.'

Beth walked off in front of me and I wondered why she was wearing a swimsuit instead of the bikini she had worn on the first day.

'We chose the worst possible day to come to the beach. We'll all have to drink lots of water and stay in the shade,' she added in her best hospital-corners voice, 'and if it gets too hot, we'll just have to go home.'

But it was too hot already and none of us was sensible enough to go home — or perhaps nobody wanted to be the first to

168

suggest it. Drunk on heat, our five bodies lay inert on their towels, subjected to the full fury of the midday sun which robbed us of even the tree's shade. The temperature wasn't so much uncomfortable as annihilating. I was sandwiched between Pierre and Christian, who, regrettably, had spent the past two hours turned towards Beth. I lay there, rigid and uncomfortable next to Pierre, like a frigid bride on her wedding night, until his rhythmic snoring finally sent me into a bright white doze.

I awoke to a disconcerting sight: the beach looked like the aftermath of a genocide, bodies lying twisted across their towels as though struck down in the midst of building a sandcastle, or putting on suncream. The babies had stopped crying, the birds were silent, even the drinks seller was nowhere to be seen. There was only the sound, incessant and haunting, of the waves beating their monotonous hymn to eternity. A pool of sweat had formed in the hollow of my breastbone, and the downy blonde hairs leading down from my navel glittered silver.

Between the twin hillocks of my bent knees I could see that there was bare sand where the teenage boys had been. Pierre was still sleeping, and there was no sound from Christian or Beth to my left. I turned on my side and imagined what the consequences would be were I to move a fraction closer and gently slip my arm around his waist. I was so close that my world was made up entirely of the skin on his back. Before I could imagine what it would be like to touch it, I watched with half-closed eyes my own forefinger running gently along the biscuit-coloured mid-section of his spine. He didn't jump, but when I repeated the gesture, made a tiny movement towards me with the lower part of his body — the kind a sleeper unconsciously makes towards his lover.

At three o'clock, Pierre caved in, and we all followed suit.

'*Ah non,*' he panted. 'It's just too hot. I don't think we should be out here any longer.'

'You're right. And we've run out of water.'

'Lets go back.'

The return journey was subdued. Pierre drove with the bad grace that follows a nap. Crowded in the back seat, I was forced against the door, while Beth and Christian slumped against each other silently, still half-asleep. Stephen was the only one attempting to be lively.

'Why don't we all go out for dinner later? Pierre, what do you say? It would be nice to try somewhere local. Do you know anywhere good?'

Pierre began eulogising a seafood restaurant overlooking the sea in Deauville. When he became excited about something, his throat whirred with enthusiasm: the phlegm accumulated from years of smoking Gauloises Blondes bubbling out greasily into words. I was keen to go out that night, but yearned first for my cool bed sheets.

Back at the house, I was surprised to find that I was the only one to retire directly to my room. The others, revived or perhaps still feverish with sun, began their evening then, despite the early hour. The late-afternoon sun was still strong enough for me to rush to close the shutters as soon as I entered my room. Even the white bedspread — exposed to its glare all afternoon — had sucked in the heat and felt uncomfortable beneath my prickling limbs. A whoop of laughter and the sounds of clinking ice rose from the terrace, while Pierre's old record player crackled out the first bars of Bing Crosby's 'Night and Day'. Pink spots danced before my closed eyes, and I tried to picture the scene below. A second burst of laughter made me think that someone, probably Stephen, had grabbed Beth, and was waltzing with her across the balcony, gracelessly dipping her, while an inadvertent snort from Pierre sprayed rosé down his shirt front. Craving sleep, but realising it was impossible until my body temperature had dropped a few degrees, I staggered into the bathroom and pulled the twin ties on either sides of my bikini bottoms, letting them slip to the floor, before switching the shower on.

I knew, without turning around, that he was behind me, though not how long he'd been there. The thin jets of water were battering the bath's enamel with enough force to drown out the noise of the door opening. Oddly, I felt no embarrassment at my nakedness. And it seemed natural, a few seconds later, to feel the damp waistband of his shorts against my stillwarm back. Twisting my neck around, still holding the shower head awkwardly in my right hand, I kissed him.

But he wasn't interested in my mouth, and was looking down at my body with greed. As he tasted it all, methodically, kneeling so as to reach me better, I became impatient, pulling his head up by the hair, untying the cord of his trunks and marvelling at the perfect symmetry, the delicate craftsmanship of that V-shaped shadow. But my dizzying desire made it impossible for me to settle on a single part of his salty flesh. Because I couldn't wait any longer, I pulled him back on the tiled floor, making my body his cushion, inhaling the burnt smell of his hair and closing my eyes. Far from being transported into another place, I could still hear the shower jets beating against the bath, feel the unexpectedly cold sole of his right foot against my ankle. And then, the suddenness hurting a little, we began to move together and I was Beth, graceful, compliant, providing a rich shelter for this body as familiar as my own. Later, while I struggled to regain my vision, with my head pressed against the curved porcelain foot of the basin, Christian leant over and slowly ran his tongue over my lips, made dry with breathlessness. I smiled at him, and the memories that were now mine for ever. He was silent. His ruffled head turned away from me, a leg still threaded between mine.

★   ★   ★

'I've given you our very best table, Monsieur Lhermite,' said the Poisson d'Avril's maître d' as he led us out on to a crowded veranda speckled with fairy lights. It was late and the sea was a sinister blanket on the horizon, hiding its wares from the sky. The other diners were already on their main courses, and Stephen was becoming peevish with hunger. The patron slapped Pierre's back a

173

great deal before allowing him to sit down, and I was grateful to be able to pour myself a glass of iced-water from the jug on the table and pass it along my burning brow. We were all lightly sunstruck. The skin on my face and shoulders felt tight, as though it had been slapped, and Pierre's nose was crimson.

I looked at Beth, who was standing behind Christian, arms loosely linked around his waist, speaking in broken French to the patron. She was wearing a dress of indefinable fabric, in midnight blue, and emanated the air of absolute calm special to women who have been beautiful all their lives.

'God, I'm starving. I wish everyone would just sit down so we could eat,' seethed Stephen in my ear.

'*Un petit Calvados pour commencer?*' suggested the patron.

'I don't see why not.' Pierre sat down noisily, and began to flick through the menu, unable to keep still. 'Sorry about him. He does go on a bit. Are you hungry?'

'She's all right. It's me you need to worry about,' said Stephen with a humourless laugh.

Beth seated herself opposite me, while Christian sat at the end of the oval table in between us. We hadn't exchanged a word

174

since our encounter that afternoon, which had left me feeling quenched, sophisticated and pleasantly debauched. As he sat down now, his knee knocking into mine, I felt a wave of heat travel through my face and neck.

'I'm not cramping you, am I?'

Beth wasn't listening, having been called on to examine Stephen's latest mosquito bite.

'No.' I laid a finger, so light it might have been a stray hair, on the muscled undulation of his thigh.

'Right, you two.'

Beth was suddenly fixing us both with her clear blue gaze.

I willed Christian to be brave enough not to pull away.

'What are we having to eat? If you want we could all share one of those things.'

She pointed to an enormous seafood platter on the next table which neither Christian nor I could have cared less about.

'No, I think I'd prefer to start with the *salade d'endive*, and then . . . .'

He was showing her now, on the badly typed menu with its slightly elevated 'r's, what he had decided on, leaving my hand resting, quite naturally, where it was.

★　★　★

We spanned many topics that night, conscious that it was our last together. We were due to leave the following evening and it felt as though we were back in Paris already. We spoke about death, Houellebecq, the French health service and Johnny Hallyday. Finally, with a kind of meandering grace, the subject turned to love.

I had said very little, Christian even less, but Pierre was gesticulating, moist-eyed as he made an impassioned yet entirely abstract speech on the subject.

'Now it's very clear to me,' he finished, 'that this little one here has never been in love.'

For all the frivolity of the atmosphere I took this badly. I thought it a rude comment to make at the time and I am still offended by it now. The reason for my indignation was that it was true. But he knew nothing about me or my past, and that night particularly, when I felt like one of them, the statement seemed like a slur. Strange that the thing we criticise most in ourselves provokes the greatest sense of outrage when pointed out by someone else. I knew that, at eighteen, my smiles were not yet backlit with secret emotion, and that when I was sad I was simply sad, without any of the sweetness that an *éducation sentimentale* provides.

Luckily, there was no call for me to respond. The subject was swiftly buried when Pierre nearly overturned the table by jumping up to ask the waiter to take a group photograph. I still have a copy of it today. Occasionally I take it out from between the leaves of the book in which it is placed and examine it, marvelling at how much information there is in a single, over-exposed snapshot. There is always one person — in this case Pierre — who, in photographs as in life, seems to be partially cut from the frame. He leans in, as though his life depends on it, grasping Stephen around the neck in an act of aggressive friendship. Stephen is red-eyed and waxy-faced — the only person out of focus. He is looking at the camera with the same polite discomfort one reserves for chance encounters with people who have long since dissolved into one's past.

The only gap in the bouquet of our five seated figures lies between Stephen and me. In retrospect this seems to confirm what I always suspected: that there was never any real bond between us. Christian sits at the centre, any dominance of the scene lost by the fact that his eyes are closed. And while my left arm is hidden behind his back (where unknown to everyone, and to the camera, my thumb was travelling slowly up and down his

177

spine), his is draped loosely around Beth's shoulders, while she attempts to hide her stomach with a casually placed hand. Next to her, I look like a gangly adolescent, uneasy in my own skin, my furtive eyes avoiding the camera. The events of that afternoon, those of the future, and the false jollity of that dinner, are there for everyone to see.

I hadn't expected to get much sleep that night and sure enough I couldn't: my tongue felt gigantic in my mouth, my limbs heavy. My lower stomach ached with the excesses of the afternoon, refusing to let me forget what had happened. Images of Beth's smiling face alternated with Christian's looking down at me, made ugly by pleasure. But I was too excited, too pleased with myself, to feel guilt.

★   ★   ★

Our last day unfolded quietly, every action tainted by our imminent departure. Beth had come down late, and sat hunched on a chair by the pool wrapped in an old Japanese kimono she had found in the cupboard in her room. I watched her and Christian above the tightly typed pages of my book, noticing how they interacted with one another, and how much more needy Beth had become. Even with her eyes closed, she kept her hand on a part of him at all times. When he spoke to her, she began to smile at the first word, unaware of what he was about to say. My thoughts dissolved as an icy jet of water burned through the base of my back, and down my bikini bottoms. It was Stephen.

'Stop it,' I cried. My book fell to the ground with a muted thud.

'I thought you looked a little too comfortable there,' he smiled.

'I didn't even hear you coming. Have you only just woken up?'

'Yes. I had an interesting night.'

Assuming Stephen was about to go into typically whingeing details about the mattress or the noises of the plumbing, and failing to register the discomposure in his eyes, I lay back down on my sunlounger and sighed with lack of interest in what I was about to ask: 'Why, what happened?'

'Well . . . I'll tell you later. Beth! Do you still want to go and get those things for your old man?'

'Yes please!'

Beth was up now, making her way into the house, the delicate silk of her kimono catching against the stone steps on the way.

'What things?'

'These boxes of crystallised fruit she saw in a confiserie next to the supermarket the other

179

day. Apparently her dad couldn't get enough of them when they once had a family holiday in Toulouse, so she wants to send him some.'

'And you're going to drive her down there? That's very sweet.'

And very convenient for me, I added to myself.

'We won't be long. I want to make the most of all this before we leave this evening.'

But there was one last impediment before I could be alone with Christian.

'Where's Pierre?' I called out to Stephen's retreating back.

'He went to get the papers a while ago. Oh, and it's true what they told us. Apparently people really are dying in Paris: it's a massive heat wave.'

I waited, so still that the pulse in the vein on the underside of my arm seemed to beat aloud, until I heard the slam of the front door and the throttle of the engine. Lying on my front, with my head turned away from Christian and my arm bent up over my face, I wondered how long it would take him to come over. Would he stroke my hair first? Or just turn me over and kiss me straight away? Minutes passed, and still I heard and felt nothing. My excitement turned to mortification: he was better at this game than I was, and he knew that I was waiting.

180

'If you want it so much why don't you come here?'

I might not have heard him, had I not been straining for the slightest sound. Submissive, forgetting my dignity, I stood up and walked over to him, sheltering the sun from my eyes with one hand. Suddenly shy, and unsure of what to do next, I perched on the edge of his chair and put a hand, tentatively, on his foot. Christian withdrew it as he pulled his body into an upright position. Seizing me with both hands by the nape of my neck he bent forward. The kiss was good: warm, not too devouring, long and tranquil. A kiss that, after the first shiver, imbued me with lethargic contentment and did not disturb the perfect equilibrium of our two bodies. A familiar wheezing noise was all the while growing louder, its source suddenly coming into view in the reflective brown irises of Christian's eyes. It was the gardener, standing perfectly still a few feet away, his eyes buried deep within their hollows.

We sprang apart, turning what should have been perfectly natural into the guilty secret that it was. There was no need to worry. He did not know which of we five were couples, and besides, I was beginning to think there was something voyeuristic about the old man.

'Can we help you?' I asked him coldly in French.

'Monsieur Pierre . . . ?'

'Is not here. I'll tell him you came by.'

The exchange was over and yet still he stood there, the pink flesh on the inside of his bottom lip slick with saliva.

'Was there anything else?' asked Christian, jerking his chin at him with unmistakable rudeness.

'No . . . I don't think so,' mumbled the old man, beginning his slow journey back to the cottage at the bottom of the garden.

We had no reason to be scared but the interruption had broken the moment, and when Pierre came back ten minutes later, we were at a respectable distance from each other. Our host, too, seemed on edge. He flitted to and fro from the kitchen all afternoon, bringing full glasses, and taking away empty ones, until Beth, relaxing after her morning's expedition, had to forcibly sit him down.

'Pierre, you've been spoiling us all weekend, now just relax. Think how wonderful it'll be when you wake up tomorrow morning and we've gone.'

'How can you say that? Do you know how much fun I've had this weekend? I'll miss you all terribly.'

182

He looked at me as he said this, and I wondered if the reason for his mood was the realisation that he would never succeed in seducing me. His extended parting hug early that evening, our bags crammed into the boot of the car and Stephen already at the wheel, confirmed as much.

'You will come back next summer, won't you?'

'Of course!' 'Yes.' 'We'd love to,' we all cried in unison, knowing full well that none of us would. Pierre's dry goodbye kiss missed my mouth by a fraction of an inch, but I managed to check my revulsion, pressing his hands and saying: 'It has been wonderful: I shall never forget it.'

For once, I wasn't lying.

★ ★ ★

I hadn't minded the fifteen-minute silence with which our drive back to Paris began, spending the time gazing unseeingly at the countryside and replaying, for the tenth time that day, the events of the night before. The truth was that I felt closer to Beth than ever before: we had tasted the same sensations and I would know now, when she spoke of Christian, exactly what she meant. After twenty minutes of no one saying a word, I suddenly remembered Stephen's cryptic comment earlier. 'So what were you going to tell me, Stephen?'

'Well, you won't believe it.'

'Tell us.'

I had never seen Stephen blush before but his forehead and the corners of his nose had begun to redden.

'Go on.'

'Ahem, well, Pierre, as it turns out — how shall I put this — wasn't interested in you, Anna.'

It was my turn to redden.

'He was interested in me.'

'What?'

Beth was sitting in the back with Christian, but I could hear the broad smile in her voice.

'No way. Stephen, what happened?'

And as we drove through the centre of Deauville, past the marble-fronted casino towards the motorway, Stephen described how, when the rest of us had gone to bed the night before, Pierre had convinced him to have one last glass of Calvados. The temperature had dropped, and they had come in from the balcony and sat on Stephen's makeshift bed in the sitting room, deconstructing a couple of their work colleagues, until, apropos of nothing, Pierre began to speak of his loneliness. His flat in Paris was too big for him after the divorce, he said, and the house in Normandy was a painful reminder of his little girl.

'You just need to find another woman to share those things with,' Stephen had attempted reassuringly.

'But that's the thing,' Pierre had replied, draining his glass with one last gulp. 'I broke up with Nicole because I realised that no woman could ever really make me happy.'

It had taken Stephen a few seconds to register what Pierre was saying, but only one to predict what was about to happen. An arm had slid behind his back, threatening to curl around his shoulder at any moment.

'Please don't say any more, please don't,' Stephen had silently prayed.

'But I think maybe you know all this. And I don't think I'd be wrong to say that it was, perhaps, the reason that you agreed to come down here?'

'But you are wrong, and it's not the reason I came here at all.' Stephen had leapt up now, appalled but full of pity for the poignant picture before him: a middle-aged man who had realised too late in life who he was, and was unable to make the transition gracefully.

We listened open-mouthed, each one of us no doubt drawing our own conclusions, no one knowing quite what to say. I was surprised, but my chief concern was that no one should remember my embarrassing pronouncements about Pierre flirting with me.

'But we all thought — well, Anna thought — that he was trying it on with her.'

'I didn't quite say that, Beth. I never said that.'

'No, I know, darling, but . . . '

'Well, Anna,' Stephen laughed bitterly. 'I guess the world doesn't revolve around you after all.'

In the rear-view mirror I could see Christian looking out of the window, smiling.

7

Confronted once again at the museum by Berthe Morisot's reproachful eyes, I had the disconcerting feeling that nothing had changed. Out of the elaborate confines of her frame she stared at me as if to say: 'Well, what did you expect?' The truth was that I had expected everything to be different. I had expected what happened in Normandy to be the beginning of something fun — if not a full-blown fling, then at least a series of amusing, secret meetings. Instead, I had returned to my sedentary job and a phone that refused to ring.

It had been nearly a week since Normandy and I'd heard nothing. I knew as much about Christian and Beth's movements as I could find out from Stephen, whom I had seen only once since our return to Paris. Apparently Christian had been working nights, and as the restaurant was nearer Beth's flat than his own she had given him a key so that he could let himself in between two and three o'clock every morning and slip into her bed. I was outraged by the ease with which their relationship had resumed its course — even progressed — in this way, not having wavered for a second, and felt confused by the permanency this new regime seemed to suggest.

'I'm not sure it's a good idea to start settling into that kind of pattern so early,' I told Beth on the phone, after enduring the description of an idyllic evening Christian had treated her to at Le Comptoir off Saint Michel — a restaurant I had planned to introduce her to. 'It'll take all the excitement out of things. I mean, you may as well move in together.'

I spat out this last part as if it were the worst eventuality I could think of, convinced that I was offering my beloved friend genuinely good advice. Wasn't she the first to say that she often became too clingy?

'Anna listen, I'm not bothered about that any more. I sort of want to move things on now. It's complicated, but you'll understand one day. He's just so easy to be with — so different to Irish guys. Have you noticed how Frenchmen don't seem to be afraid of feminine things? The other day he was actually giving me advice on some of my designs, and whenever he has a night off, he cooks for me. It's so refreshing.'

Angrily predicting that she would yet again

postpone our plans to meet, I told Beth that I had a call waiting, and hung up.

★ ★ ★

My father, sensing that all was not right, had once again offered to come and spend a weekend with me. It was the first time I was tempted to agree.

'What about Mum — would she be able to come too?'

'I'm not sure, darling. I could ask,' he added brightly, the subtext being 'although I daren't'. 'The problem is that she's got this big case on at the moment — the one I told you about — so it might be tricky this time . . .'

I stopped listening at that point, reassuring my father that I was fine and didn't need him to come out, that I was becoming quite grown-up in fact, and that he might not recognise the *jeune Parisienne* who was once his daughter.

★ ★ ★

Over the next few days a mood settled over me as grim and determined as a London sky. Again, I had been made a fool of. It wasn't the fact that I had slept with Christian that

189

pricked my vanity: it was the knowledge that, despite everything, I was still being excluded. Then I would remember that afternoon in Normandy and look around stealthily, hoping that nobody could read my mind. Blind to the tourists passing in and out of my line of vision, I developed a knack of pressing my thighs together until — unnoticed by anyone — the hard wooden seat sent a jolt of pleasure through me.

That was where he found me, one late August morning, ten days later. I had seen him coming, spotting the crown of his head as it made faltering progress through the atrium behind a gaggle of *lycéens*. I prided myself on being above girls for whom the purr of the telephone was an emotional barometer, but as the days thudded by, and that tiny corner of possibility darkened like the last chink of light against a wall, I had wondered whether this might be it: the first time something didn't go my way.

I smiled now, complacently, though with that perverse dip of disappointment that occurs when there is nothing left to wish for. Hidden by one of the Egyptian-style tombs lining the main hall, I watched him trying to find me, peering into each gallery, dwarfed by the bronze sculptures in the lobby, before finally asking an attendant. His studied nonchalance made it all the more enjoyable to watch. Doesn't the real charm of hide and seek lie in the knowledge that someone is desperately trying to find you? I knew that he would manage, eventually, and returned to my seat, assuming an unruffled attitude as I waited for him to arrive.

'How have you been?'

'Busy, you know. You?'

'Same.'

He turned and stared impassively at the adjacent still life.

'Just look at all this,' he said, sounding vaguely irritated and passing a hand behind his neck in a familiar gesture that made me queasy with longing. 'These must be worth a fortune.'

'They are. But that's not the point.'

'Listen, Anna, I just want to see you, even for a night. But it's too risky here in Paris. So I was thinking, that you and I could . . . I mean, if you wanted to . . .'

I had difficulty interpreting his scattered speech.

'I do want to. But where?'

'I've got my brother's birthday in Aubervilliers this Friday. Come with me to that.'

It was a long way from the elaborate montages I had constructed in my head. We both turned to stare at an Italian woman who had yelped with laughter a little way off, grateful for the distraction.

'She's got a work dinner that night,' he continued, 'and I've got to be back at the restaurant by seven the next morning to take a delivery. I'll just say I went out with the boys after work, and no one will ever know we've gone.'

He couldn't bring himself to say her name, and it stirred me up. I nodded, noting that the Italian lady and her noisy companion were leaving the room.

'So you'll pick me up from here at what time?'

'Six o'clock.'

'Six o'clock on Friday.'

And he was gone.

★ ★ ★

It was hard to contain my happiness. On the journey home every mundane action was gilded with excitement. I mouthed the word 'lover' to myself over and over again, enjoying the shape of it in my mouth, and revelled in the knowledge that the man selling me my bus ticket had no idea what I would be doing that weekend, treating him with undue kindness, as if to compensate for his ignorance.

There had been an awkward moment that evening when, during the course of dinner with Beth and Stephen, she had suggested that we meet up after her work event the following night to see a late-night film. Unprepared, I had made up the only thing I knew would put her off: a man.

'Ah! So you're going on a date?'

'No, no. Just a friend.'

'Well, if he's only a friend you won't mind if I join you two later on, will you?'

I looked so obviously put out that they both started laughing.

'I knew it: she's going on a date. You're a mysterious little soul sometimes, Anna, aren't you?'

Enjoying Beth's complete attention, I began to tell them the fictional circumstances in which I had met this man, borrowing details from the past and sprinkling them with a smattering from my own imagination. Satisfied I had quashed their curiosity, and pleased with my lies, I opened another bottle of Chablis no one wanted to finish. As I left and got into the lift that night I was surprised by the flushed face staring back at me in the mirror and my very apparent lack of conscience.

★ ★ ★

I hadn't doubted he would be there, parked directly outside the visitors' entrance, the hazard lights on his car causing the air around them to quiver in the heat. I opened the door and slid into the passenger seat. A gentle embarrassment, which I luxuriated in, hung in the air for the first few minutes as we decided whether to put my bag in the boot and he cleared away an accumulation of empty Evian bottles and fast-food wrappers from beneath my feet. Craving intimacy I leant across, tried to kiss him on the cheek, missed and grazed an ear. He laughed quietly, projecting little puffs of hot air against my cheek, and the knot in my stomach relaxed.

It was the last hot day of summer, and as we drove along the Seine sequins of light winked their goodbyes from the water's surface. Kicking off my shoes and putting my feet on the dashboard I pretended I was not myself, but the plaything of a married man. To complete the picture I lit a cigarette, inserting the tip of it through a slit of open window every ten seconds, watching the ash being snatched away by the wind. We had only exchanged a few words; I was beginning to feel uncomfortable, my cigarette too obvious in its intent. Deciding to empty the ashtray out of the window, I held it too close to the air current and watched helplessly as the plastic tray was ripped from my hand and carried away, as lightly as a piece of confetti.

'What have you done?' he shouted above the roar of the traffic, apologising with a gesture to the car behind.

His eyes still fixed on the road, Christian broke into a wild laugh filled with sexual impatience, unease, and exhilaration at the night that lay ahead. Seeing no alternative, I joined in.

★ ★ ★

Aubervilliers meant nothing to me, other than the recollection of an article I'd read in *Le Figaro* the first month I had arrived in Paris. A young Algerian's flat had been stormed by police a few months earlier and two miniature missiles in their initial stages of construction were discovered in his kitchen. Still, I was too curious about Christian's background to feel apprehensive.

We had pulled into the outer lane, ready to turn off the motorway, and I had no doubt that the cubist cluster of tenements looming before us was Aubervilliers. I'd heard about the concrete suburbs of Paris, but in my sheltered life, broken by spells on the Côte d'Azur and weekends in the Cotswolds, I had never had any reason to visit them. Olivier, Christian's brother, lived in one of the estates nearest to the motorway. From inside the column of flats the speeding traffic was reduced to the whirring noise of a fly. Concrete pens delineated by wire grills low enough for a child to climb over formed zoo-like enclosures, each with a single tower block in the middle.

'Here we are.'

Christian squeezed the top of my arm: the first time he had touched me since we left Paris. Bob Marley's 'Could You Be Loved' filtered joylessly from a window above us as I let him pull my face to his, keeping my eyes open as he kissed me, so that I could decipher any hint of emotion.

'*Ah, c'est joli les amoureux.*'

A crackle of retreating bicycle tyres dissolved into the rapidly descending night.

Walking up twelve floors to Olivier's flat (the lift had been vandalised) I wondered why anyone would choose to have a party at home, if this were their home. Plump red lettering scrawled across the landing read 'Fuck the police'. Christian, walking ahead of me, kept looking back with apprehensive eyes. I was flattered at the time that it was I who had been brought there, not Beth, wondering whether the whole excursion was a test, to show me where he came from and see whether I still wanted him. I now suspect that he cared too much about Beth's opinion to introduce her to the family he was embarrassed by.

★ ★ ★

There could have been more than the twenty or so people I had at first calculated were packed into Christian's brother's flat. The low ceiling made it impossible to see the walls, and clusters of smokers had capped their groups with clouds of peppered, fudge-scented hash fumes.

'*Eh, Christian! Ça va?*'

A black man with skin so dark his pores shone liquid amber in the blurred light of the room play-wrestled his hellos with Christian. I took a step back, surveying the room for anything or anyone that might be of use to me, and saw nothing. *Just do it, Feel it, Get to it* — nearly every man, and some of the women, bore the insignia of a global sports brand, preaching to the world pointlessly from chests, backs or thighs.

'Christian!'

A pretty, heavily built girl in trainers and jeans so tight you could make out the delineations of her underwear came over, raised herself on tiptoe and kissed him noisily on both cheeks.

'Eve.'

It was his sister-in-law; the eighteen-year-old mother of his baby nephew.

'And you must be Anna.'

Her smile was warm, and devoid of subtext. How had Christian explained the fact that he was bringing me? Were his family even aware of Beth's existence?

'Come with me,' she went on. 'Let's get you a drink. Christian, tell your brother to turn that down. I refuse to have to deal with that bitch from downstairs again. If she comes up, he can sort her out.'

Taking me by the hand she pulled me through a room of appreciative male glances into a cupboard-sized kitchen with slanting fittings. Pulling a bottle of muscat from the fridge she filled a Tintin-themed glass, of the kind you get free with supermarket French mustard, to a millimetre beneath the top.

'There you go. Are you hungry? There are various bits and bobs on the side there so help yourself.'

Leaning back against a cupboard and lighting a cigarette, she looked over at me with a total lack of self-consciousness.

'So how long have you known my brother-in-law?'

'Only a few months . . . '

'And you met at the restaurant?' Without waiting for an answer she went on: 'We hardly ever get to see him, he works so hard at that damned place. Still, it must be good for meeting people: Christian's come across tons of interesting characters there, and they're not all boring Parisians, you know? Which is nice.'

Back in the sitting room the atmosphere was one of drug-entranced torpor. There was only room on the floor around the coffee table for those presiding over the spliff-making — lost in the studied beatitude of their cross-legged postures — to be seated. The rest were slouched against walls or perched on sofas, talking earnestly about nothing at all. Christian pulled me down to the free corner of carpet in between him and his semi-recumbent brother, and I leant cautiously against a giant flatscreen TV, still in its box, taking short drags of whatever, periodically, came my way.

Gradually the room flatlined into a monotone whirr of a similar pitch to the traffic beyond, occasionally perforated by a high note from the speakers on the dresser or a single word I recognised. In the early hours of morning I remember Christian's hand against the skin of my back, but the rest of the night remains a blur. Still, I remember feeling relieved when at some indefinite hour, and well after most of the guests had left, Christian finally suggested we follow their example.

★ ★ ★

Pushing open the heavy metal door into the morning light, I saw that for the first time that summer it was raining. The slap of the cool air against our faces stopped us in our tracks. Despite the weather and the hour, there were now more people about than when we had arrived the night before. The diagonal shards of rain gently speared a gaggle of hooded boys, no older than fourteen, who were huddled by the swings in a partially built playground I had failed to notice earlier. As we walked past, one of the smallest turned and fixed vicious white eyes on me. I shuddered.

'Are you cold?' Christian took off his light summer jacket and put it around my shoulders. 'The car's not far.'

'Good. I'm exhausted. What time is it?'

'Nearly six.'

He turned and smilingly took my hand. The desire that had ripened throughout the evening with every complicit glance and fleeting touch opened, and I wondered if we could find somewhere quiet for an hour before beginning the journey back to Paris. Christian must have read my mind: once in the car, he collared my neck with one cold hand and slipped the other beneath my skirt. His fingertips, wet from the rain, skated across the goose-pimpled skin of my thighs which contracted further beneath his touch.

'Is there anywhere we can go?'

'Not really — and definitely nowhere around here.' He looked at my mouth as he spoke. 'We'd better get going, there'll be the usual Saturday morning tail-back as we get nearer Paris — all these bloody *campagnards* coming in to Paris for the weekend — and I've got a big delivery in a couple of hours.'

Pulling away, he started the car and I relaxed against the head-rest, watching the muscles in his thighs straining against the fabric of his jeans as he changed gears. It was raining hard now, and as the windscreen wipers whined their endless refrain, I succumbed to the insistent weights dragging my eyelids shut.

'Watch out! Watch out! Jesus. What was that?'

Steering the car back on to the road from the hard shoulder, Christian swallowed and kept his eyes fixedly ahead. We had only been driving for twenty minutes, but with the first lurching swerve my eyes had flown open.

'Sorry, sorry. God. Are you all right?'

'I'm fine.'

'Shit. I must have closed my eyes for a second.'

A hot-pink line of exhaustion was stencilled beneath his eyes, and his usually steady hand trembled on the steering wheel.

'Let's stop somewhere. I don't want to die today.'

I smiled but the flippancy of my words chilled me. I imagined a faceless policeman delivering the news to Stephen and Beth, and wondered which would take precedence in the mind of the bereaved: losing someone you love or realising that you have been double-crossed by them?

★ ★ ★

We pulled over at the first place we could see: one of the futuristic motels lining the motorways in to Paris. As soon as the engine was switched off, Christian began to breathe again. We were only forty minutes away from Paris but my concern that he was in no state to drive, and the decision I had made earlier not to walk away from our night together without quenching this empty feeling, had conspired to make him pull over.

The motel's façade, like a Mondrian painting, was a rectangular box broken up into primary-coloured squares. There were no staff. A machine by the front entrance inhaled Christian's twenty-euro note, spitting out a plastic key-card in return. This allowed us into the reception-less building, where a series of felt-lined corridors with fast-food shop lighting and passenger-ferry-style bars lining the walls led the way to our room. Number 122 (I can still remember it now) looked like a child's play-pen with a climbing frame for a bed. The rest of the details I have forgotten, but I do remember pulling, pushing and bending over those bars, in a series of acrobatic gestures that seem both obscene and ridiculous in hindsight. I remember too the synthetic feel of the sponge-like material beneath my naked flesh, and its readiness to absorb our mingled sweat. Afterwards, we lay in that peculiarly embarrassed state brought on by the utter selfishness of physical pleasure, until we fell asleep.

They say that afterwards you glow, that it makes even the ugly look beautiful — but that's a lie. Glancing at myself slyly in the windscreen mirror as Christian started up the car again, I was shocked by my reflection.

Our rough games had swollen my cheeks and lips, shined and reddened my nose, while Christian's teeth had marbled the perfect skin of my throat. No, the sex Beth had so accurately described hadn't made me beautiful, but it had stopped me caring. So I didn't care, and he didn't notice.

★ ★ ★

It was gone eight o'clock by the time we left, and the sky was willing itself to brighten through the heavy rain. As we approached Paris the clove-like smell of rubber from the motorway became stronger, the traffic thickening till we came to a gradual stop. Christian had turned on the radio, and I mouthed the words to a catchy song I disliked at the woman in the car to my left. Next to her, just visible in the passenger seat and framed by the stiff blue foam of its chair, was the downy head of a small child. She handed it something, a bottle or a toy, and I wondered, without really caring, whether you were supposed to put children beside you or in the back seat. Looking up at one of the grey bridges that intermittently broke up the motorway, I was surprised to see the figure of a girl, dramatic, standing there above us in a long black trench coat that glistened in the rain. It struck me as odd. I hadn't realised that pedestrians were allowed up on those bridges, and besides, there were no houses as far as the eye could see. Opening my mouth to voice the thought I was pre-empted by Christian's calm tones.

'Look at that girl. People are weird, aren't they? Why on earth would you choose to go for a walk across a motorway, on a disgusting morning like this? I mean there must be . . . '

Before he could finish his cursory indictment of the human race, the forlorn shape straddled the balustrade, perching a few feet above the rapid traffic moving in the opposite direction. Around us, other cars had begun to notice her. I could see the driver in the car in front of us gesticulating wildly at the shadow in the passenger seat, and instinctively I turned to the woman beside me, separated only by sheets of glass and metal. But she wasn't looking at me. In a gesture as lucid as it was graceful, she leant across to cover her child's eyes. As she did so, the girl looked down for a split second, and jumped.

In my memories, the sound of the two cars that screeched off the road to avoid her has been drowned by the dull, anticlimactic thud of her body against the tarmac. At the time I noted with a kind of clinical interest how it had broken with the impact. One leg lay at a right-angle to her torso, and a single All-Star trainer had landed upright, in a weird feat of physics, a few feet away. On our side of the carriageway, people scrabbled for their mobiles, Christian started to laugh, a shrill laugh, not quite hysterical, which stopped as abruptly as it started, before he too pointlessly dialled the emergency services.

★ ★ ★

It was the kind of experience about which there was nothing to be said. For a few minutes, I had sat petrified with fear that he might utter some banal cliché; try to make sense of it. Instead, we reached a rain-soaked Paris without exchanging a word, making a tacit pact that we would tell no one what we had seen. I sat at the little table in my flat that day, book in hand, watching the print scramble before my eyes, wishing it wasn't so cold but not able to close the balcony doors. What had happened to her that was so terrible she couldn't bear to live any more? My pristine youth could not, then, comprehend the human capacity to feel pain, and I lamented the fact that I could not call Beth, tell her what I had seen, and ask her what it meant.

8

In the period that followed I felt closer to Beth than ever before, needing her to redress the balance. The events of that night had acted as a temporary barrier to thoughts of Christian; no hypnotherapist would have been able to conjure up a more dissuasive mental connection. Even pushing aside any feelings of supersition, our night together was tainted by the girl's suicide, a disabling memory we needed time to shake off.

Confident that Christian would sooner or later turn up on my doorstep or wander through the revolving doors of the museum, I delighted in having Beth to myself again. There was a newfound fascination for me in the sheer physicality of her, and the knowledge that at night we both conjured up the same face in our dreams helped to cancel out any sense of wrongdoing on my part. I urged her now not to hold back in her sexual descriptions, recognising my own experiences in them, taking instruction even, and relishing how similar our tastes were. Our weekends had regained their initial flavour: tender, aimless, languorous days of the kind I have never experienced since. Only now there was this slow-beating sensuality infecting everything. We would discuss our common passion affectionately together, and where I had been careful to keep any of my views quiet in the past — whether real or concocted for her benefit — I was now happy to join in with the deconstructions of his character, which Beth never seemed to tire of. I have since wondered why she did not question my readiness to devote whole hours of conversation to Christian, knowing, as she affectionately did, that nothing usually aroused my interest unless it had some bearing on me. But suspicion was an alien concept to Beth. Despite the knocks she had suffered throughout her life, she had an amazing capacity to see only the good in others, naturally expecting the trust she held in them to be mirrored by those close to her.

I likened my initial meeting with Beth to falling in love. If that were the case, then those first days of September were our belated honeymoon. Splashing through the puddles of rain that lacquered the pavements of Paris and ruined our shoes, we walked from one side of the city to the next, down the banks lined with booksellers, sharing muscat grapes, soon to be out of season, from a paper bag.

She was enchanted by the discovery of

Shakespeare and Co., a second-hand book-shop on the rue de la Bûcherie where expats and ambitious young poets congregated. We would browse the shelves silently, never once buying a thing, whispering our findings to each other so as not to wake the homeless students sleeping on battered sofas at the back of the shop.

However, after the first week without him, my physical yearning for Christian became insufferable. I hungered for sensations that might appease the restlessness: going from one exhibition to the next, preparing elaborate plates of food I couldn't eat, endlessly switching radio channels unable to settle on a song I wanted to hear and struggling every night to find a comfortable position in which to sleep. My twin infatuations had become one. Watching Beth try on a trouser suit in an expensive shop on the Champs-Elysées, I sat in the communal changing room transfixed by her perfect hourglass shape from behind. I wondered if he'd ever seen the knickers she was wearing — plain black silk with a scalloped waistband — and for a moment allowed myself to enjoy the image of the two of them together.

Christian had explained this temporary period of absence from her life (and mine) claiming two of his staff were off sick. Perhaps it was true. Anyhow, it didn't matter. The idea of us becoming a couple had never even occurred to me: how would I be able to keep Beth? No, I was quite content for things to carry on the way they were.

★   ★   ★

Thursday was late-night opening at the museum, and a miscellaneous crowd filtered through the doors from six o'clock onwards; lawyers and bankers with RSI, still clutching their briefcases, escaped their computer screens to seek an injection of culture. I had missed lunch that day and glared at the forlorn suits, waiting for them to feel they had seen enough to go home so that I could run to the supermarket and buy sufficient food to fill my tiny fridge.

Franprix lit up its shoppers like mannequins in a warehouse. Guided by the blazingly cool tubes of light lining the aisles, I zigzagged past the fruit and vegetables, narrowly avoiding running over a crouching infant with my diminutive Parisian trolley. Intrigued, the four-year-old followed me at a respectful distance to the delicatessen, where I retrieved a single *oeuf-en-gelée* from a fridge shelf above his head. His quietly judgemental gaze made me uncomfortable, and, stashing the packet furtively in my trolley, I hurried on. The choices I had looked forward to making earlier on in the day now seemed mundane, with every option failing to arouse my taste buds. Catching sight of myself in a mirror above the freezer, I noticed a smudge on my cheek, and began to wipe it off with my sleeve.

'Trust you to find somewhere to admire yourself, even in a supermarket,' came a voice from behind me.

'Beth,' I said before turning, recognising that ironic Irish lilt instantly. But my surprised smile froze when I saw who was with her. 'Christian. Hi.'

He looked unflinchingly at me and allowed a polite smile to spread slowly across his lovely, blank face.

'Hello.'

'So, what are you two doing here?'

'Errrm . . . ' Beth had cocked her head to one side and was frowning indulgently at me. 'We're buying food. Why? What do you usually come here for?'

She had sensed my embarrassment and in a second would begin to wonder about the reason for it. I knew I had to say something, anything, quickly.

'Oh, I don't know. Supermarkets are amazing if you open your mind to things

. . . So what have you got in there anyway? Let's have a look.' I peered into the plastic basket Christian was holding. 'Jesus, you've bought half the shop. I hope that's not all just for you two.'

As soon as I'd said it, I realised what it must sound like: a plea to be invited for dinner.

'God, you're right. Darling we've got way too much here. Why don't you come and join us, Anna? We're making a *raclette*.'

'Oh.' I played for time. 'Isn't that meant to be a winter dish?'

'Look outside: winter's pretty much here.'

It was the first thing Christian had said to me, and I wondered whether, like poor dialogue from a romantic novel, he was referring to the end of our relationship. Suddenly the allure of the evening ahead, with all its enjoyable complications, flared in my imagination.

'Well, I have always wanted to try it. Yes, why not. I'd love to.'

'Were you just going to have a quiet one?'

She'd said it kindly, prompting them both to look into my trolley as we walked towards the checkout, but suddenly it sounded like pity.

'I wish,' I replied quickly, darting a glance at Christian to see if he was listening and hastily resting my trolley with its tell-tale contents in a corner. 'No, I was supposed to be having someone over for a drink but I might just call and tell them I'm not feeling well. I wasn't really in the mood for it anyway.'

'If you're sure,' said Beth. And, like a perfectly functioning family, we formed a conveyor belt with our groceries by the checkout counter.

* * *

Looking back on that night, I find it hard to believe that I sat between those two, my conscience calm and my hands steady, eating the dishes Beth had painstakingly prepared, laughing at her jokes, once even kissing her on the cheek at a compliment she'd paid me. I don't recall feeling any shame; initial discomfort faded as soon as we'd entered the flat. There seemed to be nothing more natural than spending the evening with the woman I adored and a man I desired. As soon as we'd walked in Beth had shrugged off her fitted Chinese satin jacket to reveal heavy breasts full of movement, the tips skimming against the thin cream jersey material of her top. Rather than feel the nudge of competition,

I remember enjoying her figure, appreciating it like a man.

'Now you two: make yourselves comfortable next door and open this.'

She was made to be a mother, I thought, bossy and tender, warm and practical. She handed me a bottle of Fleurie from the top of the fridge, and Christian a corkscrew. A wall partially separated the kitchen from the sitting room, so that as I placed the bottle on the coffee table, steadying it with one hand and twisting the metal spike into the cork with the other, we were still able to hear Beth speaking to us from next door. Amidst the gongs of saucepans and slamming of drawers, she told us she was convinced she was going to be promoted. Her boss had praised her that day on a project she'd just completed on the forthcoming season's Maoist look.

'He told me he had 'great things in store' for me. I mean, what else could he mean?'

'Here, let me do that: you're making a total mess of it,' Christian whispered, dragging his teeth across his bottom lip in consternation at my miserable efforts.

Picking my fingers gently off the neck of the bottle as though they were a bird with a broken neck, he put the wine between his knees and uncorked it in one swift movement.

'So that's all pretty good news, don't you think?'

From next door, Beth's words had been tripping over each other in their continuous sing-song rhythm without me hearing them.

'Great news,' we chorused: she had just walked into the room holding a bowl of pistachio nuts.

'If I do get a promotion, I might even move out of this place and get somewhere of my own.'

The way she looked at Christian when she said this ('of my own' not 'on my own') with a barely perceptible widening of the pupils, left no doubt as to its meaning. Unimpressed by her homely female politics, I picked up a magazine and started casually flicking through pages sticky with colour, waiting for the threat of bad humour to dissipate.

'So where's Stephen?'

'Out on a date with some girl he met on the métro.'

'Really? My God, that boy is unbelievable. How does he do it?'

'You know how he does it: you've seen him in action.'

A bubbling sound from next door had sent Beth speedily out of the room.

'Potatoes are done,' she flung back through the partition. 'Now we . . . Oh, damn.'

'What?'

'I've got oil on my top. How did I do that?'

Leaving Christian in the sitting room, I went to inspect the damage. With her chin to her chest, Beth was dabbing at the stain with a kitchen towel, darkening an already noticeable discolouration beneath her left breast.

'Take it off and put it in some cold water. I would.'

'Good idea. Keep an eye on the vegetables while I change.'

I was doing just that when, a minute later, Beth called out from her bedroom. 'Anna — can you help me with this a second?'

Facing the mirror, her hair held high above her head with both hands like a Degas pastel, she was waiting for me in a dark-green shirt of the sheerest silk, a spine of tiny mother-of-pearl buttons breaking apart half-way up her back, where she could no longer reach them.

'Sorry.'

'Don't worry.'

The skin of her neck was even paler than the rest of her, sheltered, as it had always been, by her hair. In fascination I absorbed how the subtle gradations of colour on her back became translucent where the crest of her shoulders curved into her neck. A single

216

curled wisp of hair, shorter than the rest, purer in colour and sweetly tender, had escaped her grip, and as I brushed it aside, I suppressed a furious impulse to press my lips against that unsuspecting skin.

'Anna?'

'Yes?'

'There's a hook at the top.'

'Yes — I got that.'

'Good. We'd better go and check on things next door.'

★ ★ ★

We sat in that tiny kitchen, chatting, cutting up mushrooms, peppers, ham and salami into geometric shapes which might have belonged in an infant's play box, while I waited for my moment of disorientation to pass. Later, as Beth handed out the little iron trays of bubbling cheese to us, forgetting to put one on her own plate, her eyes creasing into slits at one of her own jokes, I noticed that her benevolence actually infused the air around her, so that she took ownership of the spaces she moved in. For a moment I pictured all three of us settling into some *Jules et Jim*-style scenario, until after dinner Beth threw a look my way. The significance of that raised eyebrow and kindly set mouth from a

217

hostess is unmistakable, but Beth had never used it with me before. I was being asked to leave, which meant that I was not (as I had thought) in control of the situation: there was still something between Beth and Christian that bore no relation to me. I did not enjoy the feeling and I wasn't sure which of the two my jealousy was directed at.

Deciding to ignore her unspoken plea and delay my departure, I watched Beth scrape the plates clean of congealed cheese, each swipe of the knife making her tacit demand more insistent. When the last one had been placed in the dish-washer, I capitulated, resentful of the indelicate way I was being thrown out.

'Where's my coat?'

'It's on the back of the chair next door, darling.'

The exchange was a fraction too rapid. Christian was already crouched in front of the television, a blue screen of flickering white ants, fiddling with the channels. Were they going to watch a film together after I left? Had they, in subdued voices while I was out of the room, already decided which one to watch?

'Are you off?'

'Yeah. I've got things to do.'

'Sure you do.'

218

Taking advantage of the moment he hoisted himself up by the arm of the sofa. I kissed him peremptorily on the lips and whispered: 'When can I see you?'

'Beth and Stephen are having dinner with the old couple from downstairs next Tuesday . . .'

Terrified we would be heard, I mouthed: 'Come at eight.'

I left jettisoned by the thought that Beth had stepped into the role of the wife with tiresome friends. As the door closed I stood for a while, deciding between the elevator or a four-storey descent, determining whether or not to let this fling with Christian become something more serious.

★ ★ ★

It was on the Monday, while awaiting the arrival of two omelettes in the brasserie on the corner of quai Voltaire and rue du Bac that my phone gave a tell-tale hiccup: a text message from Stephen.

'Beth v low. Help me cheer her up tonight?'

Unable to wait until after lunch to find out more, I excused myself and rang Stephen back from the shoebox-sized lavatory out the back of the restaurant.

'It's me. Hi. What do you mean low? Why?'

'Her father, you know.' I covered my mouth with my hand, lest he should hear my sigh of relief. 'Beth's aunt rang last night: apparently he's not in a good way. Anyway, there's not much we can do, but . . . '

'Of course there is. Why don't I come over and bring some lovely take-away from Le Mille-Pâtes. That way neither of you have to cook.'

Beth, who had declined to share a bottle of wine with us that evening, stopped peeling the label off the Evian bottle for a moment and looked up with a smile.

'This is delicious, Anna. You shouldn't have — you must have spent a fortune.'

She looked lovely that night: clear-skinned and full-faced with the lights in her eyes dancing genially, the last waltz of lovers who would not be spending the night together.

'My dad rang this morning,' she'd said, as soon as she opened the door, desperate to confide her fears in me.

I pressed my lips together in silent sympathy, wishing I could stem the morose thoughts seeping from her, but knowing that the truth was inexorable, and that the guilt that paid for every carefree second she spent in Paris away from her father would curdle all that was good in her until she returned, if only briefly, to Ireland.

'Beth, why don't you take some time off work and spend a couple of weeks with him back home? I just think it's the only thing that will put your mind at rest. And I'm sure your boss would understand.'

The suggestion had been made out of friendship, but the possibilities for Christian and me surfaced amidst a wave of other thoughts.

'It's not that, Anna. I know I can go back there any time I like. But what's the fucking point? He wouldn't even recognise me. Do you have any idea what that's like? For your own father to look straight through you?'

I didn't. And I had never heard Beth swear before. I was as shocked as when, as a pious ten-year-old, I'd peered down the stairs at a dinner party my parents were holding to see my mother smoking a cigarette. It wasn't so much the fact that she occasionally smoked that had enraged me, but the sensual languor of her pose. The next morning over breakfast I'd lost my temper with her, then, quite without explanation, had burst into tears.

'Anyway, it's boring, so boring for you two to have to listen to this. Hell, even I'm bored by the whole thing. Anna, do you mind if I just go to bed? I'm afraid I'm not great company tonight.'

'Of course not.'

I made a move to hug her, but she had already got up and begun clearing the table.

'Leave that — for God's sake. Just get yourself to bed.'

We waited, eyes downcast, until we heard her bedroom door clicking shut. Stephen sighed and lit a cigarette.

'Jesus. That poor girl. Do you know how long she's had to live with this? Her whole life. I can even remember Ruth telling me that, at school, when they were both studying for A levels, Beth would have to leave early at least twice a week to drive her mother to the hospital for check-ups. The teachers all knew, of course, but she'd have to get up in the middle of their maths class, pack her things and walk out, in front of everyone. Then she had to cut short an internship with some amazing Italian designer and return home. Her dad had been found miles away from the house in his pyjamas trying to climb on to one of the neighbours' horses.'

'God.'

I was uncomfortable with details, seldom able to mould my sympathy into an adequate phrase. Giving advice or reassurance felt as unnatural to me as a foreign language: fearful of saying the wrong thing I stumbled over every word.

'I know so little about Alzheimer's . . . but

it's horrid, isn't it?'

'Yup.'

Conscious of how banal our conversation sounded, how little it helped Beth, we sat in silence until Stephen regretfully finished his cigarette and I wondered whether to leave.

'Where's Christian?'

I hadn't been ready for the question and my rushed answer sounded defensive.

'I've no idea. Why?'

'No reason. But she could probably do with a shoulder to cry on right now, and I'm beginning to wonder whether he gives her enough support about this.' Stephen closed his eyes and drew his fingers symmetrically together from the furthest edge of both cheekbones to the end of his nose in a manner that betrayed his enjoyment at passing judgement.

'Sometimes I think there's just too much history between us for me to be of any real help. I know that sounds odd, but knowing someone too well sort of makes their advice redundant somehow. Should we call Christian and get him to come over?'

I shook my head, a little too vigorously. Any jealousy I had felt towards Beth had almost entirely dissipated over the past few weeks, but there were enough taut emotions that night without Christian's presence adding to the mix.

'No. I think she just needs to have her friends around her. Besides, he's probably working. Let me go in and talk to her.'

★ ★ ★

She responded to my knock immediately, gentle though it was, and I shut the door behind me and perched beside her on the bed. She had changed into a pair of dusky pink pyjamas, decorated with bears, coffee cups and the words: *métro, boulot, dodo*. The overall effect was laughably saccharine.

'Where on earth do they come from?' I joked, placing a cup of camomile tea on the bedside table and a comforting hand on her leg.

A smile, blurred by its contact with the pillow, turned into a forced giggle.

'Aren't they hideous? My aunt bought them for me when she came over last Christmas. I think they're meant for people younger than me, probably younger than you even, but they're really comfortable, and don't worry: I keep them hidden in my bottom drawer for emergency situations like these. I would never let Christian see them.'

It was my turn to force a smile. I hated the way his name punctured every conversation, making all my words feel like lies. Her own smile faded. Her feverish cheeks and bright eyes made her look like the consumptive heroine of a Brontë novel, and I felt an almost unbearable throb of compassion for her.

'Beth . . . ' I stopped, realising I had nothing to say.

'I know. I know, my darling,' and somehow she was comforting me. 'Please don't worry. I'll be fine. It just gets to me every now and then, that's all.'

I lay down beside her on the bed for a further half-hour, turning the lights out at her request, and for the first time we discussed death, what it meant, the strangeness of it. I could no longer see her face, and unexpectedly, I found myself telling her about the girl on the bridge. I was careful enough to amend the details of course, explaining that it had been on my way back from the date I'd told her about the week before, and that I would doubtless never see the boy again. But quite abruptly, Beth stopped murmuring sleepy words of acquiescence, and fell asleep. I tiptoed out, whispering more to myself than to her:

'Just get a good night's sleep and it'll all look a whole lot different in the morning.'

I doubted that the realisation that your own father was dying could look a whole lot different. And as I kissed her forehead, unknowingly for the last time, I breathed in the mis-match of scent and lotion that I have spent every day since trying to forget.

Stephen was stubbing out a cigarette in front of a French game show in which the host spanked bikini-clad women with a giant inflatable hand. As he did so, staring at the butt as if it were to blame for his mood, a vaudeville slapping noise resonated and the studio audience guffawed with laughter.

'How is she?' he asked without looking up.

'I think she'll be all right.'

I said it because I wanted it to be true, because it made my life easier to believe that Beth would be fine. But someone else's grief is always oddly distancing. You care, of course you do, but in the end it is still someone else's grief.

9

It was just before seven by the time I got home from work. After a day of delightful anticipation, broken by twinges of concern for Beth, I'd rushed home, cursing the wiry-haired Japanese woman sitting beside me on the métro who breathed in short, whistling nasal bursts. Once through the ticket barriers, I'd broken into a semi-run. Back at the flat I changed clothes twice and sat bolt upright at the table, with nearly an hour to spare, feeling foolish in the expensive new underwear hidden beneath my jeans and T-shirt.

He was twenty minutes late, and I had remained immobile, willing myself to send Beth a reassuring text, put a CD on or turn the pages of the magazine on the table. Never before had I realised that the air around me made a noise, that you could hear silence. My paralysis was shattered only by the sound of his footsteps on the landing. I felt myself breathe again. Then that breath was mingled with his, his kisses dry, his mouth tasting of cashew nuts and red wine, so that when I finally heard the phone, I realised it had been

227

ringing for some time.

'Ignore it,' said Christian into my open mouth.

But his arms had already loosened their hold around my hips, and I got up, wrapping the duvet around myself, as if worried the caller might sense my nakedness. It was Stephen. First I wrongly interpreted his tone as bored. Then something in the flattened consonants became clearer: he was worried.

'Is Beth with you? Only I'm at Fred and Valerie's and she hasn't turned up yet. I've tried her mobile but it just goes straight to answerphone. She's an hour and a half late. We're going to have to start dinner without her.'

'She's not here,' I said quickly, filled with an irrational fear that Stephen knew, that this was all a ruse, that he was standing outside the door of my flat.

'Oh.' He sounded deflated. 'How weird.'

'She's probably just stuck in a meeting. I tell you what,' I said, keen to get him off the line. 'I'll give her a try too.'

'OK. Well, let me know if you have any luck, and I'll give Christian a call. Have you got his number?'

'No. Why would I have his number?'

'I thought Beth gave it to you that night we . . .'

228

'You're right. Maybe I do. Let me have a look.'

'No, don't worry. I think I've got it here.'

Stephen hung up and I turned to Christian, propped up against two grey-blue pillows, his face as tenderly crumpled as them. He looked like a gay man's fantasy, decadent and unravelled, his absolute good looks rendering him utterly soulless.

'That was Stephen, by the way. Beth hasn't turned up to that dinner they were going to tonight. They don't know where she is. He's going to call you.' I gestured towards his mobile, which lay expectantly on the table by his discarded jacket. 'And I think you should answer or he might think something's up.'

Nevertheless, the urgent vibrations we were both expecting made me jump.

As I was lying next to Christian, I could hear, disconcertingly, both sides of the conversation. I listened as Stephen automatically repeated the same terse phrases he'd said to me only moments earlier. Christian uttered a series of monosyllabic replies, his French accent rounding the vowels, endowing his words with a greater eloquence than mine. He was more in control than I, less wavering in his tone, and I watched admiringly. When he clipped his phone shut, two parallel lines divided his smooth brow and he swung his legs out of bed. 'Where the hell's she got to?'

He was angry now. I wondered if it were really because we hadn't had time to finish.

'She's probably forgotten and gone off drinking with people from work,' I suggested, tapping into my phone 'Where are you?' and pressing send. 'And she's always forgetting to charge her mobile, you know that.'

I kicked off a corner of duvet that was covering too much of my thigh, hoping the sight of it might bring him back to bed.

'I don't know. She's not really like that; she never forgets appointments.'

He was pulling his jeans on; I was going to have to take drastic action. I wasn't going to let Beth's delayed journey home, forgetfulness or overrun meeting ruin my moment. I propped myself on to one arm, letting the covers fall off me, and lay there naked, staring at him unflinchingly.

He stopped buttoning his jeans, his hand still on the fly, and watched me in silence. As each second ticked over, I began to feel cold and embarrassed. If I had known then what I know now, I would have felt the impropriety of our situation even more acutely. After what seemed like longer but must have been just a minute, Christian continued to dress and I let him, neither of us wanting to voice our common fear that Beth, for whatever motive, was on her way to my flat.

For that reason alone I was relieved that he hadn't stayed — though until his civil goodbye-smile I'd half expected him to. Still, I hadn't wanted our first real night together to be fraught, and I was woken by involuntary muscle spasms, which shook my body, as a sense of guilt gradually fought its way to the surface.

★ ★ ★

At St Paul métro station the next morning, the sight of a beggar sitting cross-legged on a sleeping bag soaked with his own urine, tendrils of wetness creeping towards commuters, compounded my malaise. As soon as I reached the staffroom at the museum, I texted Stephen.

'Forgot, did she?'

Minutes passed and I stared at the blank screen on my telephone, willing that little envelope to appear. And there it was.

'Still not heard from her. Am worried now.'

Someone in the corner of the room dropped something light, a pencil perhaps: Isabelle.

'Beth didn't come home last night,' I said, still looking at the phone, trying to master the

231

tremor in my voice. 'Stephen doesn't know where she is.'

Panic hit me.

'She will have been with Christian, won't she?'

I looked up at her.

'No. I . . . we know she wasn't. Where the hell is she? What on earth is she playing at?'

More people were beginning to shuffle noisily into the room, dumping bags and taking off their coats. Ignoring Isabelle, who was walking towards me with a look of concern on her face, I dialled Stephen's number and covered one ear.

'I've tried her work but no one's in yet,' he explained. 'And I can't even remember whether she starts at nine or ten in the morning, can you? I always leave before her.'

'Well, let's both keep trying her there. She'll turn up.'

I caught sight of the clock on the wall and began to stash my belongings in a locker.

'I know,' Stephen breathed deeply into the receiver. 'We'll have heard from her by this evening, I'm sure, and I'm going to tell her to have a bit more bloody consideration next time she decides to go AWOL, believe me.'

I had missed breakfast and by the middle of the day was light-headed with hunger. Shifting uncomfortably on my chair, I watched the endless sequence of tourists shuffle in and out of the room like dispirited actors at an audition they knew they weren't right for, nipping back to the staff room every hour to try Beth's phone again. There were two messages from Stephen. The first a garbled voicemail, informing me that, according to her colleagues, Beth had left work at the usual time the night before. The second a stark text message: 'We have to do something.' I rang Stephen back immediately, arranging to go straight to the flat after work. There, we would decide on 'a course of action'. Those were my words, because we were both too scared, as yet, to mention the police.

★ ★ ★

I chose to walk, and with every dull click my heels made against the sodden pavements, the reality of Beth's disappearance began to sink in. I had worked through, and rejected, every conceivable possibility, except the worst, which I refused to let my mind entertain. Until now I had been sure that she would suddenly appear, pale and contrite, but bursting with excitement at the unexpected adventure she'd had. Touched by our concern, she would apologise before launching into a detailed account of her evening. I thought about the last time I had seen her, a forty-year-old woman looking like a child in those absurd pyjamas, and my heart contracted. Suppose she had taken my advice and gone to visit her father? Surely she would not have done so without telling Stephen and me? And although I hated to admit it, the notion that she would not have rung her work to explain seemed even more improbable; Beth would not simply disappear. Minutes before I turned into Beth and Stephen's street, the rain began in earnest. My thoughts turned to Christian, who I hoped would not be there to see me with wet hair which had begun to curl at the base of my neck.

The up-beat attitude I had been simulating dissolved instantly at the sight of Stephen's eyes as he opened the door. They were hooded over, the irises turned from blue to a purulent green. He took me through to the kitchen. Dressed in crumpled beige cords spattered with ochre-coloured paint and a T-shirt bearing a butch American logo, he mechanically put the kettle on. There was a red spot forming at the wing of his left nostril, where its inward curve met his cheek.

'Still nothing?' I asked pointlessly, hanging my coat up beside a velvet jacket Beth and I had bought together at a sample sale but which she'd never worn, claiming it made her look 'wide'.

'Nope.'

On the table, a cafetière gummed up with sodden coffee stood untouched, and beside it, a half-made sandwich oozed a lip of Camembert from between two hard crusts.

'Eat something — you look terrible.'

I found his demeanour out of keeping with the situation — far too melodramatic. But it made sense: Stephen took everything personally, making everything that happened — good or bad — his. He was probably enjoying this.

'I know,' he breathed heavily as we both edged ourselves on to the high barstools he and Beth had bought on a whim.

'I just can't help thinking that something awful has happened. This is so unlike her, Anna . . . so unlike her.'

I fought the impulse to shout back at him: 'Oh for God's sake, Stephen, she's old enough to be my mother. She's probably got bored of your constant dependency, and gone to meet an old friend. Either that or fancied a bit of time on her own!' Instead I silently emptied the coffee into the sink, watching the water carry each grain down the plughole in a circular motion, like a complicated molecular diagram.

'What does Ruth think?'

'That she may be heading back home, but that it's totally unlike her not to tell anyone,' he groaned. 'She thinks we should call the police.'

The doorbell rang as if to underscore that thought, and I started.

'You see, that'll be her.' I laughed, without thinking.

'No. She's got her key. It's Christian. I told him to come over.'

As he padded down the hallway to answer the door, I pulled the kitchen blind up halfway so that I could check myself in the pane of glass mirrored by the darkness. And by the time Christian walked in, looking different, tense, like I'd never seen him, I had recomposed my face and was able to greet him with the appropriate sobriety.

'Have you checked her room?' I suggested, keen to extricate us all from the stagnant, hopeless atmosphere Stephen had created. 'I think the first thing we should do is see if her passport's there. If it's not then we can all relax: we'll know she's on her way back to Ireland to see her dad.'

We walked into Beth's light-blue-painted room illuminated only by a skylight in the slanting roof above her perfectly made bed. It suddenly seemed obscene that all three of us

236

were here. Christian and Beth had made love on that bed, maybe lain there whispering afterwards. Perhaps it showed on my face; I caught Christian looking at me with an expression of unease. For an instant I blamed Beth and Stephen for everything: for being so complacent and short-sighted that neither of them had seen it coming, for failing to spot what was going on under their noses.

'I think Anna's right: she's obviously gone to see her father,' Christian said with sudden conviction. 'It's the only thing that makes sense. He's been calling lots, and sounding more and more . . . ' he drew an invisible, unintentionally elegant semicircle in the air with his index finger. I could see that Stephen found the gesture offensive.

'What does that mean?' Stephen copied the movement, exaggeratedly, and the tension in the room rose a notch.

Christian, his voice steeled, continued, 'Well, you know . . . loopy.'

I suppressed the urge to laugh at his heavily accented use of such an old-fashioned word. Where had he picked it up from? With a rush of affection I thought of him poring over an out-of-date English phrase book as a soft-haired schoolboy. Rummaging through the drawer in her bedside table Stephen murmured, 'I think she usually keeps it here.'

And then triumphantly: 'Well, it's not here. So you're right. She must have taken off without thinking to tell us. If she has, then I'm sorry, but that's bloody inconsiderate. I don't care how upset she is, it bloody is . . . ' he added in a hurt voice, retreating to the kitchen.

We could breathe easy now. I smiled at Christian. His lack of obvious interest in me since he had arrived at the flat was making me desire him for the first time since Beth had disappeared. The situation was resolving itself: we would call Beth's father, and, if she had not yet arrived in Skibbereen, keep calling until she did. Christian didn't smile back at me. I followed his gaze to Beth's desk, where a cup was filled with the charcoal pencils she used to sketch, a single poppy peering shyly out between them. I smiled again then, convinced that Beth was all right, and reassured that I could not be a bad person if I, like Beth, always found it impossible to throw poppies away. In the ashtray on her desk a single half-smoked, lipstick-soiled cigarette had been squashed like a bent knuckle. It lay there shamelessly, delighting in its own tackiness. I couldn't remember ever seeing Beth smoke.

'Since when has she smoked?' I asked absently.

'She does occasionally, when she's really wound up about something.'

I was surprised at his authoritative tone. Did Christian imagine for a moment that he knew Beth better than I? I looked at him, disliking him briefly, and because of that, suddenly wanting him so badly that I had to sit down.

'Right. Get up. Come on. Let's go and try her father.'

I looked up at him standing before me by the bed, at the branches of lines on his palm extended towards me. He met my inviting eyes once, and then twice just to make sure, and threw my hand back disbelievingly.

'Jesus, Anna. You scare me sometimes, you really do.'

★ ★ ★

In the kitchen Stephen was holding the receiver to his ear. For what seemed like an age he said nothing, before finally speaking into it.

'Mr Murphy? Hello, it's Stephen here. Stephen. No, it's not about the television. It's Stephen — Ruth's brother.'

He rubbed at the inflamed pore on his nostril, which had budded into a tiny yellow point.

'That's right, Stephen, Beth's friend. I'm very well, but listen; I don't want you to worry, but is Beth there with you?'

A pause ensued which was long enough to make me want to grab the receiver and shout down the phone at Beth's decrepit father: 'We're all going out of our minds here! For God's sake: is your daughter with you or not?'

But Stephen was nodding patiently into the receiver, and raising an eyebrow in our direction.

'Your daughter Beth. That's right . . . OK. OK, but will you call me if she turns up? We think she was worried about you, Mr Murphy, and that she may be on her way to see you. I'm sure it's all fine, but please just tell her to call me as soon as she arrives.'

Sinking back down on to his stool Stephen put his head in his hands and laughed with relief, eventually looking up at our expectant faces.

'Right. Thank God we caught him at a lucid moment. Everything seems to be fine. Apparently he was asking her to come and see him when they spoke on the phone earlier in the week, so that's obviously what she's done. But God knows how she's planning on getting there.'

Christian and I stared at him, uncomprehending.

'I don't think you two get just how far Skibbereen is from anywhere,' he laughed. 'She'd have to fly to Dublin, get a train halfway there and then a bus. It would easily take her a day and a half from Paris — and that's if the connections are good. She's probably asleep on some coach right now. God, I need a drink, I'm going to go down to the shop and get a bottle of wine. Do you two need anything?'

As we both shook our heads I was calculating exactly how long it would take him to get there and back. By the time the front door slammed shut Christian's tongue was already in my mouth, still warm from the gulp of coffee he had just taken, his knee forcing my knees apart. I took a special delight in keeping my eyes open, surprised that far from deadening sensations it gave them an edge. I could see myself in his pupils, framed by the delicate fringe of his lashes, each dark hair thinning and lightening towards its tip.

By the time Stephen returned, we were seated on opposite sofas in the sitting room. Christian was smoking, a bored expression on his face. I was flicking nonchalantly through the TV guide. Only the most meticulous observer would have noticed that the vein in my neck was still beating fast.

241

Our concern temporarily appeased by Stephen's conversation with Beth's father, and subsequently with Ruth, the three of us talked out our conclusion that she had, in a moment of panic, decided to leave Paris immediately and make her way to Skibbereen, until our worries were entirely dispelled. But we were all pretending to each other, using any excuse to sneak out of the room and try Beth on her mobile phone, only to be greeted with the same increasingly irritating sing-song answerphone message. I had even begun to imagine that there was a hint of mockery in the upward lilt of 'and I'll get straight back to you', as though Beth were enjoying our concerted efforts to track her down. I texted her continuously, without telling the others, thinking that she might be in some kind of trouble she could only tell me about.

It was too late to go home, and when I suggested spending the night at the flat, Christian instantly concurred, adding that I could have Beth's bed, and he would sleep on the sofa. After watching the end of a badly dubbed American thriller on television, Stephen got up, stretched, and looked at his watch.

'It's past one. She'll be nearly there by now, unless she's had to stop off in a hotel overnight.'

Something in the overconfident way he was mapping her steps revived the trepidation I had felt earlier that day. What if Beth was *not* on her way back to Ireland?

'Stephen,' I cleared my throat. 'When would we know if she's, well, not heading back home?'

'It would take her a good day and a half, Anna, like I said, and Ruth said she would spend the whole of tomorrow at the farm with her father, so whatever happens she'll call us when she gets there. But we've been through this, and it all makes sense now. I mean, why else would she have taken her passport with her?'

He bit off a piece of dry skin from the side of his thumb and stood uneasily in the centre of the room like a comedian who'd forgotten his lines.

'So why the hell is her phone switched off?' Christian said without looking up.

'She's always forgetting to charge it.'

I could only remember a single instance when she had, yet I was making it a character trait.

'She obviously left in a real rush, so I really don't think that means anything. Added to which, we have to accept that none of us are exactly her first priority at the moment.'

'Still . . . ' There was a note of concern in Christian's voice.

'I think she was going mad with worry,' Stephen continued, 'and knowing her, she was probably sick of discussing it with us too. I bet she thought she was boring us with it all.'

'I'm going to bed.'

Stephen and Christian looked at me with surprise.

'I'm sure it'll all be fine,' I added in a softer tone. 'She'd probably laugh if she knew how much we were worrying. And I think we should all try to get some sleep.'

★　★　★

Wrapping myself in Beth's sheets, I was dismayed to find them freshly washed, without even the subtlest hint of her. Climbing back out of bed, I tiptoed over to her dressing table, pulled out the ground-glass stopper of her perfume and inhaled it deeply before dabbing it on my temples, wrists and neck. Her face cream caught my eye, and I gazed in wonderment at the mysterious and expensive-looking tubes and phials that I still had to try. With my fingers tightly wrapped around my mobile phone and the harmony of her scents surrounding me, I succumbed to the dulling effects of sleep.

★ ★ ★

'Anna! Anna, wake up.'

It was Christian, his face distorted with shadows, standing over me, holding something in his right hand.

'What is it?'

'It's Beth's phone.'

I sat up and rubbed my eyes, trying to fathom what this meant, and why I was lying in Beth's bed.

'I couldn't sleep — that boiler's too noisy — so I tried to shift one of the sofa pillows and found this down the back of it.'

I was finding it hard to care about the sofa or Beth's phone, but I moved across the bed to allow Christian to sit down.

'So what does that mean?'

'I don't know. It certainly explains why there's been no reply. But why wouldn't she take her phone?'

I shrugged.

'Maybe she just forgot. Or she looked for it and couldn't find it because it had fallen down the back of the sofa. It doesn't explain a whole lot.'

Christian switched it on and we both waited impatiently for the pointless swivelling motif to fill the screen and disappear. Forty-two messages. Scrolling down I saw my own name a dozen times, interspersed with Ruth's, Stephen's, a woman from Beth's work and Christian's. Noting with distaste that one of his messages began 'My darling . . . ' I looked up at him and wondered whether all this concern for Beth could be eradicated, temporarily at least, by a different impulse. At first allowing himself to be pulled in towards me, he sprang away sharply with the look of someone who has bitten into something impossibly sour.

'What the . . . ? Are you wearing her perfume?'

A few feet away Stephen slept on, and somewhere in Ireland, Beth was, no doubt, finally nearing home.

I awoke confused and ashamed, with the relevance of Christian's nocturnal visit beginning to dawn on me, in all its confused significance. I looked at the clock, wondering if it was still too early to call Ruth. By the haunted look on Stephen's face as I wandered into the kitchen I could see that he already had, and I knew that the news was not good.

'She's not there yet. How can she not have got there? It shouldn't take this long, Anna, whichever way you look at it.'

'Why? Who have you spoken to?'

'Ruth and Beth's aunt. They're at Beth's

father's house at the moment. I hung up when they started arguing on the end of the phone. Ruth thinks the old man's talking rubbish. Apparently he's been asking Beth to come and visit him for ages, and she'd promised to come, but said it would have to be sometime next month because work was too busy until then. But then Beth's aunt says she was there when he had this conversation with her on the phone — says he was perfectly compos mentis at the time.'

I sat down sluggishly, longing for the lucidity a strong coffee would bring and reaching instinctively in my mind for Beth to sort us out.

'But she might have changed her mind, Stephen. Don't you think? I mean, that night, when I came over here — the last time I saw her — I've never seen her in that kind of state before. I know it always upsets her when she speaks to her father, but that night I could tell that she was really taking it hard. And anyway, it's the only explanation.'

'But it's not, Anna, that's what I'm saying. You know it's not. It's just that we don't want to think about the others.'

I looked up, silently imploring him not to carry on.

'We can't delay it any longer. Unless we know for sure that she's gone back to Ireland, we've got to call the police.'

'He's right. We shouldn't have waited this long.'

Christian was standing in the doorway wearing only his jeans. I looked from him to the cup of coffee that sat tantalisingly on the table before Stephen. Reaching across for it seemed like an act of great significance. Raising it to my lips I closed my eyes and took a gulp. It was very perfumed, very strong, and when I opened them again, the weight of our two days of torpor lifted, and it was time to act.

★　★　★

In films people always know exactly whom to go to, what number to call, how to explain their situation, as though all their lives they'd been lying in wait for the moment when some tragedy would prompt them to march into their local police station and announce a crime. Looking very young, and holding the receiver like an object so technologically enhanced that its exact use was questionable, Stephen turned to Christian.

'Who do we call here? I've forgotten. I mean, it's not 999, is it?'

'We should call the local commissariat first,' said Christian authoritatively. 'Where do you keep the *pages jaunes*?'

The gigantic tome, lying untouched in its plastic wrapping, was found on the floor of the broom cupboard.

'Do we want general enquiries or emergencies?' Stephen said.

'Just call any damn number and get it over with,' I snapped, feeling the blood pound in my ears.

'Christian, you do it, you're French and you'll be able to explain things better than anyone else.'

As Christian tapped out the number I watched the side of his mouth twitch. Beth wasn't even here, and yet her absence was all-consuming. He paced in and out of the sitting room as he made the call, while Stephen and I sat facing one another, our elbows at right-angles to the table. The silence was broken only by intermittent '*oui*'s from the next room, as though Christian was being asked a series of very straightforward questions, without being allowed to go into detail. Finally he re-emerged.

'Right. They're coming over in half an hour to ask us some questions.' And, looking with slight disgust at the coffee pot: 'Do you have anything stronger?'

'There's some brandy up there. In that cupboard.'

A stool shrieked across the tiled floor and Stephen left the room. Christian and I sat in silence, knees almost touching, until he reached over and ran the side of his thumb across my bottom lip. The gesture made sense to me, like the answer to a question I hadn't realised I'd asked, and I wondered whether everything might still be all right.

Nearly an hour later, the doorbell rang and I heard the stupid shuffle of Stephen's Prixunic slippers against the hall carpet and his monotone: '*Bonjour. Entrez.*' The taller of the two introduced himself as Inspector Verbier. His colleague had a face and name too bland to describe or remember. He gazed blinkingly at his partner, as if born only for the purpose of complementing another human being. Inspector Verbier made up for his colleague's nonentity. A broad man in his forties with skin that should always be tanned but wasn't, he emanated a kind of slovenly sexuality. His lips were soft, feminine in their perfect delineation, and when he spoke, they parted to reveal a row of tiny yellowing milk teeth — the fangs of a sadistic schoolboy.

Declining Stephen's offer of coffee he placed himself unpleasantly near me by the table, while his blank-faced companion surveyed the ceilings and walls of the flat, as if for clues.

'So how long has . . . ' He flicked through pages of a notebook with a thick-ended thumb in search of a name.' . . . has Madame Murphy been missing?'

'Well, we're still not really sure she is missing,' I began, shocked by the seriousness of his language, 'and it's Mademoiselle.'

'Anna, can you let me deal with this, please?' Stephen cut in. 'We're really worried about her. She disappeared the evening before last, and although there *is* a possibility that she has gone to see her sick father in Ireland, it would be very out of character for her to do so without telling us. She also left her phone behind, which is unlike her.'

Stephen went on to explain at length the build-up to Beth's disappearance, including her state of mind the last time he had seen her. The inspector, I noticed, was not writing anything down but leaving the blank man to take the necessary details.

'And you're the boyfriend?' he suddenly interjected. It wasn't a question, but a rebuke.

'No. This is Beth's boyfriend.' Stephen pointed at Christian who was leaning against the wall with his head bowed.

All eyes were suddenly turned so accusingly on Christian that for a moment he looked guilty, even to me. Hot panic rose in my chest like nausea.

'And you work where?'

'I'm the manager of L'Écume, in Bastille.'

The inspector turned and gave his colleague a questioning look.

'That the place you and I went last month?'

The man nodded.

'They do a good steak there,' he told Christian magnanimously.

'Thank you.'

Christian's brittle responses to the police and a smattering of anecdotes Beth had recounted told me he was no stranger to dealing with them. The questions, initially perfunctory, were becoming barbed, Christian's answers increasingly insolent. Both men had returned to the Parisian slang that was their natural lingo, and Stephen, who had been sitting slumped in a chair across the room, looked up, his curiosity aroused by the steep gradient of their tones.

'And how were you two getting along?'

'Very well. We always got along very well.'

'Had you had a fight, or a disagreement of any kind?'

'No.'

'Not of any kind? Think carefully.'

'I think I'd remember. The answer is no,' and then more gently, 'I've been trying to think of any detail that could help.'

The room was completely still. I could hear the other man scratching his arm with the end of his pen through his oatmeal-coloured corduroy jacket. Elsewhere in the building someone was playing one of Satie's *Gymnopédies* on the piano.

'So your girlfriend, who I understand is not in the habit of disappearing, just decides to vanish one day?'

'No, because as we've just said, her father has not been well, and we think she may have gone back to Ireland to see him, only we can't get hold of her.'

Christian was enunciating each word with irritating precision.

'Ah, yes.'

A hastily scribbled comment in the book.

'So tell me: why are we here?'

'Because we thought it was the responsible thing to do.' Stephen's exasperation made him sound petulant. 'I'm beginning to wonder why we bothered,' he added, sotto voce.

Crushing his attitude with a lazily raised hand, Verbier continued, 'And you say she may be in Ireland?'

Stephen explained, again in a deliberate manner that was beginning to grate, the fact that Beth's father suffered from Alzheimer's, and that because of the illness he was not a

253

reliable source of information.

'So you see we have tried to get in touch with her,' I added, 'but we thought, now that two nights have passed, that we should really let you know so that you can make your own inquiries. Presumably you can find out for sure if she's left the country or not. Can't you?'

'Yes, Mademoiselle, we are able to do that for you. But may I suggest something?' He scratched a sardonic eyebrow in the manner of someone who was going to do so anyway. 'I think you should all sit tight, and wait for your friend to call. I have no doubt that she will.'

'Or,' cut in Stephen once more, 'she could, of course, be lying dead in a back street somewhere, which is why we've troubled you today.'

For the second time that day, I felt like laughing. I could hear myself recounting the story to Beth; I knew exactly how I would mimic Stephen's now shrill voice, and which of the policemen's attributes I would exaggerate. I could see her now, spluttering through a hand clamped to her mouth, ashamed at having put us through all this but unable to stop those mirthful eyes from creasing up.

'I tell you what. Why don't you all keep

calling her father, or anyone who lives near her father, until you find out for sure if she's either there or on her way home. That way,' he sighed, looking longingly down the hallway towards the front door, 'at least we'll know what we're dealing with.'

Mr Void had already snapped shut his notebook, signalling the end of their visit.

★ ★ ★

Feeling foolish, we remained silent for some time after the door slammed.

'Well, that told us,' I attempted, embarrassed by my own false jollity.

'I've got to get to work,' mumbled Christian.

'I guess I should go too,' I said apologetically to Stephen, minutes after he'd left. 'What are you going to do?'

'Well, I suppose I should stay here, to see if she calls, but I'm pretty surprised by how unconcerned the police seemed to be. It's sort of made me think that we might be overreacting, that it could all still be OK. It could, couldn't it?'

The question, the plea, rang in my head throughout the day at the museum, piercing the bass rumble of whispering visitors. Of course it could all still be OK. I was convinced that it would be. And yet it was totally uncharacteristic for Beth to put herself first, to disregard the concerns she knew we would all have about her safety if she disappeared without telling us. Desperately suppressing the sequences of guilt and shame flickering through my head, I gathered up crumbs of evidence from over the past few weeks which might substantiate a positive theory. Her natural gaiety had been slightly lacking of late, and she had hardly touched a drop of alcohol since we'd returned from Normandy. Normally a devoted listener, a distracted look had come into her eyes while I was telling her a story — even the kind of gossip she would normally have been captivated by. The unthinkable had, naturally, fleetingly crossed my mind: that she might know about Christian and me, but we'd both agreed that it was impossible.

'You're not here today, are you? You're somewhere else.'

It was Isabelle, peering down at me from a billowing ethnic dress the colour of seaweed, the sleeves hemmed with tiny circular mirrors.

'I'm not, no, sorry.'

I was pleased to see her. In those amorphous clothes that hid everything that was feminine about her, she suddenly

256

appeared to me as a delightfully uncompli-
cated being. It occurred to me that out of
everyone I knew she was the only person I
could be honest with — because she didn't
matter.

'How much longer do we have? I can't see
the clock from here.'

'Three quarters of an hour.'

'Are you busy later?'

Of course she wasn't. Anyone could see
that by the desperate glint in her eye.

'No.' She smiled hopefully. 'Why?'

'I thought we might go for a coffee. Or
even a real drink?'

She was crouching now, too close, visibly
excited by my invitation, probably hoping
that Stephen would join us later. People
looking straight at me, fixedly like that, has
always enervated me. It gives me a sudden
wish to escape, breeds a furious impulse to do
something with my hands, shuffle my feet,
anything to avoid that immovable glare. I
later realised that only the guilty feel that way.

'Is something wrong?'

Maybe by telling her the whole story, I
might be able to cleanse myself of the doubts
cluttering my conscience.

'Yes. And I really need to talk to someone.
If you don't mind, that is . . . '

I watched as the corners of her mouth

257

trickled into a smile.

'I'd love to help out, if I can,' she said, adding smugly, 'I knew something was bothering you.'

* * *

Against the maroon and gold backdrop of our favourite local brasserie, La Frégate, Isabelle looked more alive than she did in the museum. Her pre-Raphaelite features worked in harmony with the organic curls of the wooden banisters and snowdrop lights. And then she smiled and I should have paid more attention to the insecurities implicit in that smile. Still, I had held in my story for too long. Without lifting my eyes I told her everything.

'So,' she said slowly, after a silence so complete that I could hear the man behind me stirring his coffee. 'So, if I've got this right, you think that Beth running off might have something to do with you.'

I nodded, still staring at the lacy froth eddying in my cup, surprised at how easy it was to reduce everything to one simple sentence. But looking up I saw only a kind of pragmatism — no signs of judgement — in her face.

'Listen Anna. I don't know Beth very well,

so I can't pretend to know how her mind works, but it seems to me pretty obvious that she has just decided to take a bit of time out. You probably haven't even crossed her mind, given everything else that's going on. I bet she'll ring Stephen,' here Isabelle suppressed a smile, 'at some point over the next few days, because she's known him all her life and he's, well, closer to her age. And remember: she may see you as being far too young to understand any of this.'

I stopped in mid-nod.

'I think you've missed the point, Isabelle. I don't blame you for not understanding; it's hard to explain. Beth is the closest friend I've ever had, and I'd like to think she could tell me anything.'

'She'd probably like to think the same.'

The disingenuous eyes were wide, but the tone had been unmistakable, and she began to backtrack.

'Well, haven't you ever felt that way? When you've been going mad with worry about something that even those closest to you can't really help you with? Sometimes it's easier to just go off and deal with it on your own.'

I shook my head.

'Beth isn't like that. I mean yes, she'd hate to think of us worrying about her. She puts others first, always — I'm constantly having to tell her off for it — but we could all see what she was going through. I was even the one telling her to go and see her father so as to put her mind at rest.'

Isabelle shrugged.

'Perhaps she thinks it'll be obvious to you guys that she's gone to see him then. But Anna, I don't think you can ignore the possibility . . . ' She stopped short, looking up hesitantly at me.

'That?'

'Well, you know: that she's found out that you . . . well, that you have betrayed her.'

I knew then that Isabelle was enjoying herself. Why did the French always have to be so melodramatic? Even their modern vocabulary seemed to be borrowed from the tragedies of Racine. My behaviour may not have been impeccable, but 'betrayed'?

'Oh, come on, Isabelle. That's a pretty strong word for something which is, basically . . . ' I shifted uncomfortably on my chair, suddenly thirsty for something cold, astringent, alcoholic. ' . . . well, unimportant. And anyway, she'll never know,' I added with conviction.

'So why are you bothering if this thing with Christian is not important? Is it really worth risking everything for some guy you don't feel anything for?'

This was why I quietly got on with things, satisfying my own desires without subjecting them to someone else's approbation, without having them thrown back at me in layman's terms.

'I never said that I didn't feel anything.'

I told myself that it was like talking to a child, that she didn't understand. How could I ever have thought that she would? And the past few days, the way Christian had struggled to maintain his composure while being quizzed by the inspector, the beauty spot on his right haunch, his hand on the steering wheel, assailed me, and I wondered whether one thing explained everything and exonerated me.

'I think I might be in love with him.'

She gave a smile, newly sympathetic and sodden with sentimentality, while a tiny flame of interest was rekindled in her eyes.

'Anna . . . I must admit I'm quite surprised. I never really thought of you as the kind of girl who 'falls in love'.' She paused, searching my face carefully for signs of it. 'But well, if it is love, then that is a whole different thing.'

I had acquitted myself well, not just in her eyes but mine too, and the evening continued in a blaze of mutual confidences. When it came to discussing Stephen, I was taken aback by her honesty — and her ardour. She thought of him continually, she told me, and yet their conversations had never strayed away from the basic courtesies of two people thrown together through circumstance.

'I wish you could have fallen for someone a little easier,' I'd eventually managed, pitying Isabelle her pointless crush. 'But then I suppose none of us can really choose, can we?'

Fending off her cloying embrace on a street corner, I told her, 'Thank you for being such a good friend.'

'Always, Anna. Don't forget that: I am always here.'

As I walked off it occurred to me that I had no idea where she lived, how far she would have to walk, or whether she would get home safely.

* * *

The hallway was pitch black when I pushed open the front door of my building, and, tapping the walls, reached into the obscurity for the light switch. Had I been right to confide in Isabelle? A sense of unease crept over me as I wondered whether she was well-balanced enough to deal with the information in the right way. I wasn't sure I

262

wanted to pursue the discussion we had had that night, and suspected Isabelle might attempt to use it, revive it periodically, in a bid to intensify our friendship.

Suddenly I was in darkness. The timer had run out, and I had three more floors to go. Street lights reflected in a skylight above were enough to guide me, but as I started on the final flight, I stubbed my toe loudly on the banister. The clink of a key above made my heart quicken. There were only two flats on my floor: mine and Monsieur Abitbol's. Anxious to avoid a midnight encounter, taking two steps at a time, I reached the landing with a sense of relief, and began to rummage around in my bag for the keys.

I felt his presence in the darkness before the creaking floorboards confirmed it, and my fingers were no closer to touching the metal I so desperately needed. My keys fell from the chaos of my handbag and as I bent down to pick them up I heard a voice from behind.

'So! The little slut comes back in the middle of the night, does she?'

'Go away,' I said deliberately, marvelling at the calmness of my voice. 'Or I'll call the police.'

'What's that you say? The police? Yes, why don't you do that, you slut? And I'll tell them all about what you've been up to. I'll tell

263

them about the banging in the middle of the night, I'll tell them about the men, I'll tell them that you're charging.'

I lunged forward and swiftly inserted the key into my door. He was still babbling incoherently behind me, plucking at my clothing, but I was saved. Slamming the door behind me I collapsed against it, only to spring away a moment later when the smack of a flat palm resonated through the wood at the height of my head.

'Slut!'

Safe but scared, I automatically dialled Christian's number.

'I'll be right over. Don't move an inch. Don't even talk to him through the door. Don't do anything. Just sit tight.'

Despite the drama, I felt a smile of satisfaction break out across my face.

Disinclined to watch his arrival from my balcony, lest Monsieur Abitbol should climb out on to his, I waited, pacing to and fro the length of my tiny flat, until I heard the squeak of a trainer on the stairs.

'Anna, it's me: let me in.'

I opened the door, assuming a suitably vulnerable expression, and disguised my amusement as Christian strode across the short length of the flat, securing the catch on the window, before taking me in his arms and kissing me.

'I was so scared,' I mumbled into his neck. And I had been, quite.

'Its all right, it's all going to be all right. I want you to pack a bag, and come back now with me. The car's outside. I'm not having you stay here a minute longer. Tomorrow we'll call the landlady and get her to give you your deposit back.'

I began to put some things into an overnight bag.

'It's bloody outrageous,' he continued. 'Letting a young girl move into a place next to a complete nutter. And don't try to tell me that she doesn't know about him. You told me yourself that the whole neighbourhood knows.'

I remonstrated weakly, for the sheer pleasure of doing so, and was grateful to Christian for not worsening the situation by attempting to confront Monsieur Abitbol that night.

★ ★ ★

It was past one when we reached his flat in the sterile streets of the sixteenth arrondissement. The buildings rose higher there, as though fertilised by the riches within, but curved in at the tops, where they diminished into *chambres de bonnes*. These tiny garrets with sloping roofs that were built in the

265

sixteenth century to house the servants had since become trendy with the art and fashion world, but for all their gritty stylishness, many of them were scarcely habitable. Christian, however, had the largest of four.

'Walk in front of me,' he had insisted as we climbed the narrowest flight of stairs I had ever seen.

'Why?'

'Because then if you fall, I can catch you.'

The stairwell led to a dark, damp-smelling corridor, lined with doors so close together it was impossible to believe that they each opened into an individual living space. We stopped at the last door, and Christian let me in to a room containing only a futon, a chest of drawers with a television on top, and a chair buried beneath armfuls of clothes.

'Shall I show you the kitchen?' he asked, laughing at my astonished expression. Heads bowed, we walked into another room, a quarter of the size of the bedroom. Dirty crockery lay piled up on a windowsill, the sink being too small to accommodate it. I moved aside a turret of cups to look out over Paris, but instead of rooftops, there were only the affluent rooms of the building opposite. Because of the lateness of the hour, most were obscured by impeccably white shutters, but a single double window was lit, exposing a sitting room with walls and cushions the colour of money. There was nobody there — the owner having no doubt forgotten to turn the lights out before going to bed — but it struck me that the room would have seemed just as empty when filled with people.

He called me 'mon amour' that night, 'ma chérie', 'ma puce' and 'mon ange' and I felt the shackles of my unformed, selfish spirit loosen under so much tenderness. Perhaps love was something which, like drowning, after one last rebellious buck, you let yourself slip into. But when I awoke next morning to the sight of Christian's downy brown neck, Beth was still the first thing I thought about.

'We should call Stephen, shouldn't we? And find out if he's had any news?'

Christian moved his body, perfectly curved into the warm groove of my lower stomach, in order to turn and face me. Smeared with sleep, he nodded slowly.

'Shall I do it now? And then you can call on your way to work?'

He wandered through to the kitchen and I heard the puff of gas flower as he lit the stove.

'Really? And how does she know that? Right. Well, that's good news, I suppose. And have the police been in touch?'

Snatches of conversation reached me and I craned my neck to listen.

'Well, I think we should have faith in them, even if that Verbier guy was a Neanderthal . . . All right. Speak later.'

Wrapped in a towel he brought two bowls of coffee to bed and I propped myself up against the wall.

'Stephen's spoken to Beth's aunt again. She reckons that Beth has been in touch with her dad — thinks she may have stopped off with a friend en route to Dublin. Stephen's called Ruth though, and she hasn't heard from her.'

It was day three now, but it wasn't beyond the realms of possibility to imagine that Beth would have wanted to break up the long, lonely journey in some way.

'Christian, I know we've spoken about this and decided . . . But you don't think . . . ? No, how could she?'

'Know about us? No. There's no way she knows, Anna. This is not about us. Her father's dying and she wants to be with him. It's as simple as that. And grief makes you behave in strange ways. I think she's concentrating solely on him and has forgotten about us for the time being. I don't really blame her, to be honest.'

It irritated me that Christian, usually either silent or basic in his powers of expression, became so eloquent when speaking of Beth.

I rang Stephen myself on my way to the museum and was as reassured as Christian by his tone. He was on his way to work, and despite the fact that none of us had yet been able to get hold of Beth, things seemed to be returning to normal. I was fully expecting her, in a few days' time, to call and explain in that mellifluous voice which made everything all right that she had needed this time to herself, and would stay in Ireland long enough to ascertain what the real state of her father's health was. By the time she returned, having given me the time to feel sufficiently satiated by Christian, her liaison with him would conveniently have petered out, but our friendship would be stronger than ever. As I walked through the doors of the museum that day, I felt happier than I had done in a long time.

★ ★ ★

My landlady had been predictably hard work.
'Well, I'm sorry you've had trouble with Monsieur Abitbol,' she had said in a deferential voice. 'Of course I realise that he can be a little odd, but he's always been perfectly civil to me. He doesn't like loud music. Have you been playing loud music?'
'No, I haven't,' I stopped myself from

shouting down the receiver. 'I've not done anything wrong. And can I remind you that he nearly assaulted me last night? On my own doorstep? You're damn lucky I didn't go to the police because you'd have a job renting that place out again if I did. And I won't, but only if you give me back my deposit. He's your problem, not mine.'

We settled on a reimbursement of three quarters of a month's rent, 'because you really have left me *dans la merde*,' and I rang my father to inform him that I would be staying with a friend until I found something more suitable.

'Are you sure you shouldn't report it, my darling? That's terribly sweet of Beth to put you up.'

I had been forced to lie, not wanting to have to explain something I didn't fully comprehend myself.

That night Christian escorted me back to my flat for the last time, where we collected the remainder of my belongings. They amounted only to a few boxes, and the sight of the derisory pile by the front door, and the drooping plant I had once so cherished but which I would have to leave on the balcony, tweaked my heart. Perhaps I somehow knew that this was the moment that everything would change, that my emotional stumble, gaining gradually in momentum, would precipitate a fall.

★　★　★

Neither Christian nor I felt like cooking, so we collected a selection of savoury ready-prepared dishes destined for the very rich from the delicatessen beneath his flat. Lying on his bed afterwards amongst the wrappings, I felt perfectly content. I was at peace with the idea of Beth's temporary absence now, and felt pleasantly debauched in this flat where the walls were so thin that you could hear the Algerian man living opposite extemporising into his mobile phone.

'I love it here,' I told Christian, as he stood with his back to me scraping the remaining grains of couscous into the bin.

He turned with a look of surprise. 'Do you? You're easily pleased. If things were different, I'd get another place, but for the moment, well, it has to do.'

I hated seeing him look so serious. Choosing a sweet Turkish pastry from a box on the floor, I raised myself up on my knees and carried it slowly to his mouth, watching as an amber tear of honey fell idly on to his shirt.

'Anna,' he scolded smilingly, wiping his chin. 'It's all a game to you, isn't it?'

I was up in an instant, wrapping my arms around his waist, breathing in the scent of sweat and stale aftershave imbued in his collar. He pushed his mouth hard against mine, refusing to let me open it with my tongue, until I could no longer breathe.

10

'So how come you're staying with Isabelle?' asked Stephen, as I hung my coat up in his hallway. 'I didn't think you two were that close.'

Unprepared for the question, I feigned surprise.

'I think Isabelle's great, I always have. She's very kindly letting me stay in her spare room for a few weeks until I find another flat, and it's all working out fine.'

'What I don't get is why you'd rather stay there than here. I could really do with the company at the moment. You could have stayed in Beth's room until she gets back.'

Caught in the knot of my own lies, and excited at spending every night with Christian, Stephen's logic hadn't even occurred to me.

'Oh, Stephen.' It was perfectly obvious that I should be staying there. Of course I should. I had to think fast now. 'To be completely honest,' I began hesitantly, as though forcing myself to pronounce a difficult truth, 'the idea of staying here . . . in Beth's bedroom . . .'

He looked baffled.

'I mean she'll be coming back soon, won't she? So it just doesn't seem right.'

But he needed more.

'It felt odd, that night I spent here in her bed, sort of wrong, if that makes sense.'

A glimmer of something akin to understanding had appeared in his eyes, and I knew that I was on to something.

'Fair enough. So where is it?'

'Where's what?'

'Isabelle's flat?'

'In the sixteenth,' I replied without thinking.

'Really? Crikey, I thought the museum didn't pay very much.'

I waited for the mental connection to be established.

'Doesn't Christian live in the sixteenth? In Auteuil somewhere? According to Beth, his place is absolutely tiny. I think she only went there once. Are you anywhere near him?'

'I don't think so, it's a fairly big neighbourhood and Isabelle's on the other side.' I scrabbled around in my head for a convincing detail. 'Near the Musée Marmottan.' I had once taken Beth there to show her a darkened basement full of Monet's water lilies. 'I get off at métro La Muette, so it's not that bad a journey home from work. Here, shall we open this bottle of white or is it too early?'

'It's Beth's but I don't suppose she'll mind. Having said that, I got into huge amounts of trouble the last time you and I did that. Do you remember? It turned out it was some really special burgundy her boss had given her for Christmas.'

He gave a sad little laugh and I realised how much he was missing her.

'So you haven't heard anything more?'

'No. The police say they are finding out for sure whether she's left the country or not, which she obviously has, but it'll put my mind at rest to know for certain. As soon as they tell me that, I'll feel much better. And I think I won't even mind so much that she felt she couldn't, well, confide in me.'

'It's not just you, Stephen, it's all of us. I mean Christ, Christian's her boyfriend and she hasn't even been in touch with him.'

'I know. And when she gets back I'm going to tell her that she needs to let us in a bit more. I mean, haven't we all endlessly bored her with our problems?'

He had stopped talking and was scrutinising me with a quizzical expression.

'Look at you . . .'

'What?' I asked twitchily, getting up and

wandering out of his line of vision into the sitting room.

'Have you had your hair cut or something?'

'No.'

'I don't know. You look . . . good.'

'Don't sound so surprised.'

'No, I mean . . . different. Sort of . . . oh, I don't know. I think I'm suffering from sleep deprivation or something. Every morning I wake up just before six when I hear the water come on next door. I keep thinking she's let herself in and is having a shower.'

'Have another glass of wine: it'll help knock you out.'

Suffocated by those mustard-coloured walls and the turn of the conversation, I suggested we continue our drinking in a local bar on the boulevard St Denis. But as we walked past Beth's open bedroom door on our way out, we both fell silent.

'I miss her,' Stephen admitted.

'Me too. But she'll be back soon.'

It was while we were waiting for the lift that the call came. I recognised the brutal slang of Inspector Verbier's voice from a foot away, as soon as Stephen answered his mobile phone. The conversation lasted a mere second, before he pulled his keys from the pocket of his jeans and turned back towards the front door.

'That was the police. They've got some news apparently. They're on their way here.'

The landing seemed to shift around me as I tried to take in the significance of those three clipped sentences.

'Did they say why? Have they found her?' I put a hand on his arm: 'Stephen, they must have said something.'

'They didn't,' he said, trying to control the wobble in his voice. 'Just that — and that they'd be here in a second. OK?'

Had the news been good, surely they would have said? They would not have wanted to put us through this. The reflux of all the fears, all the suspicions I had pushed out of my head caused my legs to buckle. Leaning against the wall as Stephen struggled with the lock, I felt the unfamiliar sensation of tears needling the corners of my eyes. Stephen turned towards me, just in time to see me blot one away.

'Anna, for God's sake, don't. You're so strong, and you've been amazing over the past few days. Do you know what Beth says she loves about you? That you're young enough always to be confident that everything will be fine.'

Stephen enveloped me in a protracted, soothing hug, and for once I felt no need to pull away.

'Everything will be fine, I'm sure of it,' I murmured into his neck.

'You're right, but God, am I going to have words with that woman when she does come home.'

Minutes later the gulp of the lift, like an apprehensive messenger, informed us that they were on their way up.

'*Bonjour, Monsieur, Bonjour, Mademoiselle.*'

Verbier was alone this time, wearing a long waxed coat, like a British Barbour jacket but down to his knees, and a burgundy scarf wrapped in the kind of contrived knot that only the French can achieve, high around his throat.

'Well, I thought we should tell you that we've spoken to passport control and checked all the immigration software on our computers: there's no sign of any Beth Murphy leaving the country.'

We stared back at him.

'Is there anywhere else she might have gone? A friend or an ex-boyfriend in another part of France she might be visiting?'

Stephen was shaking his head.

'No, no, no,' I explained. 'She must have gone to see her father. It's the only thing that makes sense. If she hasn't, then this is something different . . . if she hasn't, then

278

something terrible must have happened.'

I didn't hear what the inspector said next, sitting down heavily and waiting for the cumbrous calculations of my mind to produce their result. Luckily, Stephen short-circuited the process.

'So what does all this mean, exactly?'

'It means that your friend is still in France, and most definitely a missing person.'

'But you do . . . ' My throat was dry and I swallowed hard. 'You do think she's all right though?'

It was an infantile question, full of hope and devoid of logic. I thought I saw a flicker of pity cross his face.

'Well, it's not good news, obviously. But I can assure you that in many instances of this kind there is a reasonable explanation and the person either returns home or is found safe and well.'

'How many days . . . ?' I asked falteringly. 'Because that's the way it works, isn't it? How many days before you guys accept that something has happened to her?'

The colour had drained from Stephen's face, sickly white now with frondy blond eyelashes which gave his eyes a rabbit-like quality.

'We don't like to say . . . '

'How many?' cut in Stephen.

279

'After seven,' Verbier was looking at the lino floor now, delineating a hexagonal outline with his foot, 'we generally fear the worst.'

Stephen began to sob.

I took the inspector to the door.

'Please let us know immediately if you hear anything.'

He traced a flat line through the air with his right hand, which signified 'That goes without saying', and left.

Bent over the table with his head in his hands, Stephen was whimpering now. It was the annoying, pining sound of a dog trapped. Incapable of consolation I went straight to the phone.

'I'd better call Christian and tell him what's happened.'

He was at work when I reached him, the clatter of the kitchen too loud for us to have a proper conversation. A half-hour later he stood, grim-faced, outside the front door of the flat.

'She's not gone to Ireland,' I filled him in, walking briskly in front of him towards the kitchen. 'In fact, there's no record of her leaving the country at all.'

I was aware that I sounded cold, that my speech was measured and its intonations duller than they should be. But I didn't care. If the alternative was to let myself succumb to the mawkish grief Stephen was displaying, hunched over the table as he still was, then I preferred to deal with it my way.

'Stephen.' Christian stood in the doorway with his legs apart in a way which ordinarily would have provoked desire in me. 'Stephen, look at me.'

He made no attempt to look up. I watched with fascination the blood discolouring the back of his neck in large, flower-shaped patches. In one deft movement Christian was beside him, inserting four fingers beneath his chin and jolting it sharply upwards.

'What are you crying about? Stephen, look at me. Why are you in this state? We don't know any more than we did before. So what that she didn't go to Ireland. What does that prove?'

'Everything!' His growl of rage echoed throughout the flat. A creaking door on the landing opposite answered its call, and then, hearing nothing more, slammed shut again. 'It means everything! Don't you see? It means Beth could be dead.'

Stephen's eyes were so red and sticky that it looked like the corneas were bleeding; even Christian was struggling to maintain his composure.

'Or the police may have got it wrong: they don't know everything, Stephen. They do sometimes get things wrong.'

I noted with alarm the pleading in his voice. He was asking somebody else to believe that Beth was still all right, and the realisation that he might still be in love with her, had ever been in love with her, hit me.

'He's right, Stephen,' I interjected, knowing he was wrong, wrong, wrong. 'She might still be OK. Let's try her father again, try Ruth again, try everyone — I don't believe that she can just disappear like this.'

I knew as I spoke that we wouldn't be reassured, but those few remaining minutes of hope seemed precious beyond anything.

'You all keep on asking me this question,' crackled Mr Murphy's voice on the line, 'and I'll tell you what I told the others: she's not here. She's coming to see me though. My Beth did promise she would come.'

His voice grew faint, and I suspected he had wandered away from the phone, picturing the receiver hanging limply across a dusty wooden chair in a farmhouse kitchen.

'Mr Murphy? Are you still there?'

'Of course I am. And there's no need to shout: I'm not deaf, you know, but I do wish you'd stop bothering me. She always gets back in time to do her homework. Always. What do you want my daughter for, anyway?'

'Do you understand how serious this is?' I

raised my voice, feeling my right temple beginning to throb. 'Your daughter is missing, and we've had to call the police. We're all very worried, so if she turns up, you have to tell us.'

I was preparing myself for the ordeal of reading out digits down the phone, but Beth's father had already hung up. Christian, I couldn't face, somehow beginning to feel that he was the reason for all this. I turned to Stephen. 'There's only one thing to do. We'll have to go to Ireland ourselves, speak to her dad and to the neighbours, and find out what's going on. That's what the police should already have done. I just don't think they're trying their best to sort this thing out.'

Stephen had calmed down, and began nodding his approval.

'If we leave tomorrow morning we'll be there by Friday. My boss knows what's going on but it might be trickier for you to get the time off . . .'

'I don't think you both need go,' Christian cut in with sudden authority. 'I should be around at my place in case she decides to go there, and someone should really stay here, just in case.'

'He's right.'

That night, we sat around the kitchen table planning Stephen's trip, all three of us trying to ignore the grinning photograph of Beth pinned to the noticeboard just above our heads, alongside her redundant shopping list and a flyer for a local gym she'd insisted she was going to join every week since I'd known her.

★   ★   ★

Early the following morning, Christian drove Stephen to the Gare du Nord. Even though we were taking steps to put everything right, the world around me seemed wildly out of kilter. Isabelle's constant appearances throughout the day in my section of the gallery meant that I reluctantly gave in and allowed her to become my confidante. Mid-afternoon, standing beneath the cloud-shaped awnings of the museum with my eyes on the river, I told her the news.

'Oh my God, Anna.' She raised a hand to her cheek, but the little smile was still there. 'You must be feeling terrible about everything. Sort of guilty too, I guess. It's brave of you to come into work.'

The words were there, each one picked out with care, but I began to suspect that under their bland surface was a more sinister motive. Isabelle saw herself as a friend, yet I had started to sense an enemy in her.

'Well, Stephen's gone to Ireland today to try to track her down, so things could still turn out OK.'

It sounded unconvincing, even to me, and I spent the remainder of the day cursing myself for having told her anything at all.

★   ★   ★

It was the first time I had gone back to Christian's flat alone, and the darkness of the stairwell felt desolating. Everything ordered and pure had ricocheted into another world, one where nothing made sense. I longed for my father's advice, but knew I could not call him. What would I say? Christian would be home in under an hour, so I resolved to busy myself by playing at domesticity, and prepare dinner for him. In a kitchen that size, this was easier said than done. At that point his little garret still held a residual charm. Only a few days later, those walls would begin to symbolise the prison of guilt we had built around ourselves.

I was distracted by a light going on across the street. The occupant had just seated himself low down in a velvet chair with one green corduroy-clad leg balanced on his knee. I wondered whether, if I stared at him long enough, he would sense me watching, look away from the book he was reading, stub his Gitane out in the marble ashtray on the coffee table beside him, and glance up. He didn't, and the spinach I had immersed in shallow water began to spit with annoyance. I turned it off and resumed my post at the window, determined to make the man aware of my existence.

'If he turns around,' I said to myself, 'everything will be all right, and life will return to normal.'

I stared and stared, but the onset of tears made his outline nebulous, washing the colours from the scene, and still he refused to lift his eyes from his book.

When Christian walked through the door twenty minutes later, no food had been prepared, and he would perhaps wonder why there was a mass of burnt spinach lying like a clump of dried seaweed at the bottom of the bin. I, however, was perfectly made-up, lying on the bed in one of his shirts reading a magazine. No one would ever have guessed that minutes earlier I had been pressed against the kitchen window-pane, crying about the obstinacy of a man I had never met.

'*Tu es très belle,*' he said, kissing me lightly on the mouth before putting his bag down.

I lifted my eyes from the article I wasn't

reading and attempted a smile.

'Good day?'

'Uneventful.'

Tugging harshly at the zip of his coat, he freed himself in one noiseless gesture, and squared up to me in the same way he'd confronted an Arab who had commented on the length of my skirt in a bar the week before.

'What's wrong?'

I swallowed twice, willing myself not to cry but feeling a burning sensation behind my eyes. Then his arm was round me, my nose buried in the groove of his neck.

'Promise me that it'll all be all right.'

'I promise.'

But they were only words, words you use to try to make everything better.

★ ★ ★

That night our movements were automatic, loveless, drawn out as long as we could. I turned my back to him, knowing that if our eyes met I would have to stop what we were doing. But sleep would have been impossible. Afterwards, we lay breathless beside one another, not touching. I noticed for the first time that the bed sheets needed washing, and that the damp had inscribed nicotine-rimmed

287

clouds on the walls. There was nothing poetic about the flat; it was the accommodation of a student, and that was all. Christian began to speak. He sounded strange in the murky orange dawn, and I wanted to cover up his mouth, to smother him with kisses, anything to make him stop talking.

'Is it our fault, Anna?'

'Of course not.'

Involuntarily my toe brushed against his foot; it was cold.

'You're right.' He had turned towards me now, his faultless face half buried in the pillow, a tiny bleached feather bent backwards against his cheek. 'There's no way she could have known about us.'

'Of course there's no way.' I felt impatient now, angry that he was trying to turn something that had nothing to do with us into an act of retribution, and disappointed that he would let something as absurd as superstition get to him.

'We haven't slept,' I reached for my phone to check the time, 'and it's 4 a.m. That's the only reason you're thinking like this.'

So typical, so very like a man to seek a convenient release from guilt the moment desire had been quenched — the same desire that had bred this situation to begin with. If he's not strong enough for this, I thought spitefully, he shouldn't have done what he did, and he shouldn't be lying here now.

'And if you really think that Beth is the kind of girl who would ever do anything to herself, then you know her even less well than I thought.' I shifted on to my side to avoid the intensifying dislike in his eyes.

'I know exactly how Beth felt about that, actually,' he muttered.

Refusing to give him the satisfaction of turning around, I replied: 'So you and she sat about discussing life, death and suicide, did you? How wrong I must have been about your relationship.'

'Life and death, no,' he began quietly, missing, or choosing to ignore, my sarcasm, 'but we did discuss suicide once.'

'Pillow talk, was it?' I couldn't stop myself.

'No.' A pause. 'It was the night we came back from my brother's. I know I shouldn't have, but I told her about the girl.'

He moved in closer behind me, tracing the underside of my breast apologetically with a finger. Something jarred in my mind.

'And don't worry, obviously I didn't tell her that I was with you. I'm not that stupid. No, I told her that I was out with some guys from work, that we were coming back from a big night out together when we saw it, her . . . whatever.'

I heard myself cry out — a noise that was part animal, part child.

'Jesus Christ, Anna, what is it? Are you OK?'

Memories slammed into one another, each one gathering momentum, until with agonising lucidity, I replayed the final hour I had spent with Beth, heard my own soothing voice telling her that her father's life had been rich, not cut off in its prime — not like the girl I had seen, the girl on the bridge.

'You idiot.' I was sobbing now, curled up as far from Christian as the mattress would allow. 'You idiot.'

Seized by a morbid curiosity to watch his face collapse as the realisation took hold, I turned to look at him. When I think of his expression now, it makes me flinch with sadness. The half-closed lids were drawn right back, their enchanting quality replaced by a kind of vapid disbelief, and for the first time I noticed that there were shallow lines beneath them. The idea that I had ever loved this person was laughable. Where Beth and I had seen mystery, there was only an unexceptional being painted over with our own desire. He was saying something over and over again, so quickly that at first I couldn't catch it.

'What have we done? Oh God, what have we done?'

I left him there — he wasn't talking to me in any case — and ran to the toilet. Holding my hair back with one hand, I waited. Nothing came except a small jet of saliva, which burst open in the water like a botched firework, then disappeared. When I got back a few minutes later, Christian had gone out. I was thankful to him at least for that, for realising that it wouldn't have helped either of us to have had to face each other at that moment. Still, the thought of lying there alone with my thoughts appalled me. I dressed quickly and tiptoed down the stairs into the somnolent streets below.

* * *

The digital clock outside the pharmacy on the rue de la Tour was flashing a quarter to five in the morning, and the whirring of a machine swabbing down the street unlocked a silent world. Turning to check that the figure on the opposite corner was not Christian, I almost collided with a box on wheels which completely obscured the delivery man pushing it along. Muttering '*Pardon*', and stuffing my hands in my pockets, I walked down the narrow, dawn-tinted pavements past rows of overflowing green bins until I reached the avenue Henri

291

Martin. There I felt able to breathe again, as though the width of it alone were reassuring, swallowing me in its ascetic anonymity. In Paris, even in the small hours, some bars are still open. Through a window I watched three workmen drinking Pastis, one throwing his head back with laughter at something the barman had said. I wondered how I would describe the moment to Beth. But Beth was no longer there.

Pushing open the doors of the bar, braving the workmen's stares, I settled on a banquette by the window. I can't remember how long I sat there, taking mechanical sips of the coffee I'd ordered, waiting for my imagination to uncover an escape route which might absolve me of any responsibility. But the scenes I played out in my mind only served to cement the realisation of the damage I had done. Beth had been vulnerable. She had come to Paris to start a new life, away from her sick father and the memories of a broken engagement. There she had lived quite happily with Stephen until I had appeared, falling a little bit in love with her and the way she made me feel, and wanting to take everything that was hers. Guilt and resentment flooded through me: why had she not seen me for what I was?

★ ★ ★

Did I ever truly believe that Beth might have ended her own life over the discovery? No, I never did. Perhaps because it would have made my shame unbearable, but also because I still believe today that I really did know Beth. And I knew that for all the soft lines of her face and figure, and all the tenderness she bestowed upon others, there was a kernel of toughness, bred in the hard realities of farming families. She would run from it all, yes, but I felt sure that she would start afresh somewhere else, just as she had tried to do here.

During the autumn months, at precisely half past eight in the morning, every street lamp in Paris goes out, officially announcing the end of night. Walking slowly across the pont des Invalides, nearing the museum, I had only one thought: I had to reach Stephen. The instant he returned from Ireland Christian and I would have to sit him down and tell him what we'd done. I tried to imagine his face, tried to persuade myself that he already knew, that it would not come as the shock I expected it would be, but all that was wishful thinking. Putting a hand in my pocket, I realised that I had left with nothing but my purse. Unwilling to return to the flat,

I stopped at a nearby phone box, rang Stephen, and left him Isabelle's number, thinking she, at least, would be sure to relay any message to me. That, it turned out, would be the finishing touch to my catalogue of mistakes.

★ ★ ★

Every morning, when I walked into the museum, the world instantly felt calmer. Here was a place where loud voices, dramatic gestures and violent emotions were stifled. Simply to take my place on that wooden chair, surrounded by the past and its sublimated emotions, restored some of my sangfroid. A brittle cough made me jump: for once those whispering slippers had failed to announce her arrival.

'Ça va?' She'd crept up on me, shattering the first steady heartbeat I had experienced that day. 'Oh Anna. You look terrible. Have you slept at all?'

I shook my head, willing her away. 'I'll be fine. It's quiet today, and I'd rather be here than at home, waiting by the phone. By the way,' I watched her brighten as she anticipated the favour I would ask, thinking with grim amusement that it was all coming together nicely for her, 'I gave Stephen your mobile number. I hope that's all right. It's just that I left mine at home, and he promised he'd call when he gets back from Ireland later today.'

'Of course that's fine. I'll let you know the second he calls.'

But he didn't call that morning, or that afternoon, and the fear that he had found Beth in Ireland and that she had told him everything dominated my thoughts. For some reason the idea of Stephen finding out was almost as horrifying to me as the knowledge that Beth already had. I had twice fought the urge to go and find Isabelle, and twice succumbed, only to be greeted with the same doleful smile and shaking head: Stephen still hadn't called.

I stayed at the museum as late as I could that night, desperate to avoid Christian. I needn't have bothered; he didn't come home. At a quarter to one Stephen woke me up. He was back at the flat, but his voice sounded tinny, as though he were still in Ireland.

'When did you get back?'

'This afternoon.'

'And you didn't call me? How was it? Did you find her?'

There was a pause, as though this last question — the only question I was ever going to ask — had come as a surprise.

'No. Can you get out of work tomorrow morning? I need to see you.'

He delivered the phrase in a businesslike manner. My instincts told me that he had found Beth, and that she had told him everything.

★   ★   ★

'Christian.'

I'd awoken the next morning to the sound of his key in the lock. Now he was perched on the edge of the mattress, fiddling with the remote control, the thinning grey fabric of his T-shirt stretched tight across his shoulder-blades.

'Christian.'

He was constantly fixing things: playing with electric cables, changing fuses or mending the stove. Anything to avoid looking at me.

'Yes?'

He didn't turn, so I spoke to the neck that no longer aroused me and its ladder of golden hairs.

'Stephen rang last night. I think he might know, but I'm not sure. Maybe he's just tired from the trip. Anyway, he definitely sounded weird.'

There was a pause, and the click of a fitting

296

being slid into place, before he replied. 'Does that surprise you?'

A pause. 'Why are you making everything sound as though it's my fault?' I knew, as I said this, the conversation that would ensue. But I refused to bear the burden alone.

'I don't know.' He turned to face me. 'Nothing's ever your fault, is it? But you're right: it's also my fault for not avoiding you, for giving in to you. Remember that day on the beach when you thought I was asleep? That was you, Anna. That was you starting this.'

I sat down gracelessly, terrified that I had guessed what he would say next. 'I'm not coming with you, Anna, to meet Stephen. Because if you're right, and Beth has told him, then me being there will only make things worse. Stephen has never liked me. How could he? He had Beth all to himself before I came along.'

'I can't do this on my own, Christian.'

'Yes, you can. You don't need anyone.'

In one last-ditch attempt to convince him I leant towards his face with a smile, and tried to kiss him. But he saw only the desperation in that smile. Catching my chin firmly between his thumb and forefinger, holding me up before him like a piece of fruit on a market stall, lingering over the lips and then moving up, with an expression of distaste, to the eyes, he pushed me away.

'No, Anna.'

'You're a coward.'

His head was once again hunched over the remote control.

'So are you.'

11

Stephen was already sitting on a bench by the curved stone balustrades overlooking the Palais du Luxembourg ten minutes before we were due to meet. I too had arrived early and spotted him at once, recognising the blond muss of his hair through the trees, rendered unseasonably leafless by that vicious summer.

My heart had sunk when he'd suggested we meet there: it was the backdrop to my happiest days in Paris. Instead of going straight over to Stephen, I watched him staring up into the low sky, a jigsaw puzzle of grey with one piece missing where clear blue shone through. He checked his watch, and I tried, from that gesture, and from the fact that his back was not resting against the slated spine of the bench but anxiously bent forward, to decipher whether he knew. I began my approach, with a half-smile neither too brash nor too culpable. It soon faded.

'How was Ireland? You look exhausted. Did you find anything out?'

I was aware only that I had to keep talking. 'No. No, I didn't. And when I got back last night, I tried to call you on that number you gave me.'

The events of the past few days had blurred my memory, and for a moment I couldn't remember which number he was talking about.

'I got hold of Isabelle, who told me to come over; that you'd be back at any minute. So I took a taxi round there.'

He hadn't looked at me once, still gazing upwards, as though trying to establish whether it might rain, and I looked at the blue wrist lying upturned in his lap, wondering at Isabelle's extraordinary manoeuvres.

'And I waited, and waited. But you weren't there. Which makes sense, considering you don't live there and you never have done.'

'Stephen, you know that Isabelle's a little . . . '

'So there I am, in this flat (which, by the way, is nowhere near where you said it was) talking to Isabelle, when she takes a deep breath and says she has something to tell me.'

It was pointless to try to interrupt. I could tell that he had written out the script in his head and would not stop until he had recited it all.

'And she starts this long, convoluted story, and at first I can't understand what she's telling me, and then I realise that she is only repeating things you've told her. And that it's all true. So I stop interrupting and let her finish, and at the end, she tells me that she's sorry to have to be the one to tell me, and, like a school teacher, asks me if I have any questions. And I do have one, as it happens, but it turns out that it's the only question she doesn't really know the answer to.'

'What's that?' I asked flatly.

'How long?'

He looked at me for the first time and I felt myself shrivel with humility beneath his gaze.

'How long had you two been . . . ?'

'Stephen . . . '

'I'm so sorry. Have I offended your sensibilities?'

'Listen, Stephen. It wasn't like that. And it didn't start . . . I mean, we didn't start . . . well, not until quite recently.'

'When?'

Whatever I said would have precipitated the response I got. I felt something inside me implode, softly.

'In Normandy.'

'In Normandy? Are you serious? That's not possible. While we were all under the same roof?'

'I'm not going to go into the details, Stephen. What's the point? I'm sorry that it had to happen, and I never wanted it to go this far. You've got to believe that. If I could take it all back, I would.'

'Why did it 'have to happen', Anna? That's where you've got it wrong. Shall I explain to you how most people live their lives? They see things that they want, all the time, and they accept that they can't always have them. Only you don't have that reflex, do you? And the funny thing is that from the moment I met you, I was aware of that, only it didn't matter to me, because I never thought that side of you would touch either Beth or me. Do you know how she found out?'

I nodded.

'Well?'

'I have a fair idea. But does it really matter now, Stephen?'

'You were just what she needed right now — some careless little girl to take away the only thing making her happy.'

'You make it sound like it was all me, Stephen. Christian wasn't exactly kicking and screaming. And she has plenty of things in her life: he . . . he's nothing.'

'I don't doubt that, although I'm surprised to hear you say it. But I don't give a damn about him. Some dead-beat French guy who should have worshipped the ground she walked on? No, I never held out much faith in him, but for some reason she loved him.

302

Oh, and don't be so arrogant as to think that she would do anything to herself' — he threw his head back and laughed: a mirthless, black laugh — 'because of a selfish child.'

I wasn't sure what I had expected, but it wasn't this.

'So where is she then, Stephen?'

He shook his head, unable to maintain the pitch of his anger.

'I don't know. Her father now can't even remember when he last spoke to her on the phone, let alone that whole business about her saying she was coming to see him. Meanwhile Ruth swears blind she's heard nothing from her for two weeks, but for all I know she's just protecting her.'

A jogger with bare legs ran past, spraying damp earth behind him. Neither of us spoke as the susurration of his nylon shorts retreated into the distance.

'But you know her better than anyone. You must have an idea of how she would react to . . . well, to something like this? Where might she go?'

'If I knew that I'd be there now. I've already spoken to the police today and they've promised to keep us — me — informed.'

'But Stephen, we need to forget about all the other stuff now, and concentrate on finding her. I know I've been a terrible friend, no,' I shook my head, 'worse. But I do love her and I want to help. You will tell me, if you hear anything, won't you?'

'Why should I when all of this is because of you? Do you really think that you're the kind of person Beth needs in her life? I don't think so.'

I reeled at the harshness of his words. There had to be some way of redeeming myself, some explanation I could give for the way I had behaved, some lie that would make it all go away, and yet I couldn't find one.

Placing one palm on his knee and the other on the chipped green bench, Stephen pushed himself up, looking for a second like an elderly man, and walked off.

★ ★ ★

I can bring him around. And then together we'll find Beth, and I'll get everything back the way it was before. These were my thoughts as, smiling but with tears in my eyes, I found myself wandering the back streets of the Latin Quarter an hour later, with no sense of where I was going. One thing I was sure of: I was not ready to go back to the damp, suffocating confines of Christian's flat. I blamed him for all of it. If he had not shown himself to be so weak a covert flirtation might have been our only crime. As I pictured him now, coming up behind me in Pierre's bathroom, I felt almost affronted by his aggression, and amazed at myself for giving in so readily. In the narrow street I walked down, where the cars were lined bumper to bumper, a dusty Fiat bore the daubed inscription, '*Je t'aime Nathalie*' across its rear window. I wondered whether Nathalie knew about it, whether it meant anything at all, and every question brought me back to Beth.

★ ★ ★

'But we're short-staffed at the moment, Anna. Is there any way you can come in later on?'

I had called in sick the day Stephen had confronted me, and Céline's response was typically ungracious when I called in sick again the next morning. But I wasn't lying. I did feel sick, sick at the idea of the man I had just spent the night with, the same man I could now hear brushing his teeth in the bathroom.

The previous night had been the first platonic one for us, and I still wasn't sure whether I felt relief or a terminal sense of disappointment. I had watched him getting into bed, intrigued by the lack of desire I felt for that body. But the fear, before he walked through the door at a quarter past midnight, that he might not come home at all, had reminded me that I needed him, that what we had done was forcing us, for the moment at least, to stay together.

That day I was unable to leave the flat. Stephen hadn't rung: I hadn't expected he would. At midday I had made myself a cup of coffee and, with my knees pulled into my chest, sat at the kitchen window watching the empty flat across the road. I didn't cry; I wasn't the self-pitying kind. And who would I be crying for? I believed Stephen when he said that Beth would be fine, because it suited me not to believe anything worse. One thing bothered me: I didn't see how she could have escaped the searches Stephen had informed me of, which now involved the Irish police. Perhaps she knew that by disappearing it would bring this punishment on my head.

★ ★ ★

I could not distinguish one day from another over the fortnight that followed. The rain fell incessantly. The first few mornings I rang the museum to explain that my stomach bug

306

showed no signs of abating. Then I stopped calling altogether, feeling no surprise when, finally, a message from Céline on my answerphone informed me that my services were no longer required.

⋆ ⋆ ⋆

There was only one thing left to do. Sitting in a deserted Chinese restaurant near the flat, I dialled my parents' number. When my mother unexpectedly answered, a wave of love nearly took my breath away.

'Hello?'

'Mum, it's me.'

'Hello, darling, how is everything?'

'Not so good, actually, I . . . ' but my mother's voice, imbued with that familiar note of controlled irritation, cut me off.

'Yes, I'm just coming. Anna darling? Are you there? Listen, my cab's waiting outside but I'll hand you your father.'

The immediate concern in his voice pierced the protective skein that instantly formed over my emotions during each and every exchange with my mother, and I bit my lip, trying hard not to cry.

'I've lost my job at the museum, Dad . . . '

And then there were questions, so many of them. How did it happen? When did it happen? Did I understand the trouble my uncle had gone to in order to get me that job in the first place?

Tired, and already feeling distanced from a city I was falling out of love with, I didn't even bother trying to find a suitable explanation. My mother would be disappointed, he was saying gently, but we would find a way to explain it to her. I watched three waiters out of the corner of my eye, elegantly shapeless in their pinafore shirts and drawstring trousers, converging around a large salmon that had just been delivered. Occasionally the youngest of the three threw a casual look my way, betraying a glimmer of concern that my jasmine tea was still untouched, wondering if I would ever order any food. My father had stopped talking.

'Are you still there, Dad?'

'You'd better come home. I'm afraid your mother and I can't just pay for you to be there without a job. That wasn't the idea.'

I hung up the phone and ordered a ten-euro menu I knew I wouldn't touch. It had just arrived when my phone rang again: it was my father.

'I've booked you on Eurostar. It leaves first thing tomorrow morning, 7.16 a.m. from the Gare du . . . '

'I know where they go from, Dad.'

'What?'

'I know where the train goes from.'

'Your mother's at a conference in Frankfurt until Sunday night but I'll come and pick you up at Waterloo. Have you got much stuff?'

★ ★ ★

The fact that I had given up on a job my uncle had procured for me would quietly enrage my father. But my world had capsized so completely that I no longer cared, and it was only on my way back to the flat that I began to think about what I would say to Christian.

He was still at work when I pushed the door of the flat open, and I noticed that once again, neither one of us had bothered to make the bed. His crumpled T-shirt on the floor left me cold, and I began to gather up my affairs from around the flat: some clothes, a book I had just bought and a few toiletries. The sound of his steps on the stairs made me hasten my pace.

I must have looked guilty when he walked in, flushed and pale-lipped from the wind outside. He glanced at the bag on the bed and shrugged off his jacket.

'*Tu pars?*'

Whenever we discussed anything serious,

Christian retreated to French. I had early on ascertained that this was in self-defence.

'Yes.'

He nodded slowly, unwinding the scarf from around his neck, and I noticed that he was wearing the same jumper he had worn on our drive to Normandy. A knock at the door interrupted the silence. Christian opened it just a fraction, and I recognised the voice on the other side as belonging to Saïd from across the hall. There followed an exchange that, in the circumstances, seemed surreal.

'Sorry, mate. Have you seen the rubbish bags downstairs by the door? One of them's split open all over the stairs and it's a right fucking mess. Now I'm not pointing fingers but we all have to live here, right? And I don't want to come home to a pigsty. The bin men don't even come for another two days.'

As Christian explained that he had been at work all day and was sure the occupant of 3D was the culprit, I took one last look around the room to check that I had not left anything behind. I felt no regret: there would be other men, men with equally beautiful faces, men with sensuous bodies and soft words just like him. But Beth —

Said was laughing at something Christian had said. I could see that he was trying to draw the exchange to a close, yet still their patter continued.

I picked up my bag, and walked out between the two men.

'I have to go now, Christian.'

A flicker of pain, visceral in its intensity, crossed his face.

'Anna, for God's sake. Hang on a second. Saïd, we'll have to talk about this later. Anna, don't go. Come back here.'

It would have been funny if it hadn't been so absurd. There was Saïd, still babbling about the bins, muttering 'No reason for it; there's just no reason for it' in his strongly accented French, frenzied Arab music drifting into the hallway from his flat, and Christian, stuck there, unable to say goodbye.

★ ★ ★

It felt liberating to have everything I needed in the bag on my shoulder. Not yet knowing where I would sleep, I was conscious only that it was necessary to get out of the neighbourhood quickly if I was to avoid the embarrassment of Christian coming after me. With this in mind I boarded the first métro headed anywhere central. Watching a gypsy woman and her three children work their way up and down the carriages, I fancied it might

311

be poetic to spend my last hours in Paris bidding a personal farewell to every memorable quarter, like a departing lover who kisses their sweetheart's every limb before saying goodbye. But these were spoiled memories now, irrevocably entwined with Beth or Christian. The only area free of associations were the lugubrious streets around the Gare du Nord.

★   ★   ★

I checked myself into the Hotel du Voyageur, a two-star place above an oyster bar, without even asking to see the room, and sat on the edge of the bed. The mock gentility of the place was neatly illustrated by a Monet print above the desk: it had slipped in its glass frame so that a corner of brown cardboard was visible behind it. It was only eight o'clock. I wasn't hungry and felt tempted to spend my final night in Paris in that room, waiting for morning to arrive. But there was one last thing I had to do.

★   ★   ★

'Yes, I know it's you: your number comes up on the screen.'

I hadn't expected Stephen to be friendly,

312

but the grimness of his tone cowed me for a moment.

'I just rang to say that I'm leaving in the morning. I'm going back to London.'

Nothing.

'I'd really like to say goodbye.'

He exhaled hard down the receiver. I pictured him, too tall for everything in that room, leaning with one elbow against the wall by the phone.

'When are you off?'

'Very early.'

'Are you going with him?'

'No. He . . . that's over.'

'Just like that?' He gave a sour laugh. 'Of course it is.'

'Look, it'll only take a few minutes. Can I come over now? Please?'

* * *

He looked better than he had since Beth had first disappeared. His complexion was clearer, and the mauve circles beneath his eyes had faded.

'They've found her, haven't they?' I was convinced of it. In my life, nothing had ever stayed bad for long. 'Where is she?'

'No they haven't, Anna. What makes you think that?'

'They have. Just look at you.'

'Last night I slept right through, for the first time in weeks. But only through exhaustion. Nothing else. Come in.'

I followed him meekly down the hall into the kitchen, where he turned his back to me and began spooning coffee into the cafetière.

'Instant is fine, you know.'

He turned with a dazed look.

'I fancied some real coffee. That OK with you?'

'Fine.'

'So are you flying?'

'Eurostar.'

'Right. Better, I guess.'

'Definitely.'

He placed the cafetière on the table, and we waited until it was time for him to ease the plunger down, as if it was a cue for me to speak.

'Does it help if I say that I'm sorry?'

'Not really, Anna. Does it help you?'

'No. That's not why I'm here, to feel better about myself. I just thought . . . I don't know why . . . because of everything . . . that I should say goodbye.'

The coffee was insipid. 'You're right: it does taste so much better.'

My smile was not returned. I wondered if there was anything left for me here, and whether I should leave.

'I'm sorry. I've said that already, I know, but I'm sorry for being here too, for making you feel awkward. There's no reason why you should ever have let me into this flat again.'

As I said it the thought of the night I had spent trying to tempt Christian into Beth's bed came back to me. It now seemed crazy: someone else's act.

He made no attempt to keep me there, and as we walked past Beth's darkened room, I fancied I saw her through the doorway, remembering only after my heart missed a beat that it was her dressmaker's dummy.

'I'll miss this place.'

We were standing by the door. I thought he might lean forward and kiss me on the cheek, but he made no motion towards me.

'If I tell you that I slept well last night because of a phone call I received, do you promise never to try to contact either one of us again?'

Worried I would let out the sob crushing my chest, I nodded.

'Goodbye, Anna.'

*　*　*

At six-thirty the platform of the Gare du Nord is one of the most desolate places one can be in Paris. I sat on my bags, watching a fleet of businessmen and -women with box-cases on wheels roll noisily on to the train, leaving a city that meant something quite different to them. I knew I would be back one day. But I also knew that it wouldn't be for a long time, and that even when I did return, the ghosts of that year would always be poised to jump out at me.

★　★　★

Though I longed to sleep through that three-hour journey, the monotonous noises of a video game at the back of the carriage and the clicking throat of the sleeping business-man beside me conspired to keep me awake. We sped quickly out of Paris into the suburbs, and I thought I recognised a housing estate in the distance as one Christian and I had driven past on our way to his brother's flat. Already the past three months had begun to take on a dream-like quality. To dispel it, I took my phone from my bag and deleted Beth, Stephen, Christian and Isabelle's numbers. The train gained momentum and I worked my way down the list, removing anyone connected with Paris, breathing more evenly as each person left my life for good.

The train shuddered to a halt and the

businessman's head lolled on to my shoulder. I didn't move away, oddly reassured by this human contact. He awoke with a jolt.

'*Pardon, Mademoiselle. Pardon.*'

Just before we entered the tunnel I locked myself into the toilet, to be alone for a few minutes and to wash the ashes of Paris from my face.

12

My father was standing outside the arrivals gate with the same grim expression he'd worn when he'd come home early to find me partially clothed, aged fourteen, in bed with a sixth-former from the local boys' school. For days he'd found it hard to look at me, turning his face away from mine in an attitude of false distraction, just as he did now. After brushing his cheek awkwardly against mine he put my bags wordlessly into the boot.

'Strap yourself in.'

'So how are you, Dad?'

'Your mother and I are both well. She told you, didn't she, that she's in Frankfurt until tomorrow evening?'

'*You* did, yes. But what about you: did you miss me?' I donned my most childish face, mischievous but endearing, and looked up at him in a way I knew would melt his heart.

'Of course I did. We both did. But we were rather hoping you could make this year in Paris work. I put a lot of effort into getting you that job, called in a few favours, you know.' He paused. 'To be honest, I'm disappointed.'

How is it that parents know exactly the right phrase, the one sentence among thousands that fits the bill, and is guaranteed to skewer your heart with shame?

'Dad . . . ' Against my volition, there was already an apologetic, imploring quality to my voice. 'I was really grateful for the opportunity. Honestly. But it wasn't really me.'

'Oh well if it wasn't 'you', then I quite understand,' he said, his eyes firmly on the road ahead.

Sensing the futility of my words, I turned in my seat, feeling the belt pull across my already tight chest, and looked out of the window at the Houses of Parliament, which appeared hackneyed to me after the wonders of Paris.

★ ★ ★

I went straight to my room when we got home, hoping it might bring me solace. Instead, my A level revision notes and the heavy winter coat hanging up behind my door made my feeling of estrangement keener: they were objects I no longer recognised, belonging to someone who no longer existed.

'Dinner will be ready in an hour or so.' It was my father, speaking from behind my door.

'Come in, Dad.'

But already, I could hear his slow footsteps on the stairs. Jumping off the bed and pushing open the door, I shouted down to him.

'What are we eating?'

'Lasagne. I've just put it in the oven.'

There was no hint of jollity, not a whisper of forgiveness in that tone. It promised to be a long evening.

★   ★   ★

The kitchen was just the same: nothing had moved since I'd left, and yet I found it alienating, having remembered the spaces differently in my mind. The table was surely never so narrow, and why were the worktops so clear? Laying out the knives and forks restored a soothing rhythm; so engrossed was I in my task that I did not hear my father come in.

'Is it ready?' he asked me.

'Oh, I don't know, I haven't checked.'

'Could you do that?'

'Yes, of course. I'll have a look now.'

A little overdone, but I told him it was just right, and the two of us sat down with the polite courtesy of a married couple no longer in love with one another.

'This is good.'

My father did not respond.

'Have you ever gone away with Mum to one of her work things?'

I knew the answer all too well, but was ready to try anything to break the stalemate.

'Those conferences are pretty intense,' he said, cutting off another square of pasta and putting it to his lips, 'the last thing your mother needs is me hanging around.'

The hum of the fridge seemed to be increasing in volume, but to mention it would have meant admitting to our silence. Another appliance I couldn't identify started up and began to vibrate.

'Oh for God's sake.' I put my fork down with a clatter.

My father, chewing thoughtfully, looked at me, swallowed, and looked back down at his plate again.

Unable to bear it any longer, but feeling that my limbs had lost their natural elasticity, I got up, emptied the rest of my dinner into the swing bin, and stood beside it for a while watching my father calmly finish his meal.

'I think I might go to bed, Dad. I'm pretty tired.'

Say something, I prayed quietly to myself, please just say something, or I won't be able to sleep. But as I left the room, all I could hear was the deafening roar of the fridge.

* * *

My father's disappointment had permeated the whole house, so that even in my room its molecules seemed to fill the air. After a brief attempt at sleep, an avenue of hope — as thrilling as it was unexpected — suddenly presented itself. He was my father and his love was unconditional: I would use him as my confessional, tell him about Paris, about Beth and Christian, tell him everything. Once, aged thirteen, I had stolen a five-pound note from his wallet to buy a pencil case I had been coveting for weeks. When, in a subsequent frenzy of guilt, I had owned up to him, he had listened quietly, never delivering the chastisement I expected. 'I'm glad you told me,' had been his only comment. Now, I felt confident of a similar response.

* * *

'You're still up: I thought you might have gone to bed.'

He was sitting in the olive velvet-covered armchair by the window, a glass of cognac in his hand.

'No. Can't sleep?'

'No.'

In the long, chaste nightdress my grandmother had once bought me (and which I had felt might help my cause) I sat meekly down beside him on the sofa.

'Do you remember telling me about this great French saying, one we don't have an equivalent to?'

He put down the paper he was reading. 'They have several,' he said.

'*La vie est mal faite*. That was it: life is badly made. You can't deny it, nor can you blame someone for it.'

I said these words with the inward fixed gaze of someone who lies, even to herself.

'Anna,' he put down his book. 'What's this about, exactly? Because jacking in a job is not about life or anything other than you and what you are able to make of the things which you're lucky enough to have handed to you on a plate.'

My father and I had never once discussed emotions; this was not going to be easy.

'There was more to it than that, Dad. I, well, I got myself into a difficult situation out there.'

Once I had started, it was easy. The whole story came out, all of it, although the sexual nature of my relationship with Christian was left out. And I was right: he listened without interrupting, taking occasional sips from his glass, and looking straight at me. I had nothing more to say and gave an embarrassed laugh.

'Don't know why I told you all that. Anyway, at least you know now that I wasn't just being flaky, about the job I mean, and . . . '

A chafed hand, older and more speckled with age spots than I remembered, silenced me.

'I couldn't care less about that job. I'm more worried about the fact that you haven't understood a thing, Anna. Have you?'

I didn't know what he was talking about, and my expression must have betrayed as much.

'People are fragile, Anna. They're easy to break. Haven't you grown up enough to know that yet?' He ran a finger along the rough edge of his thumbnail in a way that gave me goose bumps before going on. 'You can't take away on a whim something which may be another person's reason for everything . . . for living even.'

★ ★ ★

A month passed during which I felt as if I was convalescing from an illness. I devoted my energies to shielding my emotions from even the most remote association with Paris. Unable to listen to the radio, watch a film or read a book, in case something, however tangential, reminded me of Beth, I developed a fascination with observing my own pain, as though monitoring it made it less likely to strike when I least expected, which it sometimes did.

During that period I remember one Sunday being driven to a garden centre by my mother, who had refused to console me or discuss anything with me since my father had told her of our conversation, no doubt thinking it was better that way. Sitting in the passenger seat, wearing an old striped jumper of my father's and the tracksuit bottoms that had become my staple, I realised that that extraordinary expedition came as close as anything could to perforating my sense of numbness. I stood by self-consciously, watching her pick out obscure items from a list my father had drawn up, occasionally feeling the weight of her gaze. It was only then, in a moment so unnatural for both of us, that I sensed her unspoken sympathy.

★ ★ ★

Then, one day, my father drove me to a job interview at a London publishing house.

Unbeknown to me, he had sent off my CV a week earlier in response to an advertisment he had spotted in the paper. Because I didn't care, and because things always came easily to me, I was offered the position on the spot.

I hadn't missed Christian at all. But Beth, Beth I missed far more than I had thought possible, often wondering what she was doing and who she was with, and discovering that even in dreams it is possible to be jealous. But as her face and the contours of her body began to fade from my mind like a photograph left in sunlight too long, I reasoned that soon I would be able to convince myself that none of it had ever happened. Slowly, my life regained a purpose, and the cast populating my waking dreams began to multiply.

I saw again friends whose lives I was no longer interested in, or perhaps never had been. But I had become better at simulating curiosity, asking questions whose answers signified nothing to me. The real chore was responding to their questions about Paris, because there was nothing I could comfortably extract from my existence there. So I invented a boyfriend who bore a striking resemblance to Vincent, and friends who were nothing like anyone I had actually met in

Paris. And gradually, every time I elaborated on my fictional acquaintances, borrowing from films and books, I believed my own lies just a little bit more, resetting my memories accordingly.

POSTSCRIPT

Humming tunelessly, with a thumb in his mouth, the child pulled impatiently for the second time on Beth's coat sleeve.

'We're going to be late, Mummy, we're going to be late.'

'It's all right, darling.'

We both waited until he resumed his swinging around the nearby lamp-post.

'I was pregnant, Anna, when I found out,' she said matter-of-factly. 'I never told you — I never even had the chance to tell him — and well, it hardly matters now.' She laughed but it sounded like a yelp, or a cough. 'I wasn't sure how I was going to manage. But I did — I suppose everyone does, don't they?'

Tears of remorse sprang to my eyes and I dug my nails into the arm of my chair waiting for the dizzying wave of guilt to wash over me.

'I'm sorry.'

She gave a little laugh, dry but not bitter, and looked at me for an instant with what I like to think was a glimmer of the old affection in her eyes.

328

'But you're happy,' I flung out desperately, crying now as I took in her ringless hand on the table and the slight thickening of her waist.

'I'd really better go. I'm late,' she declared abruptly.

'But our drinks? He'll be back in a minute with them.' She signalled to the child.

'And what about Stephen?' I asked desperately. 'Are you in touch with him?'

'Of course. He's still in Paris, but you know, he's married now.'

'Stephen? Married? Who on earth did he marry?'

She smiled coolly. 'Isabelle, of course. It was always obvious those two were meant to be together.'

She rose with the particular grace I had always admired in her, and I panicked as I realised how much I needed her in my life, even after all this time.

'Just wait a minute, why don't you? Or maybe we could see each other again? Now that we've found each other . . . '

'I don't think so, Anna.'

Her response was immediate: just as much as I needed her, she needed to keep out of harm's way.

'Goodbye.'

'Goodbye then,' I replied.

I watched her walking off, until my vision was blocked by the two large glasses of white wine that had been placed on the table.

'Barman says we only do rosé in summer, I'm afraid, so I brought you this instead.'

★ ★ ★

As I went home down a street I'd walked along so many times that it had become charmless, I caught sight of something in the window of an antique shop. It was neither the silver thimbles nor the Chinese vases that arrested my gaze, but the face I saw staring back at me. It was the same face as before, heart-shaped but irregular, with the same deep-set eyes, high cheekbones and frame of brown hair. But something about it, a new depth of experience, made me catch my breath. The quality I had admired in the faces of others that resolved them, made them whole, was now etched on my own.

We do hope that you have enjoyed reading this large print book.

Did you know that all of our titles are available for purchase?

We publish a wide range of high quality large print books including:
Romances, Mysteries, Classics
General Fiction
Non Fiction and Westerns

Special interest titles available in large print are:
The Little Oxford Dictionary
Music Book
Song Book
Hymn Book
Service Book

Also available from us courtesy of Oxford University Press:
Young Readers' Dictionary
(large print edition)
Young Readers' Thesaurus
(large print edition)

For further information or a free brochure, please contact us at:
Ulverscroft Large Print Books Ltd.,
The Green, Bradgate Road, Anstey,
Leicester, LE7 7FU, England.
Tel: (00 44) 0116 236 4325
Fax: (00 44) 0116 234 0205

THE SNOWING AND GREENING OF THOMAS PASSMORE

Paul Burman

Something strange has happened to Thomas Passmore. Waking from a warm Australian beach, he finds himself at Heathrow Airport on a winter's morning, only he can't remember getting there. Burdened with emotional baggage and a sense of deja vu, Thomas pieces together fragments of his life by walking through the shadows of his past. Haunted by his father's suicide, his mother's rejection and by memories of his first love, his increasingly bizarre journey takes him into a world where one man's struggle to live again, as timeless as the battle of the seasons, becomes a choice between loss and life.

ILLUMINATIONS

Eva Hoffman

Isabel Merton is a renowned concert pianist. At the height of her career, she feels increasingly torn between the musical realm she inhabits, and her fragmented life as an itinerant artist, with its frequent flights and anonymous hotels. Away from her New York home, on a European tour, Isabel meets Anzor Islikhanov, a political exile from war-torn Chechnya, who is driven by his desire to avenge his people. When their paths cross in several cities, they become drawn to each other — until a menacing incident forces Isabel to re-evaluate his actions and her own feelings, throwing her into a creative crisis . . .

LEAVING GAZA

Margaret Sutherland

Ruth, an Israeli writer who grew up amid gunfire and grenade, startles the genteel artistic world of Barbara and Heath Barnes. Barbara still lives and paints in her Australian hometown. Ruth's arrival coincides with Barbie's declaration of war on a life she now sees as subservient and controlled. Heath misunderstands Barbara and Ruth is drawn in to fill the growing rift. But following a crisis, Barbara's future lies in ruins. Peace is a hard-won trophy — and, like her admired early Australian women painters, she sets out on the road to freedom and the right to become herself.

NOVEL ABOUT MY WIFE

Emily Perkins

Tom Stone is madly in love with his wife Ann, an Australian in self-imposed exile in London. Expecting their first child, they buy a semi-derelict house in Hackney despite their spiralling money troubles. But soon Ann becomes convinced that a local homeless man is shadowing her — she spends hours cleaning the house, and sits up all night talking with a feverish passion. As their child grows, Tom senses an impending threat. Their home seems beset with vermin, smells and strange noises. On the verge of losing the house, Tom makes a decision that he hopes will save their lives.

THE SERVANTS

M. M. Smith

Things are unreliable. Things break. Things fall apart. Eleven-year-old Mark knows this all too well. And when he moves out of London to the wintry Brighton seaside, the situation is already bad. His mother is ill, and Mark hates his new stepfather. There's nothing to do and the new house feels nothing like home, filled with odd sounds and hidden rooms . . . and a strange old lady in the basement. Shadows gather — life goes from bad to worse — Mark must do something, but he doesn't know what. And the only people who might be able to help him — may not exist.

```
501  502  503  504  505  506  507  508  509  510  511  512  513  514  515
516  517  518  519  520  521  522  523  524  525  526  527  528  529  530
531  532  533  534  535  536  537  538  539  540  541  542  543  544  545
546  547  548  549  550  551  552  553  554  555  556  557  558  559  560
561  562  563  564  565  566  567  568  569  570  571  572  573  574  575
576  577  578  579  580  581  582  583  584  585  586  587  588  589  590
591  592  593  594  595  596  597  598  599  600

601  602  603  604  605  606  607  608  609  610  611  612  613  614  615
616  617  618  619  620  621  622  623  624  625  626  627  628  629  630
631  632  633  634  635  636  637  638  639  640  641  642  643  644  645
646  647  648  649  650  651  652  653  654  655  656  657  658  659  660
661  662  663  664  665  666  667  668  669  670  671  672  673  674  675
676  677  678  679  680  681  682  683  684  685  686  687  688  689  690
691  692  693  694  695  696  697  698  699  700

701  702  703  704  705  706  707  708  709  710  711  712  713  714  715
716  717  718  719  720  721  722  723  724  725  726  727  728  729  730
731  732  733  734  735  736  737  738  739  740  741  742  743  744  745
746  747  748  749  750  751  752  753  754  755  756  757  758  759  760
761  762  763  764  765  766  767  768  769  770  771  772  773  774  775
776  777  778  779  780  781  782  783  784  785  786  787  788  789  790
791  792  793  794  795  796  797  798  799  800

801  802  803  804  805  806  807  808  809  810  811  812  813  814  815
816  817  818  819  820  821  822  823  824  825  826  827  828  829  830
831  832  833  834  835  836  837  838  839  840  841  842  843  844  845
846  847  848  849  850  851  852  853  854  855  856  857  858  859  860
861  862  863  864  865  866  867  868  869  870  871  872  873  874  875
876  877  878  879  880  881  882  883  884  885  886  887  888  889  890
891  892  893  894  895  896  897  898  899  900

901  902  903  904  905  906  907  908  909  910  911  912  913  914  915
916  917  918  919  920  921  922  923  924  925  926  927  928  929  930
931  932  933  934  935  936  937  938  939  940  941  942  943  944  945
946  947  948  949  950  951  952  953  954  955  956  957  958  959  960
961  962  963  964  965  966  967  968  969  970  971  972  973  974  975
976  977  978  979  980  981  982  983  984  985  986  987  988  989  990
991  992  993  994  995  996  997  998  999  1000
```

M/c 3318